Big Lake

By Nick Russell

Nick Russell
1400 Colorado Street C-16
Boulder City, NV 89005
E-mail: Editor@gypsyjournal.net

Also By Nick Russell

Fiction
Big Lake
Big Lake Lynching
Nonfiction
Highway History and Back Road Mystery
Meandering Down The Highway
The Frugal RVer
Work Your Way Across The USA
The Gun Shop Manual

Author's Note

While there is a body of water named Big Lake in the White Mountains of Arizona, the community of Big Lake and all persons in this book live only in the author's imagination. Any resemblance in this story to actual persons, living or dead, is purely coincidental.

Prologue

While the rest of the world may see images of cactus, barren rock mountains, vast deserts, and the Grand Canyon when thinking of Arizona, there is another, lesser known topographic character to this southwestern state. The Mogollon Rim is a massive upthrust shelf of mountain country, stretching nearly 200 miles, from Prescott in the central part of the state, and on into New Mexico to the east.

Here lies the world's largest Ponderosa pine forest, snow capped peaks climbing to over 9,000 feet, dozens of lakes filled with trophy rainbow and brown trout, and the White Mountain Apache Indian reservation. The forests are home to bear, mountain lion, elk and deer. The dozen or so rustic small towns scattered along the Mogollon Rim have experienced a growth surge in recent years as crime weary residents, fleeing the smog and stresses of big city life, have discovered the high mountain paradise.

Stretching along the base of the Rim, as it is called locally, is another little known secret outside the state's borders - the Salt River Canyon. This smaller version of the Grand Canyon, a deep gorge winding nearly 50 miles long, is as scenic as its famous big brother, but has been tamed by U.S. Highway 60, a two lane thoroughfare meandering more or less east-west across the state. Between the pine country of Show Low and the high desert of Globe, Highway 60 dips southward briefly, to cross the Salt River Canyon in a series of hairpin turns and steep downgrades.

The highway is a major route for travelers and commerce between the high country and the rest of the state. As Highway 60 descends off the high country of the Rim, the terrain changes from alpine to desert, majestic pine trees are replaced by mesquite and cactus, and sagebrush takes the place of grassy open meadows.

Chapter 1

Early on a Monday morning in late November the canyon was deserted, weekend visitors to the high country back at their desks in air conditioned offices in Phoenix and Tucson. A lone hawk rode the thermals through the canyon, sharp eyes alert for prey. Below, a small ground squirrel cautiously peered out from under a prickly pear cactus, wary of danger. Sensing none, after a long scrutiny it scampered across the inside lane of blacktop. The hawk, alerted by the movement, began a downward plunge, razor sharp talons extended in its dive toward an easy meal.

Unaware of the danger from above, the ground squirrel suddenly paused as a low growl and slight vibration simultaneously alerted its senses, telegraphing danger signals to its brain. With a frantic scrambling of nails on pavement, it made a hasty u-turn and retreated hurriedly back to its cover, seconds before the hawk could pounce on it. Frustrated, the winged predator reversed its plunge as the sound of a heavy engine grew louder.

Casually steering the armored car with one hand, Phil Johnson stuck a cigarette between his lips and thumbed the striker on his old Zippo lighter, a well worn souvenir he had carried every day since picking it up in a Saigon post exchange back in his Army days. Through a blue cloud of tobacco smoke, he looked sideways at his partner and grinned. "So, you gonna take that little teller, Tanya, to lunch while we're in the city?"

Mike Perkins' face reddened. "Come on Phil. You know I'm married. I don't mess around."

The driver leered, enjoying the younger man's discomfort. "Yeah kid, but that'll change. That little gal sure has the hots for you. Ever notice that every time we make our drop off at the bank, she makes it a point to check us in? And she's always giving you the eye. I tell you... a man would be pretty dumb to pass that up. Great ass and everything else that goes with it."

"Yeah, maybe so. But a man'd be even dumber to mess up what I've got at home. When you got prime rib waiting on the table, why stop for a hotdog?"

Johnson chuckled and nodded his head. The inside of the truck had warmed up, and he took off his uniform hat and hung it over the barrel of the 12 gauge pump shotgun mounted vertically in a rack attached to the dashboard, then shrugged out of the heavy jacket he had worn when they began their route two hours earlier in the high country. Perkins reached over and guided the wheel with one hand to make the chore easier for his partner. "Thanks, kid," Johnson said as he pushed the jacket onto the seat beside him and reclaimed the steering wheel. "Guess I can't argue with you on that one, Mike. I just wish that little cutiepie would give me the chance, since you're going to disappoint her"

"I'll put in a good word for you," said the younger guard. "Maybe you can..."

"What's this?" interrupted Johnson as they rounded a curve, nodding toward a Jeep Wagoneer pulled into a scenic turnoff, its hood up. "What's she doing way out here?"

" Pull over."

"Hey kid, you wanna get us fired? You know we're not supposed to make any unauthorized stops."

"Bullshit, Phil! Pull over. This doesn't make sense."

The armored car pulled in beside the Jeep and stopped. Perkins opened his door and stepped down onto the ground. "What are you doing here?" he asked the woman who stood next to the upraised hood.

Before she could answer, a figure slipped around the back of the armored car and a sharp crack broke the early morning air. The bullet slammed into the back of the young guard's head and pitched him face forward down into the dirt, blood spraying the side of the armored car. The woman shuddered for an instant, then looked into the face of the gunman. "Come on, we don't have time to waste!"

Phil Johnson holstered his Smith & Wesson .38 and looked down at his dead partner, awestruck. "Damn! Twenty years in the Army and I never killed anyone...."

"Hurry up, baby," the woman said. "Someone might come along any time."

Stepping over the body, she hustled the guard to the back of the armored car. His hands shaking, Johnson fumbled a set of keys off his belt and unlocked the two sets of locks, then swung the doors open.

Inside, neatly stacked, were twenty canvas money bags, each secured by a metal hasp. The receipts of a long ski weekend in the mountains, destined for the holding bank in central Phoenix.

Throwing open the rear tailgate of the Jeep, the man and woman quickly transferred the money, alert for the sound of an approaching car. The job only took a few moments, and when the last bag was in the Jeep, the woman wiped perspiration from her forehead with the back of her hand. "Let's get going. Mexico's waiting."

Johnson grabbed her by the back of the head and pulled her face close to his for a kiss. "Oh, girl! It's going to be so good."

"Not if you don't move your ass," she urged. "Get busy so we can get out of here."

Johnson walked back to the body of Mike Perkins and bent over. He hesitated, then took a deep breath and, grabbing him by the boots, dragged the dead man to the back of the armored car, trying to avoid looking at his mangled head. Grunting, he managed to manhandle the body through the steel doors, all the time fighting down nausea. "Come on, damn it," said the woman nervously.

Johnson crawled inside and dragged his partner's lifeless body in far enough to be able to close the doors. Then he stepped over the corpse and started to climb out of the armored car. The sight of a snub nose .38 revolver in the woman's hand stopped him. "What the..."

"Sorry, baby," said the woman, a smirk distorting her features. "But with all this money, a dirty old man like you would just slow me down, don't you think? Thanks for the help." Johnson's scream was cut short by three quick gunshots. He tumbled backward onto the body of the man he had killed. A heavy weight settled in his chest and it became impossible to keep his eyelids open, no mattered how hard he struggled.

Before his life's blood had stopped pumping out of him, the Jeep was gone and silence once again filled the canyon. The hawk, soaring high overhead, watched the Jeep's progress until it disappeared around a curve, then went back to the hunt.

Chapter 2

Jim Weber was a cigar smoker. Though he knew it was socially unacceptable, Weber loved cigars, favoring vile, evil looking black cheroots that produced thick clouds of offensive blue smoke that drove ladies away and could make the stomachs of even strong men queasy after a night of heavy drinking. Bowing to social pressure and the demands of his physician, Weber had cut back on his cigar consumption lately, lighting one up only when he was alone in his patrol car or relaxing at the end of a long day's work; or sometimes, when he was under intense pressure and felt the need to pamper himself while he punished the world around him. But the habit of having a cigar stuck between his lips was so ingrained that, though Weber smoked them less these days, he frequently chewed on an unlit one, just to keep himself in practice and the world at bay.

Today was an intense day, and though it was before nine o'clock in the morning, Weber puffed great clouds of toxic smoke that hung thick in the air and formed a halo around the mounted mule deer head hanging on the wall above his gun rack. He rummaged through several neat piles of forms, receipts, and reports on top of the battered old roll-top desk in his office, leaving mayhem in his wake. "Mary! How the hell can I find anything in this mess? Get in here and give me a hand!" he shouted.

"Jesus Jim, calm down," answered a voice from the outer office.

A moment later an older woman stepped through the door, a steaming mug of coffee in her hand. Even in a red flannel shirt and jeans, it was evident that she was an attractive woman, her shapely figure belying her 60 years. Mischievous blue eyes sparkled under a thick mane of graying hair. "Damn! It smells like you're burning old tires in here," she complained, batting at the smoke with one hand and thrusting the mug in Weber's direction with the other. "Here, have your coffee. You're such a grouch in the mornings!"

"I don't want coffee," he said, while accepting the mug anyway, "I just want to find the damn maintenance forms for the patrol cars. You've got everything all screwed up in here. I can't find a damned thing!"

"Well, I guess that huge mess on your desk was just easier to deal with!" Mary Caitlin shot back sarcastically. "If you'd marry that nice girl over at the Thriftway, maybe you'd get a little civilization into your life! Turn you into a more organized man. Might even clear up your complexion, who knows? 'Course, you'd have to give up those nasty cigars, because no woman I know could tolerate them! "

"Ahh... Mary, not again," said the sheriff with a shake of his head, spurning his administrative assistant's latest effort to find him a bride. "If I've got to choose between a woman and a good cigar, I'll take the cigar every time. At least I know what to expect from a stogie. Besides, I told you, I'm waiting for Pete to die so I can have you," he said, giving her rump an affectionate pat. "Anyway, you mess things up enough for me around here. I don't need some woman losing everything in my house too!"

"Forget it, lover," Mary said, punching him on the arm as she picked up a folder from the desk. "It'll be a long wait. Pete's just too damn mean to die. Besides, I'd hurt you, youngster! Here's your maintenance forms, right under your nose."

As the sheriff took the folder from her, the outer office door banged open, bringing in a waft of cold, pine scented air. Deputy Tommy Frost entered the room, stomping snow off his boots. "I swear, it must have gotten down to zero last night! Sorry I'm late Jim, my damn car wouldn't start again this morning. Shelly had to give me a jump." The deputy took off his Stetson and uniform coat and hung them on a hall tree next to the door.

"I'm going over the maintenance records this morning," replied the sheriff. "I'm going to
try and convince the Council we need at least two new vehicles. These old clunkers are nickel and diming us to death."

The telephone rang and Tommy lifted a receiver from the phone on the nearest desk. "Big Lake Sheriff's Office, Deputy Frost speaking," he said as he perched on the corner of the desk. He listened for a moment or two, his face growing pale. "Okay, yeah. I'll tell him. He's on his way."

The freckle-faced young deputy hung up the phone and turned to the sheriff, his eyes wide with shock. "Jesus Christ Jim, that was the Highway Patrol. They want you to go to the Salt River Canyon. Your brother-in-law has been shot!"

The town of Big Lake, Arizona sits, appropriately enough, along the shore of Big Lake, a three mile long body of deep, cold mountain water, teeming with fighting trout that draw anglers from across the southwest. At 9,000 feet, the community is a popular summer getaway for desert dwellers and a winter destination for skiers.

Main Street is the center of activity in town, housing a myriad of small shops catering to both the tourist trade and full time residents, several restaurants, and most recently, an art gallery or two. The Sheriff's Office is located in the middle of town, with the Big Lake Town Offices located next door, across a small parking lot. The Post Office and the small quarters occupied by the town's newspaper are directly across the street. Looking south, Main Street seems to end at the foot of Apache Mountain, an imposing monolith that towers over the town, but in reality the street turns left sharply at the last minute and connects with the state highway a mile away, completing a loop begun on the north end of town.

Big Lake's year round population of 4,000 triples in summer as the weekend homes of part time residents fill up, along with the area's numerous motels, lodges, and tourist cabins. Over the past decade, hundreds of small cabins, as well as many expensive custom homes, have been built in the area as the upper middle class and wealthy of Tucson, Scottsdale, and Phoenix have discovered the mountain retreat, along with refugees fleeing California's earthquakes, mud slides, wildfires, and urban violence.

Longtime residents, while often secretly appreciating the extra dollars these newcomers bring to town, publicly decry the loss of small town atmosphere and quality of life they've long enjoyed. In winter, life takes on a slower pace during the week, but when the snow piles up, cars and sport utility vehicles carrying ski racks bring crowds of powder lovers to the mountains.

Siren screaming, red and blue lights flashing, Sheriff Jim Weber pushed his Ford Bronco through town and down the winding mountain road at top speed, thankful that there was no fresh snow to deal with. The shortest route to the Salt River Canyon was through the White Mountain Apache Indian Reservation, and the lawman thumbed his radio microphone. "Apache Tribal Police dispatcher, this is Sheriff Weber from Big Lake. Do you copy?"

A reply came through the static. "10-4 Sheriff, but you're breaking up a little."

"I'm on Highway 260, on an emergency run. I'll be coming through your area on Route 73, code three."

"Okay Sheriff. Do you need assistance?"

"No, I just wanted to let you know I'm trespassing."

Unlike some white law enforcement agencies, the Big Lake Sheriff had a good working relationship with the Apache Tribal Police.

"10-4 Sheriff. We'll be watching for you. Please be careful through Hon-Dah and Whiteriver."

"10-4. Thanks."

As his Bronco shot out of the forest, into the clearing that was the tribe's new hotel and gambling complex at Hon-Dah, Weber eased off the accelerator. Making a right onto Route 73, he sped up as soon as he was clear of the casino area. The big V-8 engine ate up the 25 miles to the tribal capitol at Whiteriver, where he again slowed down. An Apache police car sat alongside the road as he entered the small town, and pulled out ahead of the Bronco to give him an escort through town.

"Sheriff, this is Andy Bacca," spoke a voice over his radio from the car ahead. "What's going on?"

The sheriff picked up his microphone and answered his friend. "Highway Patrol called. Mike's armored car was hijacked in the Canyon. He and Phil Johnson were both shot."

"Oh Christ," replied Bacca, ignoring radio procedure at the news of the tragedy. "I'm sorry Jim! Let's get you moving."

The tribal police car's siren screamed, roof lights came on, and both police vehicles picked up speed. Only when they were well outside of Whiteriver did the Apache Police car pull over, and Weber heard his friend call "Good luck" over the radio as he sped past.

South of Whiteriver, the land was more open, rolling hills replacing the mountains, and pine trees giving way to desert vegetation. Weber pushed the Bronco over 100 miles per hour until his route intersected with Highway 60, where he turned south for the final 20 mile run to the Salt River Canyon. Radio traffic crackled over the speaker in his Bronco, and as he entered the canyon, he encountered several cars and recreational vehicles backed up on the highway.

Slowing, Weber eased his Bronco into the left lane and used his siren to warn oncoming traffic. Nearly a mile into the canyon he spotted red flares burning on the road, and a uniformed Department of Public

Safety officer directing traffic. He waved Weber on, and around the next bend the sheriff came upon the crime scene.

Several DPS and county squad cars were on the scene, and the armored car sat behind a cordon of yellow crime scene tape. Technicians worked through the area, taking photographs, measurements, and making notes. Paul Simpson, a longtime friend and Highway Patrol veteran, met Weber.

"How bad is it, Paul?" the sheriff asked, though the ambulance sitting silent alongside the road answered his question.

"Bad, Jim. They're both dead. Whoever did it killed them and made off with all the money they were carrying. A trucker coming down the Canyon spotted the armored car and stopped at the store at the bottom to call it in."

Weber stepped over the crime scene tape and walked to the open doors of the armored car. The coppery smell of blood was overpowering. Weber had to blink twice to clear the roaring inside his head. Simpson laid a steadying hand on the sheriff's shoulder. "We haven't moved anything. This is Gila County jurisdiction. Their Detective Loraz is in charge of the scene." Simpson indicated a Hispanic man in Levis and blue work shirt walking toward them, an automatic pistol riding high on the right side of his belt.

"Sheriff Weber? I'm Raul Loraz," he said, offering his hand. Loraz' grip was firm, his face serious, expression sympathetic. "I understand one of the victims is a relative of yours?"

"The younger one," Weber said, nodding toward the gore inside the armored car.

Loraz grimaced. "Sorry for your loss."

Fighting down the bile rising in his throat, Weber backed away from the opening. In fifteen years of law enforcement, he'd seen a lot of broken, bloodied bodies. As sheriff of a small rural town, many of those bodies had been friends and acquaintances. But this was the first time he'd had to experience what violence or accident left of a family member.

"What can you tell me?" Loraz asked, tipping his straw cowboy hat up on his forehead.

"Mike Perkins, my sister's husband. The other one is Phil Johnson. Phil's been with Southwest Armored for about three years. Retired Army lifer. Mike's only been on the job a year or so. Both lived in Big Lake."

"We've called the company," Loraz told him. "They're sending some people up. They said the truck made pickups at Sunrise ski area, Hon-

Dah, and several stops in Pinetop-Lakeside and Show Low. They figure they were carrying at least a quarter million."

"Yeah," Weber said. "They make the run every Monday and Thursday. Never any trouble before."

"Always that much money?"

"I doubt it. But with the skiers and all, the mountain is busy."

Traffic had begun to move slowly, drivers pausing to gawk at the scene, getting their vicarious thrill. The uniformed officer directing traffic slapped the hood of a big Suburban that had stopped. "Come on, move it," he ordered a rubbernecking driver.

"Did your brother-in-law mention anyone trailing them lately?" Loraz asked.

"No," Weber replied. "If there had been, I'm sure they'd have told the company and had a tail car."

The crime technicians finished with their work, and ambulance attendants began zipping the bodies into plastic body bags and loading them onto wheeled stretchers. A heavyset, balding man in light blue coveralls walked over to the two lawmen, wiping perspiration off his florid face with a large handkerchief.

"Sheriff Weber, this is Charlie McNally, our chief crime scene investigator," said Loraz. "What have you got for me, Charlie?"

McNally shook his head. "It's weird, Raul. The younger one was shot once in the back of the head, close range, almost execution style. From the blood in the dirt next to the truck and the blood spray on the side of the cab, along with the marks in the dirt, it looks like he was killed outside the truck and then dragged inside. The older guard took three shots in the chest, not as close. From what I see, he was shot inside the truck. But his body is laying on top of the first victim."

The sheriff voiced a thought that had been nagging him. "Something's wrong here," Weber said. "Those guys aren't supposed to stop for anything. What made them pull over?"

"Good question. You knew them both, you tell me. What would make them break company policy and pull over out here in the middle of nowhere?" asked Loraz.

"Company regulations don't even let them stop for an accident without radioing in first. Of course, here in the Canyon, their radio and cell phone probably wouldn't work. But they'd go down to the bottom and stop at the store."

"No evidence of an accident," observed McNally with a shake of his head. "Not a scratch on the truck, no fluids on the ground. It wasn't an accident that made them stop."

"Any other ideas?" prompted Loraz.

"Nothing that I can think of. Mike was a stickler for following the rules. I just can't see him pulling over for anything."

"Well," said Loraz, sticking a cigarette into his mouth, "Something, or someone, sure did. And these boys paid for it with their lives."

All three turned at the sound of the officer in the roadway, as he shouted at a heavyset woman in a U-Haul truck that had nearly run him down while she stared at the bodies being loaded into the ambulance. "Christ, lady! Watch where you're going before you kill somebody!" Chastised, the woman picked up speed and passed. Violent death seemed to enthrall everyone who saw it.

Weber looked back toward the truck. "I need to get out of here. I need to tell my sister. I don't want her hearing this from someone else."

"Okay," agreed Loraz, offering a business card. "I'll be in touch. We're not prima donnas here in Gila County. Whatever I find out, you'll know as soon as I do. And since their run covered so many different jurisdictions, we all need to work together on this."

"Thanks Loraz," said Weber, taking the card. "Let's get these bastards. I want whoever did this to burn!"

Only when the sheriff was back in his Bronco and well away from the crime scene did he pull his vehicle over to the side of the highway and allow his emotions to break through. Weber covered his face with shaking hands and great sobs wracked his body.

"Debbie," he said aloud. "Oh kid, how am I going to tell you this? How *can* I tell you this?"

Driving out of the Salt River Canyon, Weber tried to force his numb mind to work. Debbie would be in Show Low today, completing her final exams. His sister had been pursuing a degree in early childhood education through Northern Arizona University's extension classes. Through hard work and persistence, she had completed the normal four year course requirements three semesters ahead of schedule, and once finals were behind her, was slated to graduate with the winter class in just two weeks. Weber couldn't imagine how the terrible news of Mike's murder would impact her at what was supposed to be such a happy time in her life.

When John and Patricia Weber were killed in a traffic accident, they left behind a small ranch, a thousand head of cattle, and two children. Army Corporal Jim Weber had just arrived at his new duty station at Fort Campbell, Kentucky when news of his parents' death reached him. He took emergency leave to fly home to Arizona to settle his parents' affairs and make arrangements for his twelve year old sister. The young soldier faced an overwhelming task, and though he loved his job as a military policeman, he soon realized he couldn't run the ranch and raise his young sister from afar. He applied for and received a hardship discharge, only six months into his second enlistment.

But ranching and livestock had never appealed to the young man, and he soon remembered why he had joined the Army. Before two years had passed, Weber had sold off the cattle, leased out the acreage, with the exception of the family home and surrounding ten acres, and taken a job with the Big Lake Sheriff's Office. When Pete Caitlan retired as Sheriff, Weber was his handpicked successor.

Debbie Weber grew from a beautiful young girl into a beautiful woman under the watchful eye of her older brother. Tall and lissome, with long blonde hair, sparkling blue eyes, and a vivacious personality, she soon had the attention of young men for miles around. Jim Weber did his best to intimidate the young bucks who showed up on his doorstep, but before long Debbie was caught up in her own world of parties, school dances, and other teenage activities.

Playing the dual roles of both father and older brother, the young deputy waited up past many a midnight for his popular young sister to get in from her many social functions. Most testosterone-driven young suitors were intimidated by the gruff greeting they received from Weber and soon went off in search of easier pickings. But one young ranch hand refused to be put off. Mike Perkins showed up at the Weber door one evening to escort Debbie to a dance, and no matter how forbidding the girl's brother seemed, he came back again and again to take Debbie to dances, picnics, and dinner. Over time, Weber became accustomed to, and then actually fond of, the tenacious young Romeo, and when, in her nineteenth year, Debbie came to him to show off her brand new engagement ring, Weber was nearly as delighted as she was.

The drive to Show Low was shorter, less than fifty miles up Highway 60. Weber had managed to compose himself by the time he reached the community college campus where Debbie took her classes. He parked the Bronco and went into the registrar's office to locate his sister. An efficient young woman at the receptionist's desk checked her computer screen, quickly typed in a few bits of information, then smiled at the sheriff as she brushed a wisp of unruly hair out of her face.

"Looks like she's over in building C. Would you like me to call and ask her to come over here?" she offered.

"Please," Weber asked. "Is there a conference room or something we can use? I need to give her some bad news."

"Oh no! Of course. Right here. I'll bring her right in, Sheriff." She showed Weber to a brightly lit room across the hall, decorated with Southwestern themes and plants. Ignoring the sofa and chairs, Weber stood and tried once again to think of any words that would make the terrible news he had for his sister any easier to accept. He had never felt so inadequate as at that moment.

All too soon the door opened, and Debbie walked in, looking perplexed. Her long hair was hanging loose over her shoulders and she was wearing a heavy sweater under a green down vest. A heavy canvas book bag hung off one shoulder. Weber caught just a hint of perfume as she approached him.

"Jimmy? What are you doing here? What's going on?" she asked.

"Sit down, Debbie," Weber said, leading her to the sofa. "We need to talk."

"What is it, Jimmy? I don't want to sit down. Tell me." She looked deeply into his solemn eyes. "What is it, Jimmy? You're scaring me!"

"Debbie, something terrible has happened." He took a deep breath and plunged ahead. "Mike's gone."

"Gone?" Her big eyes seemed to grow even larger. "What do you mean, gone?"

Weber put his arms around her and pulled her close to him, wishing his body could absorb her pain and shield her from what he had to say.

"There was a robbery. Mike and Phil were both shot, Debbie. Someone killed them both."

Her scream echoed across the campus, starting as a high pitched exclamation and drawing out into a long wail of anguish. As the receptionist poked her head in the door, a look of dismay on her face, Weber held his trembling sister and cried along with her.

Chapter 3

"How is she?"

Mary Caitlin stood in the doorway of Weber's cabin, a look of deep grief etching her normally cheerful face.

Weber shook his head. "She really lost it. Doc Carson came over and gave her something to help her sleep. I just got her into bed."

"How about *you*? Are you okay?"

Weber massaged his face and red rimmed eyes with his fingers. "I feel like someone's got a grip on my guts and won't let go. I just can't believe this."

Mary pulled the sheriff close and embraced him. "I think you need some rest too. It must have been horrible for you to have to see them like that. What can I do to help?"

Weber could smell her perfume and shampoo, feel the softness of her shirt on his cheek, but all his mind could see was the terrible sight of the two bodies sprawled amid the blood in the back of the armored car. Finally, he pushed himself away from the comfort of his friend's embrace.

"I need to get back to the office. I imagine there must be a million calls coming in. I unplugged the phone so it wouldn't wake Debbie."

"Phoenix and Tucson TV stations, newspapers, friends all calling to see what they can do to help," said Mary. "Tommy and Chad are covering the office. You need to rest."

"I can't right now, Mary. I need to be moving, *doing* something! Will you stay with Debbie?"

Jim Weber had been more than a deputy to Mary's husband during his long tenure as sheriff, and then as her employer. He and his sister were also the children Pete and Mary Caitlin had never had.

"Of course I will. You go do what you need to do."

Weber's deputies greeted him with sorrowful eyes when he walked into the Sheriff's Office. "You all right, Slugger?" Chad Summers asked.

Even though Weber was his boss, the long-time deputy still insisted on calling him by the name he had called him since he coached Weber's Little League team years before.

"Yeah, Chad. Good as I can be, I guess."

"Phones have been going crazy," said Tommy Frost. "I fielded most of the media callers, just told them it was a Gila County case and referred them down there. A lot of townspeople have been calling, too. It's slowed down a little bit in the last hour or so. Damn Jimmy, what happened?"

"I don't know, Tommy. Someone got them to stop in the Canyon, and then shot both of them. I can't figure it out."

"Doesn't make sense," Chad said, as he poured a mug of coffee and handed it to Weber. "They knew better than to stop for *anything*. As much as Mike knew about police work, I can't see him taking any chances. And Phil was ex-military. He spent his life obeying the rules."

Mike Perkins had wanted to follow Weber into police work, and as a teenager had spent nearly as many hours hanging around the Sheriff's Office or riding along on patrols with Weber as he had courting Debbie. But a heart murmur discovered during his physical had prevented him from wearing the uniform. Still, he had performed many hours of volunteer work with the Sheriff's Office over the years. The job as an armored car guard was the closest he would ever get to becoming a law enforcement officer.

While they were talking, the door opened, and Paul Lewis, the editor and publisher of the weekly *Big Lake Herald,* walked in. Lewis was a roly-poly, good humored little gnome who peered out at the world from faded blue eyes that hid behind wire rimmed glasses. He huffed his way across the office and gripped Weber's arm. "You okay, Jimmy?"

Weber nodded at his lifelong friend and smiled weakly. "I'm coping, Paul. Have you talked to the guys yet?"

Lewis nodded and said "Chad filled me in on what you've got so far. I'm not here officially, I just wanted to see if you were okay. How's Debbie?"

"Doc gave her a sedative," Weber said. "She's sleeping."

"Listen, Jimmy, if there's anything I can do...."

The ringing of the telephone interrupted him, and Tommy answered it, then turned toward Weber.

"Jim, it's the FBI. A Special Agent Parks, from Phoenix."

"I'll take it in my office."

"Sheriff Weber, this is Larry Parks, with the FBI office down here in Phoenix," said the caller as Weber sank into his chair. Parks' voice had a Southwestern drawl. Weber guessed Texas or Oklahoma. "Since the armored car was carrying federally insured bank deposits, I've been assigned to the hijacking. How are you holding up? I understand one of the guards was your brother-in-law?"

"Yeah, Mike Perkins. Do you have anything yet?"

"Not much more than you already know. I just got off the phone with Detective Loraz. He tells me there'll be autopsies on the victims some time tonight. The armored car office told me they were carrying just at $300,000."

Weber rubbed his eyes. It felt like they were full of gravel.

"From what I've got from the company, both men were pretty well trained. No one seems to know what would have made them stop, especially in an isolated place like that. It was against every rule in the book."

"I've been wracking my brain for a reason too," Weber replied. "I keep coming up with a blank."

"How's your sister doing?"

"We had to have her sedated. She's sleeping."

"I won't keep you," Parks said. "Just wanted to touch base. I'll probably need to talk to your sister when she's up to it, Sheriff. Find out if her husband mentioned anyone following them lately, that sort of thing."

"Mike and I were close," Weber said. "I had dinner with them just last night, he never mentioned anything."

"Nothing in their reports to the company, either," said Parks. "I want you to know, Sheriff Weber, this has our topmost priority. Whatever it takes, we'll get these guys. You hang in there and take care of that little girl. I'll be up that way tomorrow or the next day."

"Thanks," Weber said, and hung up the phone. It rang immediately.

"Sheriff Weber, this is Raul Loraz."

"Any news yet? I just hung up from the FBI."

"That's one of the reasons I'm calling; to tell you they've stepped into the case too. Also... something else. Something real weird."

"What?" asked Weber.

"Johnson's gun had been fired. There was one empty casing in the cylinder. The autopsies are scheduled for tonight, but I asked the medical examiner to do a quick test on his hands. It showed he'd fired a gun recently."

"Do you think he managed to shoot one of them?" Weber asked, straightening up in his chair, suddenly on full alert. If he did, and they showed up at a hospital..."

"We've got the word out to every hospital, medical office, and clinic in the state," said Loraz. "But I keep wondering, if they got into a gunfight, why was his gun snapped into its holster when we found them?"

"Nothing about this case makes sense." Weber rubbed his eyes again. His head throbbed. "Maybe he shot at a coyote or something. Hell, your guess is as good as mine."

"The guy was retired military," said Loraz. "You'd think a guy like that would understand firearms discipline."

"How about Mike? Did you check his weapon?"

"Yeah," the detective replied. "His gun was fully loaded. We tested his hands too, just to see. Came up blank."

Weber cupped the telephone between his ear and shoulder, and tried again to massage the pressure out of his forehead. "Now what?"

"We'll have the autopsy reports some time tomorrow. That may tell us something. I'm sending a man into Phoenix tomorrow to interview employees of the company they worked for, to see if anyone has anything that might help us. You could help the investigation a lot if you'd cover some ground up there for me. Talk to the people around town who knew them. Maybe they mentioned something to somebody that might give us a lead if they were being tailed. And if you'd talk to the people where they made their pickups. You know the routine."

"You got it," Weber promised.

"How's your sister?"

"She's not handling it very well," Weber replied. "Who can blame her? Our local doctor gave her something to help her sleep."

"Okay. Well, keep in touch. I'll call back as soon as I have anything at all," Loraz promised, and rang off.

Weber hung up the phone and tried to ignore the pain inside his skull. All he wanted in the world was to go back to has cabin and hold his grieving sister, to pour out his own hurt and frustration. But the lawman inside him wouldn't let him. There were people to interview, information to be gathered and sorted. Weber knew that every crime had a solution, and many times the first step toward that solution was some small, seemingly insignificant bit of information from someone connected with one of the parties in the case. It might have been a casual comment, an observation, or just a memory of something that seemed out of place, but unimportant at the time. Wherever that pivotal first piece of information was, Weber knew it was out there, and he was determined to find it.

It was late in the day when Weber left the office, after his telephone conversations with Loraz and Parks. He drove back to his cabin to check in on Debbie, and Mary Caitlin reported that his sister was still sleeping. From there, Weber drove out to Pine Cone Road, a winding, narrow lane that serpentined up the side of Bobcat Mountain before ending at a Forest Service fire lookout tower. Several rustic cabins, some not much more than shacks, were located along the road. In one, a small one bedroom cabin built years before as a weekend cottage, Phil Johnson had lived.

Weber drove past Johnson's cabin and pulled into the driveway of a larger two story house a quarter mile up the road. The white frame house sat toward the back of a snow covered yard. A wide front porch, complete with wooden swing, was more reminiscent of a Midwest farmhouse than a mountain dwelling. While most local cabins were surrounded by tall pine trees that shaded out any grass, Weber knew that in summer, this house had a large, well trimmed lawn. Weber parked, and an old yellow Golden Retriever ambled through the snow to meet him, a large stick in its mouth. It dropped the stick at Weber's feet and wagged its tail at the sheriff.

"How you doing, Charlie?" Weber greeted the dog, and bent over to scratch its ears. Charlie arched his back with pleasure. "You're a good old boy, aren't you?"

"Who's out there?" demanded a voice from the direction of the house. Weber looked up to see the door open, and an elderly woman sitting in a wheelchair. He threw the stick toward the edge of the yard for Charlie. and walked toward the porch.

"Miss Lucy, it's Jim Weber. How are you today?"

Grey eyes regarded him, and Weber was briefly reminded of a bird, as she ever so slightly tilted her head in the direction of his voice. Miss Lucy Washburn was regarded by some in Big Lake as matriarch, by others as an eccentric. Her father, Big Mike Washburn, had been one of the earliest settlers in the Big Lake country, back in the 1880's, carving a large cattle ranching and logging operation out of a wilderness while he battled hostile Indians, rustlers, squatters, and, later on, increasing pressure from government agencies that attempted to regulate the empire he had created with grazing leases, forestry policies, and taxation.

Big Mike defeated them all, and became a legend in the mountain country of the West. A century later the survivalist movement would look toward him as a role model, a man who wouldn't be controlled by Washington or Phoenix bureaucracies, who stood alone against Big Brother.

Big Mike Washburn was a hard working, hard drinking, hard living man, who refused to give in to anyone or anything until the very end. On his seventieth birthday, in 1937, he downed most of a bottle of Jack Daniels, ate a huge steak from a steer he had butchered himself, and then climbed onto the back of a dappled stallion none of his cowboys could break to saddle, and told them to watch how the old man taught a horse a few manners. The stallion proved to be a stubborn student, and threw Big Mike into a corral post, breaking his neck.

Big Mike's only child, Lucy, was born late in his life. She was thirteen when she watched her father die in the dirt of the horse corral. Her mother Sarah was a frail thing, who needed a man to help her run the empire Big Mike had created. She promptly married a local hard case, named Eddie Franklin. Eddie was more interested in gin and women than in livestock, and he proceeded to drink himself into oblivion most days. When he wasn't passed out, he was trying to find another woman to conquer.

One day, three years after Big Mike's death, in a drunken stupor, Eddie noticed just how pretty his young stepdaughter was. Sarah was off to town, selecting a bolt of blue cloth from which to create a dress for her only child. Eddie tried to pin young Lucy against a wall in the hallway outside her bedroom, while his hands roamed over her supple body. The young woman fought back viciously, and in the struggle, she tripped over a small table at the top of the stairway, pitching headfirst down a flight of stairs, severing her spine and fracturing her skull in the process.

Eddie claimed the girl had fallen while he was outside tending to a sick horse, and since Lucy was still unconscious, there was no one to dispute his claim. But Sarah knew what had happened. She had caught the way Eddie Franklin stared at her daughter's developing figure.

Once she made sure Lucy was in good hands, in a Phoenix hospital, she returned to Big Lake, retrieved Big Mike's old .44 Colt, the same one he had used to battle Indians and dispatch crippled livestock with, from it's place in a chest full of his things stored in the attic. She marched Eddie Franklin to the top of the same steps he had caused her daughter to tumble down, where she unceremoniously shot him dead. Then she went into her bedroom, wrote a long letter of apology to Lucy, a shorter note explaining her actions to her attorney, and turned the big Colt on herself.

Many people questioned why Lucy insisted on coming back to the home that had held so much tragedy, after her long recuperation and nearly a year of therapy. But she did. There was sufficient money to convert the house to accommodate her special needs, she hired a housekeeper/companion, and began to prove herself nearly as shrewd a businessperson as her father had been.

America had just entered World War II and manpower was hard to find, but she managed to hold on, and Washburn beef and timber proved essential to the war effort. After the war, the country was on the move. Lucy sold the logging operation and began dividing the ranch holdings into smaller portions, which she developed. Much of the present town of Big Lake was former Washburn land. She had built several cabins for weekend rentals, and Phil Johnson had lived in one of them.

"How are you, Jim? Come sit and talk to an old lady a bit."

She rolled her wheelchair out of the doorway, and Weber stepped inside. The wide entrance hall was decorated with old branding irons, steer horns, and Navajo rugs. Weber followed the wheelchair into the big front room and perched on the edge of the overstuffed chair Miss Lucy indicated.

"I heard about your sister's husband. Terrible thing."

"Yes, it is," Weber agreed. "Miss Lucy, I need to get a look at the cabin Phil Johnson rented from you. Is that all right with you?"

At the mention of Johnson's name, she frowned. "Now Jim Weber, you know that I always speak my mind. And I know that it may be wrong to speak bad of the dead. But that Phil Johnson was a bad man!"

Weber looked at her. "What do you mean, a bad man?"

"He was a drunkard, for one thing. Whenever he came up here to pay his rent, I could smell the alcohol on his breath. I hate a drunkard!"

"I can understand that," said Weber. "But was he ever a problem to you? Did he ever give you any cause to dislike him, except for the alcohol on his breath?"

"Why? You think I shot him? My mama was the one who shot drunk men around here!"

Weber felt his face color, and she seemed to take delight in his discomfort.

"Of course not, Miss Lucy. I just..."

"Don't you think I can't take care of myself, Jim Weber! I still have Daddy's old Colt in my nightstand, and I can use it!"

"I'm sure you can," Weber said. "Miss Lucy, I'm just trying to get a handle on the man. You see, there was no reason for them to stop down there in that canyon. It was against every rule and everything they were taught. Now, I know my brother-in-law, Mike Perkins. I can't see what could possibly cause him to stop. But I didn't know Johnson very well. I need to see if I can learn what might make him stop way out there in the middle of nowhere."

"Only three things motivate men," replied Lucy Washburn, with conviction. "Greed, booze, and sex. Sometimes all three. All you have to do is figure out which ones got those boys to stop."

Weber shook his head and grinned, in spite of himself. "Come on Miss Lucy, we're not all that bad, are we?"

"You're damn right you are," she said forcefully. "Even you, Jim Weber! I've known you since you were a boy. And you and I have had some similar things to deal with. We both took on our family ranches after our parents passed on, and we both sold them off. I've always liked you. I remember when you was just a kid and I'd hire you to work around this place, or one of my rentals. You've grown into a fine man. But when it comes right down to it, your weaknesses are still the same as every man's."

"You think so?"

"Yep. I've never heard of you boozing it up, but I imagine there's some gal out there you'd get silly over. But those aren't your weaknesses, Sheriff. With you it's greed."

Weber was taken aback, and didn't know how to reply.

"It's not greed for money," Miss Lucy went on. "It's greed for revenge, right now. You want to get whoever killed those boys, because one was your family. Whoever did it hurt your sister, and I know you love that little girl to death. And because that's your job to get them. But it's more than the job. You need to get them to satisfy your sense of right and wrong."

Weber nodded. "You may be right, Miss Lucy."

"Of course I'm right! A man does what he has to do. You'll get them, Sheriff. Just remember what I told you. Booze, greed, and sex. That's all you need to look for."

Phil Johnson's cabin reflected the fact that he had been a career military man. It was neat; everything in its proper place. The living room held an old sofa, recliner, color television, and a stereo system. The cassette tapes and compact discs in the rack next to the stereo were mostly country. The only thing on top of the end table next to the recliner was a *TV Guide* and an ashtray. At one end of the living room was a small kitchen nook. A clean coffee cup sat perched upside down in the dish rack. Weber opened the refrigerator. It was nearly empty, containing just two bottles of Budweiser, a half full quart cardboard carton of milk, and a package of bacon.

Weber went into the bedroom. The bed was made, with the corners of the covers tucked in, in crisp military style. A dresser sat along one wall, nightstands on either side of the bed. One held a small lamp and an ashtray. Inside the drawer was a short barreled Smith and Wesson Chief's Special .38 revolver and a flashlight. The other night stand was bare on top. The only things inside the drawer were a road atlas and local telephone book. Weber noted that there were no photographs on the walls in either room, no sign that someone lived within these walls. The cabin was as impersonal as a motel room.

The dressers contained some carefully folded underwear, a box of military ribbons, paperwork relating to Johnson's service and retirement, and a bank book from the Timber Savings Bank in Big Lake, showing that Johnson's account balance was just over $200.

The closet held more clothes, a few pairs of jeans and slacks on hangers, several uniforms for the armored car company, and western shirts. Two nylon travel bags were sitting on the closet floor. Weber carried the bags to the bed, sat them down and unzipped them. They were packed with clothes, a shaving kit, and deodorant. It looked like Johnson had been planning a trip.

Weber went into the bathroom. Nothing out of the ordinary. As he stepped back into the bedroom, something caught his eye. Something that he had missed before. He bent over next to the bed and picked it up. An empty foil condom wrapper, dropped casually on the floor at the side of the bed. "So, you had a girlfriend, did you Phil?" Weber asked aloud. "Was that your weakness?"

It was dark by the time Weber locked the door of Johnson's cabin, after finding nothing else of importance. He drove back to his own cabin. Mary Caitlin's Blazer was still in the driveway. When he stepped inside, Debbie was sitting on the sofa, drinking a cup of tea. She quickly came into his arms.

"How you doing, kitten?"

She buried her face in his shoulder and shook her head. "I don't know, Jimmy. I think I'm numb."

He hugged her and nodded. "Me too. Did you get any sleep?"

"She just woke up a few minutes ago," said Mary, as she came out of the kitchen and handed Weber a cup of coffee. "How are *you* doing, Jim?"

"About the best I can, Mary. Look, you need to get home. Pete's probably growling about his dinner."

"Oh, that old bandit thinks gourmet cooking is a cup of coffee and a handful of donuts," Mary replied. "He can manage."

"Really," Weber insisted. "We'll be fine. I need to get some rest, and tomorrow's going to be a long day."

"Okay then, if you don't need anything else," she said.

Weber walked her out to her truck, and she turned to him just before she climbed in, placing a gentle hand on his cheek. "You'll get them, Jimmy. Get yourself some rest."

"I will, Mary," he promised.

As he walked back to the cabin to comfort his sister, Mary wasn't sure if the sheriff's last words referred to rest, or revenge.

Siren screaming, Weber steered the big Bronco at high speed down the narrow two lane canyon road, the big tires squealing as they tried to hold on through the sharp turns, at speeds the Bronco was never intended to handle, even with its police performance package. He wrestled the steering wheel as he began to lose control on a particularly treacherous curve, felt the rear end start to fishtail, but managed to get the 4x4 straightened out, and punched the gas pedal. The big V-8 engine responded with a roar, the tires gained purchase on the pavement, and the Bronco shot through the short straightaway and into the next turn. Up ahead, Weber spotted the safety pullout, the big armored car sitting with its rear doors open.

The sheriff jammed on the brake pedal, and the Bronco slid to a grinding stop in a cloud of dust behind the armored car. Mike Perkins glanced at his brother-in-law as he stepped out of the rear cargo door, and a big grin split his face. A heavy canvas money bag hung from each hand. Behind him, in the semi-darkness of the armored car's interior, Weber could see the body of Phil Johnson, sprawled on the floor.

"Hey Jimmy. What's up?"

"Get out of here," shouted Weber, as he jumped out of the Bronco. *"Go Mike!"*

Perkins looked confused for a moment, and as he delayed, a dark figure snuck up on him from behind, a massive handgun in its fist. Like a deadly viper searching for prey, the barrel wavered for a second, then centered on the back of Perkins' head.

"No!" screamed Weber, as he dragged his .45 Colt from its holster. The world went into slow motion mode, the big semi-automatic seemed to take forever to clear leather. Before Weber could bring it to bear on the assassin, the gun in the dark figure's hand roared, an explosion of fire blasting out of the barrel. The bullet slammed into Perkins' skull, and his expression went from carefree to confused in an instant, then Weber watched the life go out of his eyes, and Perkins collapsed into a heap at his feet.

As the bullet exited Perkins' skull, blood and bits of bone and brain sprayed over Weber's face and shirt, partially blinding him. He frantically wiped his eyes clear and centered his gun's sights on the dark figure as it casually walked up to Perkins' body and aimed at his crumpled form. Before Weber could pull the trigger, another bullet tore into the man on the ground, jerking the body with its impact. Weber squeezed the trigger, the big Colt roared and a 220 grain hollow point bullet punched into the assassin's torso.

The big bullet would knock a horse off its feet, but it seemed to have no effect whatsoever on the killer. Ignoring his wound, he fired again into the dead man. Weber screamed in rage and jerked the Colt's trigger as fast as he could, the pistol bucking in his hand. He watched the bullets tear into his target, without effect. The killer just kept shooting Perkins again and again, even as Weber's bullets ripped through him.

With his last shot expended, the slide on Weber's gun locked open. He used his thumb to push the magazine release and grappled with his left hand to free another magazine from the black nylon pouch on his belt, never taking his eyes off his target.

As he jammed the fresh magazine into the well at the bottom of his pistol, and released the slide to chamber a round, the dark figure finally stopped shooting Perkins, and turned away without a glance at Weber, walking casually toward the front of the armored car.

"Stop, you son of a bitch!" Weber ordered, in a trembling voice, but the murderer ignored him. The sheriff aimed down the barrel of his pistol and carefully squeezed off another shot. He watched the bullet tear a big chunk

of cloth out of the killer's shirt, but he kept walking away, without so much as flinching to acknowledge the bullets the sheriff had hit him with.

Weber was crying in rage and frustration as he shot the retreating form again and again, emptying the seven round magazine. As the Colt's slide locked open a second time, the mysterious killer disappeared around the front of the armored car. Weber screamed out his anger and impotency through the haze of gun smoke. Tears stung his eyes, the acrid smell of cordite burning his throat. Bellowing in frustration, Weber threw the Colt in the direction the killer had gone and sank to his knees in the dirt.

"Jimmy, are you alright? Jimmy!"

Weber shot upright in bed, confused and thrashing wildly. His heart was pounding, and a low pitched sound, a combination of moan and animal growl, filled the room. Debbie grabbed his flailing arm as it grazed her face. Her voice rose in alarm.

"Jimmy! Wake up! It's me, Debbie!"

Weber realized the alien sound was coming from himself. He managed to gain some control and stopped thrashing. Debbie's eyes were wide with alarm.

"Jimmy?"

"Oh Debbie! I'm so sorry! I tried... I couldn't make him stop!"

Debbie crawled onto the bed and pulled him close, her own sobs shaking her body as Weber's convulsed him.

"It's okay, Jimmy! It was only a dream. It's okay."

Brother and sister held each other, letting their grief take control of them. Weber couldn't contain it any longer, and the emotional dam holding back his sorrow burst. For long moments he leaned into Debbie, soaking her nightshirt with his tears. Finally, her own face wet, and eyes red, Debbie pulled away slightly, and looked solemnly at her older brother.

"Jimmy, listen to me," she said forcefully, "there was nothing you could have done to stop what happened! Nothing anybody could have done. It was a terrible thing, and I hate it. But you couldn't have known. No one could have. Don't blame yourself. You couldn't do anything!"

Weber knew her words were intended to ease his pain, but they did little to help. He looked into her worried eyes and nodded his head in reluctant agreement, more for her benefit than his own.

Finally he lay back down and Debbie snuggled into his side. After a time Debbie's breathing became slower as she fell into a deep sleep.

"I have to be strong for her." Weber told himself silently. *"She just lost*

her husband, and I'm falling apart on her. I need to get control of this thing, so I can help her through this."

He kissed the sleeping woman's forehead tenderly, and made a silent vow to be the strong big brother she had depended on for so long. But it was a long time before he finally fell back asleep.

Chapter 4

A light snow had fallen overnight, softening the edges of the world. Debbie insisted on going back to her house, the big family home they had grown up in. When she and Mike Perkins had married, Weber had built the smaller cabin he lived in, careful to locate it a couple of miles away to give the newlyweds plenty of privacy. He was reluctant to let Debbie go off on her own, but she kissed his cheek and pulled on her coat.

"Jimmy, I know you have trouble believing it, but I'm a big girl. Sooner or later I'm going to have to face that house without Mike. I *need* to be in my own house, surrounded by the things Mike and I lived with. Does that make any sense to you? Marsha will be there. I'll be okay. I promise." She gave him a sad smile. "After all, I'm Jim Weber's sister, you know. You didn't raise me to be a wimp!"

Weber smiled in spite of himself and brushed a wisp of blonde hair off her forehead.

"Okay, kid. I'll stop by later."

She gave him a final squeeze and was out the door.

Mary Caitlin met him at the door of the Sheriff's Office.

"I was just going to get on the radio and try to raise you. Your phone must still be unplugged."

"It is," Weber remembered. "What's going on?"

"That Detective Loraz from Gila County has phoned twice. He wanted you to call him the second you get in."

Weber went into his office and dialed the telephone number on Raul Loraz's business card. A secretary answered the phone and quickly routed the call to Loraz.

"How are you this morning, Sheriff?" Loraz asked.

"I'm okay, Loraz. What do you have?"

"Well, I don't know what to tell you. This damn case just gets weirder at every turn. We got a ballistics match on the bullet that killed Mike Perkins. It came from Phil Johnson's gun."

Weber jerked upright in his chair, spilling the mug of coffee Mary Caitlin had just placed in front of him. Alarmed, she grabbed a handful of tissues from a box on the top of the desk and blotted up the mess.

"No way!"

"Yeah, perfect match."

"What the hell.... you think Johnson shot Mike?" Weber asked, in disbelief.

"I don't know, Sheriff. But his gun was the murder weapon. And we *know* he had fired a gun sometime fairly close to the time he was killed."

"What about the slugs from *his* body," Weber asked.

"Different gun, different type of bullet. The .38 bullet we recovered from Mike Perkins was a jacketed hollow point, 158 grain. The three we took from Johnson's body were solid lead. And the markings from the barrel are different."

Every firearm leaves its own signature on a bullet fired through its barrel. These minute scratches from the lands and grooves inside the barrel are as individual as a person's fingerprints.

"You still there, Sheriff?" Loraz asked.

"Huh? Oh, yeah,... sorry," Weber apologized. "Just blown away."

"Like I said, it just gets weirder and weirder," Loraz repeated.

Weber's head was spinning from the news. He realized Loraz was asking him a question.

"I'm sorry, Detective. What were you saying?"

"I was asking if you had found out anything on your end yet?"

"Not much. I did a quick search of Johnson's cabin. He was going on a trip. I found a couple of packed suitcases."

"Hmm.... that makes him look even more suspicious." said Loraz. "But if he was planning on killing his partner and splitting with the money, why were they still in his place? How could he have planned to get back there and pick them up?"

"I don't know," admitted Weber. "But... I'm just wondering about something."

"What's that?"

"Assuming that he *did* shoot Mike, we still don't know who killed Johnson. Someone had to do it, *and* take the money. Maybe whoever did that was supposed to bring his stuff to him and they were going to go away together."

"So he kills Perkins, and gets double-crossed by his partner," mused Loraz. "Makes more sense than anything else so far."

"Yeah, and that means whoever the killer was, they're from right here in Big Lake, or close by," said Weber. "You can bet your badge on one thing, Loraz. Whoever did it, I'm gonna own their ass!"

Weber spent most of the day retracing the dead men's route of the day before. He didn't learn anything that would indicate they were being tailed. But he *did* get a clearer picture of Phil Johnson.

Joyce Taylor, the manager at the Timber Savings Bank, frowned when Weber asked her about Johnson.

"I never felt comfortable around him, Sheriff. He was creepy is all I can say!"

"Creepy how?" Weber prompted.

"He was one of those men who made a woman feel naked every time he looked at her. He was a starer."

"Did he ever make any inappropriate remarks or do anything?"

"No, and if he ever did, I'd have called his office and reported him. He just made you feel dirty whenever he looked at you."

The bank manager was in her late 40s, short and plump. Not exactly a sex object in most men's eyes, Weber thought to himself. But he had known her for a long time and knew her to be a level headed woman. If she felt threatened in some way by Phil Johnson, Weber didn't doubt she had good reason.

The pretty young girl in the finance office at Sunrise Ski area had an entirely different opinion of Johnson.

"Oh, Phil was just your typical dirty old man," she giggled. "Harmless, but always flirting. He was always telling me he was going to come around some day and run off with me. I mean, I liked him, but run away with *him*?" She broke into another round of giggles.

Walking through the parking lot to his Bronco, Weber shook his head at the different way the two women reacted to Johnson. But, considering the source, he wasn't really all that surprised that the young woman's reaction was so opposite Joyce Taylor's. He was sure Johnson's attention was an ego boost to the woman he had just left.

Johnson's affect on women seemed to be noticeable at every stop Weber made. A cashier at the vault at Hon-Dah Casino admitted that he had asked her out on several occasions before she finally gave in. She described Johnson as "not exactly a gentleman."

When Weber pried deeper, her face colored. "Look, the guy wanted more than I was willing to give him, okay? He made a pass, I said no. We had a little wrestling match in his car. It was no big deal!"

At his final stop, at a bank in Show Low, Weber got his first solid clue in the case.

"Phil Johnson was going somewhere, and he expected to do it with money," said the branch manager.

"How do you know that?" Weber asked.

"He came in here last week and cashed in $7,000 in CDs. Converted them into international money orders."

"Did he give you any indication where he was heading?" Weber inquired. "Was it going to be a vacation?"

"No, he wasn't coming back."

"What makes you say that?"

She looked around to be sure no one was within hearing range, then leaned closer and lowered her voice.

"Sheriff, what I'm going to tell you is confidential. I could lose my job. I could lose a whole lot more. Do you understand?"

Weber nodded. "It stays right here."

She sighed sadly. "Phil Johnson was a charmer when he wanted to be," her faced turned pink. "Sheriff, I'm married. But a year or so ago my husband and I separated for a few months. Phil and I.... well, we had a little fling." She was clearly uncomfortable with the revelation.

"It only lasted a couple of weeks, and I broke it off. But he didn't want to let go. He asked me to get together a couple of times afterwards, and I kept telling him it was over. He really resented that. When he came in last week, he bragged that he had a new woman, someone much younger and prettier. He said she was coming into a lot of money and they were leaving the country. I just figured he was trying to get to me, so I ignored it until all this."

She looked at Weber with pleading eyes.

"Please, Sheriff. Danny and I patched things up between us, and he doesn't know about Phil. If he ever found out..."

Weber gave her hand a gentle squeeze.

"Like I told you, it stays here. Thanks for your help."

Driving back to Big Lake, he was convinced that the answer to the mystery of what had occurred in the canyon was directly connected to Phil Johnson and his mysterious girlfriend.

The duties of a small town sheriff don't take time out for personal tragedies or major investigations. Weber's radio crackled when he was five miles outside of Big Lake.

"Sheriff Weber? Do you read me?"

"I copy. What do you need, Robyn?" he asked the part time dispatcher.

"How far are you from the Thriftway? Ernie Miller's over there causing trouble for his ex-wife again."

"I can be there in about ten. Who's on it?"

"Tommy and Buz. But they need you. He's getting pretty wild."

"10-4, I'm on the way."

Weber hung up the mike and hit his lights and siren, picking up speed. Ernie Miller was one of the local losers the Sheriff's Office had to contend with on a regular basis. A mean-tempered bully who liked his whiskey straight and plentiful, Miller delighted in beating up anyone who crossed his path when he was hitting the bottle.

After several years of suffering abuse at his hands, his wife had finally taken their two children and moved out. Miller had appeared at the grocery store where she worked as a cashier on a number of occasions, pleading with her to return home, making threats and causing a scene. The last time, the store's manager had given Elaine Miller an ultimatum - get a court order prohibiting her estranged husband from coming around, or lose her job.

Weber only encountered one other vehicle on the road into town and was able to reach the grocery store quickly. It was obvious that the situation had escalated since Robyn's radio call. A crowd stood in the parking lot, peering in the big display windows and the automatic doors. Big Lake's two other patrol vehicles, a battered Chevrolet Caprice and an S-10 Blazer, were canted across the sidewalk. From inside, Weber heard the sounds of voices raised in conflict.

"Out of the way folks! Make a path," Weber ordered, as he plowed through the crowd to the door. The inside of the store was a mess, broken bottles and groceries littering the floor in front of the three checkout stands. Tommy Frost was leaning over a counter, using his hand to try to stem the flow from a bloody nose. His uniform shirt was ripped down the front and his right eye was rapidly turning purple. Buz Carelton was beside Tommy, his feet planted shoulder width apart, holding his .357 magnum Colt Trooper in both hands, upper torso bent forward slightly in the classic Weaver combat stance. A livid red welt covered Buz's left cheek.

The object of Buz's attention was a big, panting man, his tangled shoulder length red hair matted with perspiration. The stomach of Miller's filthy red checked flannel shirt bulged over the biker belt holding up grungy blue Levis. From thirty feet away, Weber could smell the alcohol he reeked of. He gripped a wooden baseball bat in his right hand, slapping it into the palm of the other as he taunted the deputy.

"Come on you skinny-assed piece of shit! You don't have the balls to shoot me. Come on over here and try to put your goddamned handcuffs on me! I'll bust your ugly head wide open."

Elaine Miller sat on the floor, blood seeping from a cut on her forehead. Frank Harrelson rushed up to Weber as he stepped inside.

"Do you see this mess?" he shouted. "I want that maniac arrested! Do something, Sheriff!"

Weber used one arm to brush the store manager aside as he strode up to his deputies, his boots crunching over dry dog food that had spilled out of a broken bag on the floor.

"You guys okay?"

"What's it look like, Jimmy?" asked Tommy Frost, managing to straighten up. "I think the crazy bastard broke my ribs!"

Weber faced the drunken man squarely.

"Miller, drop that club and put your hands up now!"

"Screw you, Sheriff! You stay out of this. I'm tired of this bitch's bullshit. Ain't no goddamned piece of paper going to keep me away from my woman!"

Elaine Miller flinched when he waved his hand in her direction, scooting back against the wall.

"Look Miller, I'm tired, I'm hungry and I'm pissed off! Now, you drop that damned thing or I'm going to let Buz here shoot you right in the gut. Then I'm going to take that baseball bat away from you and shove it so far up your ass you'll have to have it surgically removed!"

"This is between my wife and me! You guys just get the hell out of here!" Miller took a half step forward and Buz cocked the magnum.

"Ernie, please! You're going to get yourself killed. Would you please stop it!" Elaine Miller pleaded.

"Shut up, bitch," Miller shouted. "This is all your goddamned fault anyway. If you'd get your ass back home where it belongs none of this would have happened."

"I'm not going back there. I told you that a hundred times! It's over, Ernie."

"Shut up, you slut," Miller roared. "I'll knock your damned head off!"

He turned to shake the baseball bat in his wife's face and Weber saw his opportunity. In three fast steps he closed the distance between himself and the troublemaker and snatched the club out of his fist. Miller spun around and the sheriff swung the bat underhand hard, jabbing the grip end deep into Miller's solar plexus. The air whooshed out of the bearded man and he started to sink to his knees, his eyes rolling up in his head.

The violence seemed to trip a switch inside Weber, and the sheriff gave vent to his rage over the murders, over the sight of his battered deputies and the abused woman, and the mess Miller had made of the Thriftway. The bat clattering out of his hands, Weber grabbed Miller by the shirt and slapped him once, twice, a third time across the face. Blood and mucus flew.

"You son of a bitch! I'm sick of you beating on people around here! How does it feel? You like it? You want some more?"

Strong hands pulled the sheriff off the beaten man. Weber struggled until Buz's words penetrated the red cloud in his head.

"Come on, Jimmy. Stop it! He's had enough."

Weber let go of Miller and the man dropped to the floor, pulling himself into a fetal position.

"You can't treat me that way," he whined. "I got rights. You can't do that!"

Weber stood over the cowering man, trembling from the adrenalin rush. He took several deep breaths, fighting the urge to sink his boots into the bully's body. He shook his head and took a step back.

"Handcuff this worthless slob and get him to the jail," Weber ordered. "Call Doc Johnson to come over to the jail and check Tommy out."

He turned and headed toward the door.

"That's it, Elaine! You're through here. Get out," Harrelson ordered the woman who still crouched on the floor. "I've had it!" The man's voice was shrill.

Weber waved a hand in the direction of the store manager.

"Let it go, Frank," he said. "It's not her fault."

"I don't care, Jimmy. I want her gone!"

Weber shook his head resignedly and walked over to the man. He draped an arm over Harrelson's shoulder. The manager's normally pasty complexion was flushed with emotion and agitation.

"Look, Frank. I'm locking the guy up. He'll do at least six months for this. Give her a break, okay? She's got two kids to support."

"Forget it. I said she's fired!"

Weber took another deep breath. His heart had slowed its pounding and he suddenly felt exhausted. When he spoke, his voice was barely above a whisper. "Frank, I can't make you change your mind. I know that. But let me say this. In a night or two, it's going to be my turn to go out on patrol. Now, I bet if I were to drive out by Nelson's Point, I'd find a few neckers parked out there. It's a real romantic spot, don't you think?"

The manager's face turned a deeper crimson.

"And you know what, Frank? I bet if I looked real close, I might find a married middle aged businessman playing nasty with a certain younger female employee who just got out of high school last summer. Now, if I were to see anything that looked suspicious, like let's say, a breach of the public decency, I just might have to arrest that businessman, Frank. And call his wife to come down and bail him out. Now Frank, don't you agree with me that would really suck? Especially when that guy's wife's daddy owns the store he manages? You following me on this, Frank?"

By then, Harrelson's face was pale. He seemed to shrink in stature and lose the fire in his demeanor.

"I knew a nice guy like you would understand how Elaine needs this job, and would get off her back," Weber said. He dropped his arm from Harrelson's shoulder and headed for the door. "Have a good day, Frank," he said over his shoulder. "And you might want to call a stock boy to clean up a little in here. This place is a mess."

Chapter 5

Weber wanted desperately to go home and lie down on his bed for a year or two. But when he left the Thriftway, he drove to Debbie's house. Marsha Perry met him at the door.

"Hi, handsome! Come on in."

Weber gave Marsha a tired smile and went into the living room. Debbie sat on the sofa, a glass of soda in her hand. Weber bent and kissed her cheek.

"How you doing, Princess?"

Debbie gave him a wan smile. "I'm okay, Jimmy. Marsha has been playing mother hen. How are *you*?"

"I'm fine, kid. It's just been a rough day."

Marsha sighed dramatically and rolled her eyes. "Some things never change. *I* didn't get a kiss!"

Since they were little girls, Debbie and Marsha had been best friends, though they were complete opposites. While Debbie was slender, well built, blonde and beautiful, Marsha was short, plump, and dark haired. As a teenager, Debbie's personality ranged through the full spectrum, from moody to vivacious, on an hourly basis, while Marsha was ever the same smiling, bubbly girl.

Weber had always suspected that Marsha had attached herself to Debbie early on in an effort to ride her coattails to social activities and friends she knew she would never acquire on her own. Not that Marsha hadn't been a loyal friend to Debbie. They were closer than sisters, and Marsha had helped Debbie through the loss of her parents, had encouraged and supported her when she started college, and had even stepped in to prepare Mike's meals on evenings when Debbie had late classes.

Weber and Marsha had always had a teasing, comfortable relationship. The little girl crush she had on her best friend's big brother had matured into a comfortable adult friendship. Marsha owned an antique shop called Yesterdays, and spent hours scouring towns throughout the region in search of merchandise, hitting every yard sale, flea market and junk shop for miles around. Her efforts proved successful; her old pieces of furniture, Depression glassware, and other reminders of the past were popular with the tourists, and she had built a successful business that provided her with a comfortable income.

"Hell, Marsha, last time I kissed you, you pinched my butt and I had bruises for weeks," Weber declared. No matter how down and melancholy a person was, Marsha was always able to coax a smile out of them.

"Just testing those buns to see if they were ripe yet, big boy," she leered. "I'm a comparison shopper, you know."

"Any word on anything yet," Debbie interrupted.

"Some things have developed, Debbie. But first, let me ask you a question. How well did you know Phil Johnson?"

Debbie's eyebrows wrinkled. "What do you mean?"

"Well, I've talked to several women who knew him, and I came away with the opinion he was something of a ladies' man."

"Yeah, right," Marsha snorted. "More like he *thought* he was a ladies man! In his dreams, maybe!"

"What do you mean?" Weber asked.

"Oh, you know Marsha," Debbie explained. "She's always writing checks she can't cash. Phil was here one day and she started flirting with him. He took her up on it and she got offended."

"That's not the way it was, Debbie! You know that," Marsha cried. "He was a dog!"

She turned to Weber. "Yeah, I was teasing him. You know how I am, Jimmy. That's just my way! But later he got me alone in the kitchen and I thought I was going to have to deck him to make him leave me alone."

"He came on to you?"

"Came on's not the word for it. He tried to grab a quick feel, and I pushed his hand away. Next thing I knew, he was all over me! Slobbering and pawing... what a creep!"

"*Honestly,* Marsha," Debbie exclaimed. "I think you're making a mountain out of a mole hill! I knew Phil pretty well, and he was *never* anything but a perfect gentleman to me. I think you just bit off more than you could chew that time. Stop being so dramatic!"

It was obvious Debbie's words stung her friend. Marsha's face colored.

"Well, I don't know what to tell you," Weber interrupted, hoping to avoid a confrontation between the two friends. "But it looks like Phil may have been involved in the hijacking in some way, Debbie."

Her jaw dropped. "Involved? What are you saying, Jimmy?"

"Debbie, the bullet that killed Mike was from Phil's gun. And tests show he'd fired a gun sometime before he was killed."

"I can't believe that! Phil and Mike were friends. It's impossible!"

"I know. But there's more. I found two packed suitcases at his cabin. And last week he cashed in a bunch of certificates of deposit and bragged he was going away."

Debbie was speechless.

"Holy shit," Marsha said. "Then who killed Phil? And where did the money go?"

"We're still working on that," Weber replied.

"He was our friend," Debbie said in disbelief. "My God, he ate at our table. He went with us when we went to Las Vegas last month! I'm sorry, I just can't believe it."

The ringing of the telephone interrupted her. Marsha answered it and then held out the receiver to Weber.

"It's your office."

"Jimmy? Agent Parks from the FBI is here," said Robyn.

"Tell him I'm on the way," Weber replied.

Special Agent Larry Parks could have stepped right out of a recruiting poster for the Federal Bureau of Investigation. Average height, average build, wearing a dark blue suit with light blue shirt, and darker tie. His brown hair was trimmed close.

"I thought I'd come up and see what we could find out from this end," Parks said. "Have you learned anything yet that might help us get to the bottom of this thing?"

Weber sank into his chair. "You heard that Mike Perkins was killed by Johnson's gun?"

Parks nodded. "I talked to Loraz first thing this morning. He thinks Johnson set your brother- in-law up, and then got himself double-crossed for his trouble. What do you think?"

"Could be," Weber agreed. "I know he was bragging about running off with some woman, and he cashed in some savings and bought travelers checks. And when I went through his place, I found two packed suitcases."

"Any idea who the woman might be?" asked Parks.

Weber shook his head. "From what I've been able to gather so far, it looks like he made a move on every woman he ever met, with the exception of my sister, who swears he was always a perfect gentleman around her."

"Makes sense," Parks observed. "If he was planning this thing all along, he wouldn't want to do anything to rile Perkins up or to rock the boat."

"Okay, I've told you mine, you tell me yours," Weber said. Most local law enforcement in the United States is under the impression, sometimes for good reason, that the Federal Bureau of Investigation is more than willing to pump them for information, but is less forthcoming with what they learn about a case. Many police officers believe the FBI is happy to let them do all the grunt work, then step in to claim the credit when a case is solved. Weber didn't have enough experience working with the feds to have formed an opinion one way or the other.

Parks held up a hand and shook his head with a smile.

"Hold on there, hoss! Don't go getting your defenses up on me. I told you I'm going to work *with* you to solve this thing. There won't be any inter-agency rivalries around here, okay? Whoever killed them boys needs to be caught up with. I don't give a darn about the glory. I just don't like back shooters and robbers. So let's not get off on the wrong foot, okay?"

Weber nodded. "Sorry, it's been a bad couple of days."

"No offense taken," Parks assured him. "We'll get 'em, Sheriff."

He opened a manila folder that was sitting on the floor at his feet.

"I ran a complete background check on both guards, just to see what we could dig up. You already know Perkins. Small town kid, wannabe cop, seems as honest as the day is long. I don't think there's anything there. But Johnson, he's another story. Retired Army, joined in 1970, just as Vietnam was winding down. Got out as an E-6. I'd have thought after 20 years, he'd make more rank than that, and it looks like he did. But he got himself busted three different times. Last time they pulled the plug on him and made him take his retirement."

"Busted? What for?"

"Guess," Parks grinned slyly. He read from his notes. "Let's see... the first time was in 1978, he lost a stripe and forfeited 30 days pay when he got himself accused of getting rough with a girl who was married to one of the enlisted men in his platoon. That was at Fort Campbell, Kentucky. The lady claimed he tried to get into her pants and she wasn't interested.

The record doesn't say he actually *tried* to rape her, but it must have come pretty close."

Weber thought about what the cashier at the casino had said. *"He wanted more than I was willing to give. We had a little wrestling match..."*

"Let's see here," Parks continued. "In 1986 Johnson was stationed in Germany. He apparently got involved with another married woman, this time the wife of an officer. He got charged with conduct unbecoming a non-commissioned officer, and got a reduction in rank and they shipped him back to the States." He looked up. "I kind of think they wanted to cover up the whole mess. Dirty laundry, don't you know?"

Weber nodded.

"Okay then, the last time, and the most serious one. According to the record, a young WAC at Fort Jackson, South Carolina accused Johnson of date rape. She claimed they had been at a party and she got drunk and passed out in a spare bedroom. When she woke up, he was on top of her."

Weber whistled. "He did get around, didn't he?"

"Seems he just couldn't keep that old zipper up," Parks agreed. "Guy must have had a case of raging hormones that would read right off the Richter scale."

Weber related what he had learned from the women he had interviewed that day, along with the information Marsha Perry had given him.

"Well, I think we both know what we need to do," Parks said. "If we find this woman Johnson was supposed to be running away with, we may just find out what happened down there in that canyon."

"That's assuming Johnson was actually tied into this thing," Weber said for the sake of argument. "I guess there could always be some other explanation."

Parks shook his head in denial. "No Sheriff, it's like my old Daddy used to always say... when a guy lets the little head do his thinking for him, trouble will always follow. And from what we know about Phil Johnson, that little head was in total control all of his life. She's out there. And she's the key to solving this case."

Weber insisted Agent Parks bunk in his spare bedroom. After stowing his overnight bag at Weber's cabin, they drove to the Roundup Steakhouse, Big Lake's most popular eating spot. On weekends the place was always packed, but on this midweek evening, they had their choice of tables. Once the pretty waitress in cowgirl outfit and boots seated them and took their drink order, Parks looked around him. The rough cedar walls were decorated with western memorabilia, old saddles, steer horns, and branding irons. Several old Winchester rifles hung from hooks high up on the walls.

"Man, I'd love to get my hands on one of those old lever actions," Parks said. "I collect old guns. If the Bureau would let me, I'd carry an old long barreled six shooter as my duty weapon."

"I like the modern stuff more," Weber said. "I tend to favor a Colt semi-auto."

".45?"

"Yeah, I've got three. And a ten millimeter."

"Hard to beat," Parks agreed. "I wish they'd let us carry them. I just don't like the double action Glocks and Sigs. They're good guns, but I'm a traditionalist."

The waitress returned with their drinks. Weber had ordered his standard Coors, while Parks had a Screwdriver. The FBI man held up his glass.

"Here's to you, Sheriff. I know this case is personal to you. But like I said, we'll get 'em."

Weber tilted the mouth of his bottle toward Parks, then drank.

The steaks were perfect, thick slabs of medium-rare beef cooked over a mesquite fire, accompanied by heaping mounds of wedge cut potatoes, ranch beans, and fresh baked bread. Parks obviously savored every bite.

"Man, you can't get food like this at those chain restaurants in the big city," he complained. "I think I've died and gone to heaven!"

Their pleasant meal was interrupted when a big mountain man wearing camouflage fatigues stormed up to the table.

"What the hell you doing thumping my baby brother around and locking him up?" demanded the intruder in a loud voice.

"Evening, Jesse," Weber said. "Go away."

The giant leaned thick arms on the tabletop. Hair the texture of steel wool poked out of the open collar of his shirt.

"You got no right, Jim Weber! I hear you beat him with a baseball bat!"

Weber sighed and pushed back his chair. "Look, Jesse, your brother tore up the Thriftway, he smacked his wife around, he roughed up two of my deputies, and he defied a court order. I told him to drop that baseball bat and he wouldn't do it. My deputies would have been within their rights to shoot him."

The big man scowled and opened his mouth to speak. Weber cut him off.

"You're right, I did take that baseball bat away from him and used it on him. Then I slapped the shit out of him. And do you know what he did, Jesse? He curled up on the floor like a baby and whined like the coward he is. Now, I'm sitting here with my friend having a quiet meal. If you want to file a charge against me, go see Judge Ryman in the morning. Or go home and call the mayor and the town council members. But get your ugly face out of my sight before I drag your sorry ass back there into the kitchen and have Andy throw you on the grill!"

The bearded man leaned into Weber's face and sneered down at the sheriff. "You haven't heard the last of this, Weber! I'm going to stomp your ass one of these days. You're gonna pay for this. Just you wait and see!" His hand strayed dangerously close to the steak knife laying on Weber's plate as he spoke.

Before the sheriff could respond, the big man's eyes bulged and he sucked in his breath sharply. Larry Parks dug the barrel of his semi-automatic pistol deeper into Jesse Miller's groin.

"Mister, you just threatened a police officer in the presence of an FBI agent. Now, it's a big world, and I imagine there's some ugly old gal out there somewhere who might even be hard up enough to jump between the sheets with your sorry ass some day. It's gonna be kind of hard to satisfy her with your scrotum gone, don't you think? How about you take the man's advice and get the hell out of here?"

There's something about cold steel against warm testicles that calms down even the most hostile aggressor. Jesse straightened up cautiously, raised his hands and backed away from the table.

"You have yourself a nice night, sport," Parks called after him. "Go home and brush your teeth. I bet there's a lonely sheep out there some place."

Weber fought to keep from laughing out loud as Jesse fled the room.

"You do have a way about you, Agent Parks! I think I'm going to like working with you."

Parks grinned back as he slid his pistol away.

"Friend of yours, Sheriff?"

"Local bad ass. One of those militia types. His brother got out of hand this afternoon and took on a couple of my deputies."

"You actually smack him with a baseball bat?" Parks asked.

"Well hell, Parks! Softball season's five months away! A man's got to keep in shape."

Both lawmen chuckled at the black humor.

On the drive back to Weber's cabin, he lifted the microphone from its hanger on the dashboard. "Just need to check in," he told Parks. "Big Lake, this is Unit One. Copy?"

In a moment the voice of Dolan Reed, Weber's fourth deputy, came back over the air.

"10-4, Sheriff. What can I do for you?"

"Just checking in before I head home. Anything going on?"

"Oh, Ernie Miller's raising hell, threatening to call in the FBI if we don't let him out. Says we violated his civil rights."

Parks grinned across the Bronco's cab at Weber. "Those boys are real big on their rights, aren't they?"

Weber laughed, then keyed the mike. "Who's on patrol?"

"Tommy was supposed to be, until midnight, then Chad was going to take over. But the doc wanted him to get some rest after today, so Chad came in early."

The sound of loud cursing came over the radio, accompanied by banging.

"What's that?" Weber asked with a frown.

"Miller, going off still. You can hear him way out here in the front."

"What say we bring him his FBI agent?" Parks suggested with an evil grin.

"You want to?" Weber replied, laughing.

"Let's do it!"

Weber hung up the microphone and stepped on the gas.

The Big Lake jail's two holding cells were located in the rear of the Sheriff's Office, at the end of a long hall and through the booking room. From the front reception area, they could hear the sound of Miller ranting. Weber led Parks down the hall and into the cell area. Though the whiskey he had consumed had worn off, Ernie Miller's disposition hadn't improved a bit. He was so busy with his tantrum that it took him several minutes to notice their presence.

"Who the hell are you?" he demanded of Parks.

"Special Agent Parks, Federal Bureau of Investigation," replied Parks, holding his identification case up to the bars. "You wanted to see me?"

"You're damned right I did! This Nazi assaulted me and then locked me up in direct violation of my civil rights! Now your ass is gonna hang, Weber!"

"He assaulted you?" Parks asked in indignation. "Sheriff, did you assault this man?"

"Well, I guess I did, sort of." Weber said, looking chastised.

"You're damned right you did," Miller retorted. "He hit me with a baseball bat!"

"A baseball bat? You're kidding me, right?" Parks asked, appalled.

"He had it first, I just took it away from him," Weber whined.

"That's it," Parks declared. "Sheriff, you're relieved of duty! Give me your weapon and badge. Deputy, open this cell." he ordered Dolan Reed.

Weber hung his head and stripped off his gun belt and laid it on a chair behind him. He slowly unpinned his badge and placed it gently in Parks' outstretched palm. A confused Deputy Reed unlocked the cell door.

Grinning widely, Miller started out the cell door. Parks placed a hand on his chest and halted him. "Whoa, fella, where do you think you're going?"

Confusion clouded Miller's face. "You're letting me out, ain't ya?"

"I can't let you out," Parks explained. "That's going to take a court order. And since we're talking a violation of your civil rights, it has to be a federal judge that releases you. Probably can't get one up here for at least a week or two. No... I'm locking Sheriff Weber up with you. Anyone who would treat a citizen like you the way he did belongs in a cell."

"Well, put him in the other cell!" Miller demanded.

"Can't do that," Parks said, shaking his head. "We have to keep that cell open for female or juvenile prisoners. Federal law, you know. I'm afraid you boys are just gong to have to be roommates until I can get a federal judge to come up here."

"No way!" protested Miller. "Don't lock that psycho son of a bitch in here with me. He'll kill me!"

"He'd better not," warned Parks. "Killing a federal witness is a crime! He'll get at least five years." He took Weber by the arm and began to guide him into the cell.

"Forget it," pleaded Miller. "I don't want him in here! Get him out of here."

"You sure?" Parks asked. "I really think we need to get him off the street, not only to protect your rights, but the rights of all those other citizens out there."

Miller backed to the rear of his cell, his hands held out in front of himself, palms up, as if to ward off a blow. His quavering voice begged Parks to change his mind. "No, no... I don't want to file no charge. I don't want no judge. I just want him out of here!'

"Well..... that's your right too, I guess. You sure?" Parks asked a final time. "I could leave my name in case you change your mind."

"No, get away," pleaded Miller.

The three lawmen had to choke back laughter until they were outside on the sidewalk in front of the Sheriff's Office. Once in the cold night air, they doubled over with convulsions and roared. Finally, Weber wiped tears from his eyes and managed to straighten up, until he saw Dolan's hands upraised in supplication. At the sight, another wave of hysteria overtook him.

Chapter 6

When Parks came out of Weber's guest bedroom Wednesday morning, the blue suit had been replaced by Levis and a blue denim shirt. The FBI agent wore western boots instead of the low cut shoes he had worn the day before.

"My, my... aren't we looking western today," Weber teased.

"Well, when in Rome and all that," Parks retorted. "What's on the agenda today?"

"We need to find out who this woman was Johnson was seeing," Weber said. "And maybe find out if he told anyone around here where he might have been heading off to."

"Doesn't seem like a man planning to go on the run would leave that much of a trail," Parks suggested.

"Maybe so," Weber admitted. "But he seemed to be a bit of a braggart. You never know."

"So where do we start?"

"I think we're going to go see a lady," Weber said as they climbed into the Bronco.

Miss Lucy Washburn met them at the door of her home. "Jim Weber, you keep coming around here like this and people are going to start talking," she warned.

Weber smiled and introduced Larry Parks.

"Well, he sure don't look like no J. Edgar Hoover to me," Miss Lucy said. "Not that that's all bad. Old J. Edgar was pretty fat and homely, as I recall."

"Miss Lucy," Weber began, "We're still trying to learn more about Phil Johnson. I know you told me a little about him before, but is there anything else you can remember?"

"What, you think I'm getting senile, Jim Weber? I'll tell you something, young man. I may be crippled up, but my mind is as sharp as a tack! There's not much that gets by me."

"I don't doubt that," Weber acknowledged.

"Miss Washburn, did you ever talk much to Johnson?" Parks asked.

"No I did *not*, young man! I do not choose to squander my time talking to drunkards. And the man was a drunkard!"

"We understand that," Weber said. "But he rented your cabin for almost three years. Surely you must know something that could help us."

"I know he was a drunkard," Miss Lucy retorted. "I know he was a tomcat. Always had some woman or other down there at that cabin. Remember what I told you, Sheriff. Booze, greed or sex. Sometimes all three!"

"Yes ma'am," Weber replied. "You said something about women. Did he ever mention women to you?"

Miss Lucy's icy glare could have frozen water. "Certainly not! I'm a lady and I wouldn't have tolerated such talk."

"Then how...."

"Follow me," Miss Lucy said and rolled her wheelchair into the big kitchen. She rolled herself up to a broad, low mounted window facing down the hill. A pair of ten power Bushnell binoculars sat on a stand next to the window.

"Why, Miss Lucy! You're a Peeping Tom!" Weber exclaimed.

"Watch your mouth, Jim Weber! I'm a bird watcher. It's not my fault that from here I can see my cabin so clearly. Besides... a person has a right to know what's going on right on their own property!"

Weber was tempted to tell her that when she rented the cabin, it became Johnson's property, at least for the duration of the lease. But he held his tongue. Instead he picked up the binoculars and peered through them. Phil Johnson's cabin leapt into sharp focus through the thin screen of trees. He realized it would have been easy for the elderly woman to spy on Johnson's comings and goings.

"Did you recognize any of these women who came to visit Johnson?" he asked.

"Might have, might not have," Miss Lucy replied.

"What does that mean?" asked the sheriff.

"It means I'm not in the habit of discussing other people's sins. Lord knows I have enough of my own to cope with!"

"Miss Washburn, this is a police investigation," Parks explained patiently. "Two men are dead. A lot of money is missing."

"I know that, you Junior G-Man," Miss Lucy shot back. "Jesus, it's my legs that are crippled, I keep telling you! My brain is in fine shape!"

"Then help us," Weber pleaded. "Who all did you see down there, Miss Lucy?"

She shook her head in exasperation. "I'll never get over how dumb women can be over some no account man! And it seems the worse they are, the more women flock after them! Maybe that's why you're still single, Jim Weber. You're just too good for your own sake."

Weber grinned. "Could be, Miss Lucy. Or it could be that I've just never met a woman who could hold a candle to you."

She slapped his hand. "Don't sweet talk me, young man! I may be crippled, but I'm not senile!"

Parks smiled kindly at the woman in the wheelchair. "Miss Washburn, you may be handicapped, but you're obviously one of the sharpest women around Big Lake."

"I'm not *handicapped*," she declared, "I'm *crippled*! If I was *handicapped*, some sanctimonious fool would be on the boob tube holding a telethon for me and interrupting my afternoon talk shows!"

She backed herself away from the window and turned to face the two lawmen.

"Candy Phillips from the bakery was a regular for a while. That was months ago. Haven't seen her there lately. Margo Prestwick was around off and on. She's the heavyset blonde who works at the Antler Inn."

Weber pulled a small notebook from his shirt pocket and jotted down the names.

"Then there was Betty Zalenski, the woman who rents my cabin down on Lakeview Road. Her husband ran off a year or so ago. Can't say she traded up when she got involved with Johnson."

"Anyone else," Weber asked.

"There were two or three others. I don't know them all. Oh... I *do* remember another. Elaine Miller from the Thriftway."

Weber almost dropped his pen, but managed to hide his surprise. He couldn't picture Elaine Miller having an affair. But he had been a policeman long enough to know that everyone had their own closet full of dusty skeletons.

"Anyone else?"

"Like I said, there were some I didn't know."

"Thank you, Miss Lucy," Weber said. "We really appreciate your help."

She saw them to the door, and as they were walking down the ramp from the porch, Miss Lucy looked Weber in the eye and spoke again.

"Sheriff, you're a man. Don't judge those women too harshly. Sometimes the nights get long, and a woman just aches to be held...."

She suddenly realized she may have been revealing something about her own needs and clamped her lips in a thin line. Weber looked into her eyes a long moment and she slowly closed the door.

A towheaded little boy with a runny nose answered the door of the dilapidated single-wide mobile home, and led them into a sparsely furnished but clean living room. A band-aid closed the abrasion on Elaine Miller's forehead. She shooed the boy away and he ran into a bedroom, where the sound of cartoons came from a television. Weber wasn't sure how to begin interrogating the woman. While he was sympathetic to the problems she had experienced, he needed answers.

"How's Ernie?" she asked after Weber and Parks were seated.

"He's hung over," Weber said. "He'll see the judge this morning and he'll get a trial date. I imagine he'll make bail."

"Jesse will bail him out," Elaine said. "What if he comes around here?"

"I think even he's smart enough not to do that," Weber said. "But I'll have a deputy keep an eye on the place for you. And if he does show up, don't let him in. Call us right away."

She nodded and Weber leaned forward.

"Elaine, I have to ask you about something. Something personal. I don't want to put you on the spot, but I need to know about you and Phil Johnson."

A small vein jumped in her neck and she paled visibly. Her mouth worked a couple of times, but nothing came out. Her expression reminded Weber of a deer caught in a car's headlights. Then she started to shake her head in denial.

"Whatever you tell us stays right here." Weber assured her. "But I have to know."

Elaine closed her eyes for a moment, and when she opened them again, a look of defeat took over her face and she sighed heavily.

"It was stupid, Sheriff. I knew it when it started, but I was just so...." She shook her head and looked toward the ceiling. "I just got so tired of Ernie's abuse. Always cussing me out, beating on me. It gets old."

Weber and Parks remained silent, letting her tell it her own way.

"Anyway," she continued, "Phil came into the store all the time. I had moved out... this was the first time, back last summer. I was living with my sister out on Porcupine Trail."

She reached for a can of Pepsi on the coffee table and took a long drink.

"You have to understand, Sheriff. I dropped out of school in the tenth grade when I got pregnant with Carrie. I never had much in the way of job skills. And over at the Thriftway, you can't get more than minimum wage and thirty hours a week, unless you're willing to play footsie with Frank Harrelson. Phil was a gentleman at first. And let's be honest, that Army pension sure looked good to me at that point."

Weber wondered how many desperate women were willing to trade their self-esteem for something they called security.

"So anyway... we got together a few times. I was trying to convince myself Phil Johnson was my knight in shining armor. It didn't take long to learn he was like every other man. I wanted to believe there was a future for us, but that future only lasted until the next woman caught his eye."

She shuddered. "Like I said, I knew going in it was stupid. But what can I say?'

She shook her hear ruefully. "I will say one thing for Phil Johnson though."

"What's that," Weber asked.

"When he wanted to be, he was one hell of a lover! He taught me things about myself I wouldn't have believed possible!"

"Elaine... I have to ask. When it ended, were you upset?"

She looked at him and smiled sadly. "Sheriff, one man or another has been upsetting me all my life. From my drunken Daddy to my drunken husband to Phil Johnson. What you really want to know is, did I kill him? No I didn't. If I was the killing type, Ernie Miller would have been buried a long time ago! Sure, Phil used me. But I used him, too. At least he didn't slam me into the wall when he was done."

Back in the Bronco, Parks shook his head as Weber backed out of the driveway.

"You know, Sheriff, it's a good thing someone killed Johnson. Otherwise I think some husband would have shot him dead for sure."

"Well, one thing's for sure," Weber replied. "I don't know if it was a jealous husband who killed him, but Phil Johnson is going to leave an empty spot in a lot of ladies' lives."

"Yeah, but it sounds like at least a few husbands will be sleeping easier around here," Parks observed.

The multi-faceted reactions of women to Phil Johnson didn't disappoint Weber and Parks as they talked to the other women Miss Lucy had referred to. While it appeared Johnson definitely had a way with women, a darker side to his personality also came through.

"I really fell for him," Candy Phillips admitted ruefully. "He'd been around the world, served in Vietnam, he knew how to treat a woman like a lady. Always opening doors for me, sending me flowers..." she sighed, "Not like the local yokels around here who think the zenith of chivalry is not spitting their tobacco juice on your living room carpet! I mean, face it Sheriff, my life is cinnamon rolls and glazed donuts. Phil added a new dimension."

"How long were you seeing him?" Weber asked.

Candy absently wiped a towel across the top of a glass display case filled with pastries.

"Let's see, we started out last February. I remember that our first date was Valentine's Day. He brought me a dozen red roses. No one has ever bought me roses before." There was a wistfulness to her as she recalled her relationship with Johnson.

"Where did it go from there?" Parks asked.

Candy smiled conspiratorially. "To bed. Real fast!"

She didn't seem the least bit embarrassed by the confession.

"Phil didn't believe in wasting any time when it came to the chase," she said. "I've never been one to jump into bed with a man on the first date. But I did with Phil Johnson."

"How long did the affair last?" Weber asked.

"Until I walked in and caught him in bed with Laura Wilson. I remember the exact date. June 15th."

"Laura Wilson?" Weber asked incredulously. "Roger Wilson's wife?"

Candy nodded her head with a sad smile. "The one and only."

Roger Wilson owned High Country Realty, one of the most successful real estate agencies in that part of the state. He was rich, handsome, and could have his choice of any woman, Weber thought. His wife Laura was a stunning redhead, with the supple body of a movie star, and perfect skin that Weber himself had fantasized touching more than once. The couple always seemed blissfully happy, and lived in a magnificent log home perched on the top of Saddleback Mountain, with a commanding view of the valley and lake below. Weber couldn't picture Laura Wilson being attracted to a man like Phil Johnson.

"How did that come about?" Weber asked, trying not to let his surprise show through in his voice.

Candy shook her head and sighed again. "Oh, I think I knew all along that Phil was seeing other women. He told me going in that he wasn't ready to be tied down. But like they say, love is blind. One day last June he told me he had to go over to Flagstaff for the day. I decided to go over to his place and surprise him. I had this vision of him walking in and finding a home cooked meal on the table and me waiting in something flimsy." Again the rueful smile.

"Well, there was a vision, all right! When I got there, I saw Phil's Jeep in the driveway, which surprised me, because he said he'd be out of town. But then I figured he might have gone with someone else. I let myself in and heard noise coming from the bedroom. He and Laura were really having themselves a good time. It took them a while to even notice I was there."

"What did you do?" inquired Parks.

"Oh, I didn't make a scene, though I was pretty crushed. They finally saw me, Laura ran into the bedroom and Phil acted like I was a cat burglar or something. He got all mad and told me to get out and not come back."

The faint smile was replaced by a film of tears in her eyes, but Candy blinked them away.

"Was that the end of it?" Weber asked. "Did you see him after that?"

She shook her head. "It didn't work that way with Phil. Once he was done with you and had found a new toy, it was over. I called a time or two, but he just hung up on me. I guess you could say he threw me away like day old bread."

"How'd you feel about that?" Weber asked.

He knew it was a stupid question even as he asked it. Candy didn't spare him any embarrassment.

"Well gee, Sheriff, I was just tickled pink! What do you think? I was humiliated, I was hurt, I was angry!"

"Candy," Weber asked hesitantly, "how angry? Angry enough to kill him?"

She threw back her head and laughed, and when she spoke, her words surprised the sheriff.

"Oh, I probably was mad enough to kill. But not Phil Johnson. Like I said, I knew what he was deep inside myself. No, if I was going to kill anyone, it would have been Laura Wilson. I mean, she's got it all... beauty, money, a fancy house and expensive cars, a rich hunk for a husband. Why did she have to take what I had too? If you find her some day with a bread knife stuck in her back, come see me. But I didn't kill Phil Johnson."

Margo Prestwick was an overweight bleached blonde with a bad attitude. When they walked into the Antler Inn, she was drawing a glass of beer from a tap behind the bar. When the glass was full, she slapped it down in front of a skinny cowboy perched on a stool, sloshing beer onto the bar. She moved away with no attempt to clean up the spill. Weber figured most customers at the Antler Inn weren't all that finicky about neatness anyway.

The tavern was housed in a square cinder block building situated two miles outside of Big Lake, on the road to Round Valley. The scarred wooden bar ran along one wall, vinyl coated booths patched with silver duct tape taking up the other side. A pool table with torn felt sat toward the rear of the room, near a jukebox and cigarette machine. The decor leaned heavily toward neon beer signs and pinup calendars, all floating in a thick haze of blue cigarette smoke. The place wasn't going to win any Beautiful Business awards from the Chamber of Commerce. The clientele tended to be a rough and tumble lot, and Weber's deputies responded to the establishment on a regular basis, to break up fights between the patrons.

"What can I get you?" Margo asked indifferently when she walked to the end of the bar where the sheriff and Parks stood.

"Margo, this is Special Agent Parks with the FBI office in Phoenix," Weber said and nodded at Parks.

The barmaid rolled her eyes disdainfully. "Okay, I'm impressed. What do you want?"

"We'd like to talk to you about Phil Johnson," said Weber. "I'm sure you know by now that he and Mike Perkins were killed Monday."

"Yeah, so I heard," Margo sneered. "Big loss."

"Miss Prestwick, we understand you had some sort of a relationship with Johnson at one time," Parks said. "We need to know about that."

Margo's laugh wasn't friendly. "*Miss* Prestwick? Damn, Sheriff, where'd you get this character? Next thing I know, he'll be kissing my hand. Well, you can kiss my ass while you're at it! I don't have anything to say to you about Phil Johnson or anyone else!"

"Come on, Margo," Weber said. "There's no need for the attitude, okay? We're just trying to get to the bottom of this case. We're talking to anyone who knew Phil Johnson."

"Yeah? Well, hire me a lawyer and arrest me if you want to talk to me! I don't tell cops nothing!"

Weber didn't try to hide his irritation. He grabbed the woman's fleshy arm as she turned away. "Listen, Margo, we can do this a couple of ways. I don't care. The easy way is, you answer our questions and we go away. The hard way is, I post a deputy outside the door and we bust every drunk staggering out of here. Meanwhile I make a call to the State Liquor Board and they send an agent up here to talk to you about how important it is to check everyone's identification to be sure they're of age when they drink in here. Oh, and did I mention how I go through all the incident reports my deputies have filed about this place, and how I take them to the Town Council to have this dive considered a public nuisance and the doors locked?"

"Screw you, Weber! I told you I got nothing to say," she snarled and tried to shake her arm out of Weber's grip.

"There some kind of problem here?" asked a burly truck driver, as he came around the corner of the bar.

"That's entirely up to you, buddy," Parks said, stepping into his path. "How do you feel about jail food? Because if you don't get back to your Coors and mind your own business, you're going to spend the next six months bunking with a nasty con named Sweaty Eddie, who is gonna think you're pretty cute. Especially when I tell him you're funny that way."

The trucker shrugged his shoulders and did an about face. "I don't need this shit!"

"Okay everybody, listen up!" Weber shouted above the music. "This place is now closed down by order of the Big Lake Sheriff's Department! You've all got two minutes to clear out. Anyone who doesn't go peacefully can go to jail. It's your choice!"

There were curses and grumbling from the patrons, but they picked up their change and started for the door.

"Jesus Christ, Sheriff," Margo cried, "You'll ruin my business!"

"Like I said, there are two ways to do this, Margo. What's it going to be?"

"Oh shit!" she said in surrender, "What do you want to know?"

"How long were you seeing Johnson?"

"I don't know. A few months."

"When did it end?"

"It ended when I got tired of his bullshit," she replied, massaging her arm where the sheriff's fingers had dug into the fat. "Back in October or September. I don't know for sure."

"Why did he drop you?"

"What makes you think he dumped me? Maybe I dumped him!"

"That wasn't his style," Weber told her. "He got tired of his women and went on to someone else."

"Okay, God damn it! He dumped me, so what? One day he just stopped coming in. Stopped calling. Whenever I called him, he hung up on me. The next thing I knew he was in here with some skinny little skirt from over in Nutrioso. I was tempted to mop up the floor with her, but she wasn't worth it. Neither was he."

"When's the last time you saw him?" Weber asked.

"I don't know. Some time around Thanksgiving, I think. He was in here and got into a shoving match with Ernie Miller."

Weber glanced in Parks' direction. "Ernie Miller? What happened between them?"

"Who knows? Just drunks acting tough, I guess. I was about ready to call the cops when Jesse broke it up. He and Phil sat down in that corner booth over there and seemed to settle whatever it was all about."

"Margo, did you kill Phil Johnson and Mike Perkins?" Weber asked.

"Yeah, right," she snorted, and laughed, her foul breath making Weber blink. "If I did, you think I'd still be pouring beer for the slugs in this dump? I'd be on a beach somewhere spending all that money!"

"You take me to all the best places, Sheriff," observed Parks as they were driving away from the Antler Inn. "What's next, the Salvation Army soup kitchen?"

"It's a small town," Weber replied, shaking his head. "We only have one homeless guy, and he's probably up at the ski slope, taking the day off."

"So what do you make of the thing with Ernie Miller?"

"Well, it could be like Margo said," Weber suggested. "Just two drunks trying each other on for size."

"Yeah. Or maybe Miller found out Johnson was humping his old lady and took offense. I've never believed much in coincidence."

"Yeah," Weber replied. "You think our killer is sitting right there in my jail even as we speak?"

"Well, only one way to find out. Hit it, Bubba."

Weber turned the Bronco in the direction of town and stepped on the gas.

Mary Caitlin told them Deputy Chad Summers had taken Ernie Miller over to the courthouse for his arraignment on various charges, including assault, two counts of assaulting a police officer, disorderly conduct, violating a court order, and resisting arrest. Chad was just pulling out of the parking lot of Big Lake's tiny court building when they arrived.

"He's gone," the deputy informed them. "His brother posted his bail and took off with him."

"Seems Jesse spends a lot of time and energy handling Ernie's problems," Parks observed. "Any idea where they went?"

"Jesse's a survivalist," Weber told him. "One of those home grown militia types who thinks the government is corrupt and out to get him. He's got a compound outside of town a ways. You know the type of place I mean.... pit bulls and barbed wire."

"Well hell, Sheriff Weber, of course the government's corrupt!" Parks said. "How else could it afford to pay me that princely salary I live on? But they're not out to get him. They're too busy trying to stick it to *you*. That's really why I'm here!"

"No use heading out there right now," Weber decided. "Let's finish up with the women on our list first. The Zalenski woman's place is just around the corner."

"Let's see," Parks said, weighing the alternatives, "hairy legged survivalists with green teeth or lonely women. Yep, I'm on your side. Let's go see the lady."

Weber grinned at him as he turned onto Lakeview Road. "Obviously you've never gotten a good look at the legs on some of the grizzly bears that pass for women around here!"

Betty Zalenski's cabin was a pretty redwood structure, small but neatly kept. She seemed to expect Weber to show up on her doorstep sooner or later. Without a word of greeting, she turned and led them into her kitchen, where they sat at the table. She didn't offer them coffee or even wait to learn why they were there.

"I didn't kill Phil Johnson or Debbie's husband," she said before Weber could get started.

Her direct approach took Weber by surprise.

"I went to school with Debbie and Mike, I liked them both. I'd never do anything to hurt either one of them."

The sheriff noticed she didn't say she wouldn't have hurt Johnson. But before he could put the thought into words, Betty surprised him again by taking the initiative.

"I won't lie to you, Sheriff. I would have killed Phil in a heartbeat if I'd have had the chance."

"That's not the smartest thing you could tell us right now," Parks suggested.

Betty was a tall, thin woman. Small breasts, narrow hips. She wasn't exceptionally pretty, plain was probably the most generous description anyone would ever have for her. She reached a hand up and toyed absently with her lifeless brown hair.

"Like I said, I won't lie to you. I wanted Phil Johnson dead. He didn't deserve to live. But I didn't kill him. Oh, I thought about it! One night I even sat outside his cabin with my ex-husband's old deer rifle, waiting for him to come home so I could blow his head off. But he never showed up."

"Murder's pretty serious business, Betty," Weber said. "Why did you want to kill Phil Johnson?"

She looked the sheriff directly in the eye and said "Because he raped me."

There was silence in the little kitchen for several seconds. Finally Betty Zalenski looked toward the ceiling, took a deep breath and continued.

"I met Phil a while after my husband left. I waitress over at the Roundup on weekends when they're short handed. He came in a lot and we got to talking. He asked me out, but I wasn't in any frame of mind to get involved with anyone at that time. He kept coming around. He was always a gentleman, but persistent. Finally I gave in and we went over to Pinetop for dinner one night. When he brought me home, he tried to get romantic, and I told him no. I could tell he didn't like it much, but he didn't push the issue. In fact, the next day he called to apologize."

"What happened then?" Weber asked.

"Well, like I said, he was a gentleman... and persistent. I figured he got the message when I turned him down the first time. After a week or two, we went out again. That time he was on perfect behavior. He walked me back to my door, shook my hand and walked away. Same thing the next two or three times. I guess I let my guard down. And he was just waiting for the opportunity."

She recounted the story like she was telling them the plot of a movie she'd watched on television the night before. No emotion, no recrimination, just the facts.

"Anyway, I'd been up to his cabin a couple of times. And he was always careful not to make even the slightest move out of line. But the last time, I'd gone up to return a couple of books I'd borrowed from him. I was running late and had to get to the Roundup. Phil said I could use his bedroom to change into my uniform, and I figured "no problem." I trusted him by then."

"That's when he raped you?" Weber prompted.

"Yes. I had just gotten undressed when he came in and started to put his hands all over me. I told him no and pushed him away, but that only seemed to turn him on more. The next thing I knew, he was shoving me onto the bed...."

Again, she looked steadily into Weber's eyes. No wavering, no plea for pity or sympathy. Just the facts.

"Why didn't you report it?" Weber asked her.

"I don't know," she shrugged. "Maybe because I was ashamed. Maybe because I figured people would see it as a newly divorced woman getting undressed at a man's place and figure she just asked for it. Small town, small minds."

Weber reached across the table and took her hand in his. She didn't pull back. But there was no response either.

"I wouldn't have thought that way, Betty."

She smiled a tiny smile and gently pulled her hand free.

"No, Sheriff, but let me ask you this. Would you have been standing in line to ask me out once the word got around town?"

He had no answer for her.

As they were leaving, Betty surprised Weber a final time.

"You want to know something ironic, Sheriff?"

"What's that, Betty?"

"I had already made up my mind to sleep with him. In fact, I was going to ask him that night if I could come over and spend the night after work. All he had to do was wait a little bit longer."

Chapter 7

The Wilson home sat at the end of a long driveway and was screened from the road by a thick stand of pine and spruce trees. Parks whistled when the sprawling two story house came into view. Most of the front was glass, affording generous views of the valley, town, and lake that sat at the bottom of the mountain.

Parks whistled. "Somebody's making money," he observed.

"Roger Wilson is Big Lake's golden boy," Weber told him. "Born with a silver spoon in his mouth, worked hard to turn it into gold. His old man was some kind of retired investment banker who dropped out early to live the good life. His first car was a Porsche, when he turned sixteen. High school and college football star, real estate speculator, land developer, and all around success story. Rumor has it he'll make a bid for state senator in the next election."

"What about the loving wife?" Parks asked.

"His perfect partner. Drop dead gorgeous. Daddy's a rich homebuilder from down in Tucson. Went to finishing school, did some acting before Roger came along and saved her from the evils of Hollywood. A real knockout."

"So why would she be involved with a loser like Johnson?"

Weber shook his head. "Partner, if you ever figure out what goes on in women's minds, throw that tin badge of yours away and hit the talk show circuit. You'll make a zillion bucks!"

Parks laughed out loud as Weber shut the Bronco off in front of the house. A white Ford Expedition and a red Jeep Wrangler sat in the driveway. The door to a three car garage was closed. The place was silent. Weber noted that there wasn't any smoke coming from either of the house's two chimneys.

"Wonder if anyone's home?"

"Let me show you a trick they taught us in FBI school," Parks said. He stepped past Weber and pressed the button for the doorbell. From inside came the faint sound of chimes. After half a minute, Parks rang the bell again. Still no response.

"Well, sometimes it works and sometimes it doesn't," Parks shrugged.

"Let's roll by the office and give Loraz a call," Weber suggested. "See what he's got by now. We can stop back here later."

"Sure you don't want me to kick in the door?" Parks asked, playfully raising a size ten boot. "We learned that in FBI school too."

"Get in the car, class clown," Weber ordered.

It took several minutes to make a connection with Loraz, and when he came on the line, Weber switched the call to a speaker phone.

"I hope you guys have good news for me," Loraz said, exasperated. "we've about hit a brick wall down here."

"Well, it seems Phil Johnson had a real knack for getting women," Weber reported, "married or otherwise."

"Yeah, that seems to come up here too," Loraz told them. "I talked to a bank manager in Globe where they made stops regularly. She said she had to discipline two different tellers for acting like horny schoolgirls around the guy."

"We need to learn his secret," Parks put in.

"I did turn up one thing," Loraz continued. "He apparently bragged to a woman at one of the banks they picked up at that he was about to come into some heavy money. No specifics, just that he wouldn't be spending his time driving an armored car very much longer."

Weber related what they had learned from their investigation so far, and they all seemed in agreement on several points - that Johnson had probably killed Mike Perkins, that he had in turn been killed by a person or persons acting as accomplices, and that the identity of the unknown killer(s) most likely was to be found in or around Big Lake. They ended the conversation with an agreement to hold another telephone conference in two days, unless something pertinent came up before then.

"Well, now what do you suggest?" Weber asked.

"How about we have a visit with your sister?" Parks suggested. "With what we've picked up, maybe it'll trip a switch in her head someplace and she'll remember something her husband might have said.... maybe another woman who Johnson was messing around with and told Mike about. Or maybe he bragged to Mike about his upcoming trip. It's worth a shot. What do you think?"

"Okay." Weber was reluctant to interview Debbie, with all she'd been through. "But if she starts getting too upset, we back off, okay? The funeral is tomorrow and she's dealing with a lot right now."

"I understand that," Parks said. "Last thing I want to do is add to her grief. Good thing for her she's got a brother like you to lean on."

Mary Caitlin stopped them as they were heading for the door. "Jimmy, I just had a call from Margo Prestwick over at the Antler Inn. She wants you to call her right away."

"This out of a woman who doesn't talk to cops," Weber said, turning back into his office and picking up the telephone.

Margo answered on the third ring. The sound of the jukebox was loud in the background. As Weber identified himself, drunken laughter came over the line. The Antler Inn was busy.

"Listen, you prick, Ernie Miller was in here a little while ago," she said, obviously agitated. "He was all pissed off because he thought I was cooperating with you, and talking about him and Johnson getting into that fight here. You leave me out of this, you hear me? I don't need any grief from that clown!"

"Just relax, Margo. How could he have known we talked?" Weber asked.

"Jesus Christ! You can't sneeze in this hick town without three people saying 'God bless'! You really can't be that stupid, are you? You creeps come in here and hassle me in front of everyone, and wonder how word got out?" Margo said in a shrill voice.

"What did he say, exactly?" Weber asked.

"I don't know *exactly*," Margo shouted. "Something about don't cross him or I'd wind up just as dead as Phil Johnson. To keep my mouth shut or else."

Weber couldn't imagine that loud mouth shut for long, but it was a pleasant thought.

"Anything else?"

"Yeah, he said Johnson and him just had a little disagreement. That it was no big deal and that they were buddies. Said Johnson even had a thing going with his sister Tina. Look Sheriff, I don't want any part of that crazy bunch. I'll go out to my car some night, and that'll be it! Boom!"

Weber knew the Millers' had a reputation that intimidated a lot of people around Big Lake.

"Okay, Margo. Thanks. I'll be sure your name doesn't come up."

"It better not, or I'll come down to that jail and kick your ass myself, badge or no badge!"

Weber hung up while she was still screaming into the telephone. He decided that he and Parks needed to track down Ernie Miller as soon as possible.

Debbie answered their knock at her door wearing a black dress, her eyes red and puffy.

"You okay, kid?" Weber asked, concerned.

She gave him a big hug and wiped her eyes with the back of a hand and smiled weakly.

"I'm all right, Jimmy. Just trying on my dress for tomorrow. I just..." her voice broke.

Weber pulled her close again. "Hey, Princess, we're going to get through this, okay?"

She nodded and pulled away, then turned to Parks. "I'm sorry, you must be Agent Parks?"

"Yea ma'am, Larry Parks. I'm so sorry for your loss."

"Please, come in. I'm forgetting my manners." Debbie led them to the living room, where Weber dropped into a chair and Parks took the end of the sofa. Debbie sat at the other end of the sofa and turned toward them. "I finally convinced Marsha to go over to her store and check on things," she told Weber. "Heather has been filling in for her."

"Mrs. Perkins, I know this is a terrible time for you. But I need to ask you some questions," Parks began.

"Call me Debbie. I don't know what I can tell you that I haven't already told my brother, but go ahead." Debbie's eyes were vacant, her voice dead.

Parks pulled out a small notebook and looked toward Weber, who nodded for him to continue.

"Now Debbie, are you sure that Mike didn't mention anything out of the ordinary?" Maybe a car that had been following them, or someone watching them when they made their stops? Some citizen who tried to strike up a conversation. *Anything* at all?"

"No," Debbie shook her head. "Jimmy's asked me that two or three times already. Mike didn't say anything about anyone acting suspicious. If he had noticed anything, he'd have reported it and the company would have sent a tail car."

"Debbie...." Parks seemed hesitant to bring up the subject, but plunged ahead. "you know that we suspect Phil Johnson of being a part of all this. All the evidence we have so far seems to indicate that Johnson shot your husband and then whoever he was working with shot him. It seems like he was involved with a lot of different women. You were close to him, what can you tell us about him?"

Debbie shook her head slowly. "I still find it hard to believe. I mean, Phil was our friend! He ate here with us, we went on a weekend trip to Las Vegas together, he and Mike were friends. I just don't...." her voice trailed off.

"Sometimes we think we know someone, and then we find out that they're an entirely different person," Parks offered.

"Yes," Debbie said with a nod. "I guess I can't argue with the evidence you have, but it just seems impossible, knowing Phil the way I did."

"Debbie.... like I said, Phil was a ladies man.... did he ever..."

"Come on to me? No way!" She shook her head vehemently. "I've already told Jimmy, he was always a gentleman to me. There was never the slightest hint of a pass or anything inappropriate." Her voice had risen and she seemed to catch herself. "God, I sound like I'm defending the man who may have killed my husband! But I keep thinking there must be some other explanation. I keep thinking I'll wake up and this will all have been a nightmare."

She reached for a pack of cigarettes on the coffee table, shook one out and lit it. Inhaling deeply, she blew a cloud of smoke toward the ceiling. Then she turned back to Parks.

"When we were in Vegas, the three of us shared a double room to save on expenses. Mike and Phil were down in the casino and I had gone up to take a nap because we'd stayed up late the night before. I couldn't get to sleep and decided to take a shower. Phil came in to get some more money he'd left in his suitcase just as I was getting out of the shower. He walked in on me naked. I think he was more embarrassed than I was! I mean, he was mortified! He kept apologizing; he even went down and apologized to Mike. Does that sound like a man who was chasing every girl he could and then killed his friend?"

"No," Parks admitted, and changed his line of questioning. "What about any girlfriends? Did he ever bring anyone around? Ever talk about a girlfriend?"

"Oh, I'm not saying he wasn't popular with the ladies," Debbie acknowledged. "He had several casual acquaintances and he probably even mentioned one or two of them. The only one I can really remember meeting was Tina Miller. He brought her when we all went on a picnic one

Sunday last summer. And I think that's only because I kept wondering why he was with *her*. I mean, she'd be pretty enough if she ever cleaned herself up, I guess. But that family...ugh!"

Weber and Parks exchanged subtle glances.

"Tell me about that. How did they seem together?"

"Gosh.... just normal, I guess. I mean, she's as wacky as her brothers, she spent most of the day talking about how the government is oppressing all of us, and we had to be ready to fight back. I remember Mike told her she was exaggerating and she really went ballistic on him! Called him a lackey and said it was people like him that deserved to be slaves to the system. Phil seemed embarrassed by the way she acted. I never saw them together after that, though I think Mike mentioned that Phil had talked about seeing her occasionally."

"Did Johnson say anything about going on a trip?" Parks asked.

"No. He took his vacation time back in July. I remember, because he went back east somewhere to visit his brother. I can't see how he could have gotten any more time off. The company was real stingy about time off."

"You said you went to Vegas. Did Johnson spend a lot of money there?"

"Oh, I think we all did," Debbie said. "Doesn't everyone in Vegas? The bright lights, the sound of the slot machines. It's easy to get carried away."

Parks raised his eyebrows. "Did Johnson get carried away?"

"No, not really. He probably spent three or four hundred dollars. But he wasn't exactly a pauper, you know. He had his job and his military retirement. He had more to spend than Mike and I did. With me going to school and all, we were stretched pretty thin most of the time."

Weber could see that the interview was beginning to wear on his sister, and he was relieved when the door opened and Marsha swept in on a blast of cold air. "Hi Jimmy! Who's the hunk?"

Debbie shook her head in wonderment at her friend. "Marsha, have you no shame? My God!"

Marsha shook her head and grinned at Parks. "What can I say, someone has to be the town vamp, might as well be me!"

Parks grinned self-consciously and flipped his notebook closed.

"We'll get out of your way," Weber said. "I'll pick you up first thing in the morning, okay?"

Debbie saw them to the door and patted her brother on the back.

"Thanks Jimmy. I don't know how I could get through all this without you."

"Sure you don't want to come back to my place for the night?" he asked her.

As she shook her head, Marsha piped up "Can I, if she won't?"

As the two policemen stepped out into the evening air, Debbie was shushing her friend. Opening the door of his Bronco, Weber was glad Debbie had Marsha to help her through this crisis.

Chapter 8

Big Lake's non-denominational church was housed in an imposing cedar and stone building with long stained glass windows high on the side walls. The church was filled to capacity for Mike Perkins' funeral. Weber sat in the front pew with Debbie. Mike's sister Rachel, a stunning raven haired woman who worked as an insurance agent in Phoenix, was on her other side. Their father had disappeared in search of greener pastures when Mike was a baby and their mother was an invalid confined to a nursing home in Phoenix. Pete and Mary Caitlin shared the seat with them. The plain gunmetal grey casket was surrounded by flower arrangements. Parks sat in the back of the church.

As the minister read Mike's eulogy, Debbie squeezed Weber's hand and sobbed quietly. Weber's own eyes were wet as the service closed and the Big Lake Sheriff's Office deputies and uniformed representatives of Copperstate Armored Transport moved silently down the aisle of the church with the casket. Weber and his group led the mourners outside. The crowd stood silently as Mike's body was loaded into the waiting hearse. In the back of the limousine for the ride to the cemetery, both Debbie and Rachel broke down. Weber did his best to console the grieving women and they managed to gain some degree of poise before the big car stopped near the grave site.

The cold winter day chilled everyone as the minister recited a short prayer, then Debbie stepped forward and carefully laid a single red rose on the casket. She bent to kiss the cold metal, then stepped away, her eyes lingering for one last look. Rachel held her arm as Weber, then his deputies, stepped forward and each executed a smart salute. From a small grove of spruce trees, a lone bugler began playing *Taps*, the melancholy notes drifting over the cemetery.

As the crowd began to disperse, the grave diggers waited discreetly to begin the interment. Weber paused for a final moment with his friend. "Mike, I promise you, I'll take good care of Debbie. And I promise you,

I'll find out who did this and I'll avenge you." Grief and rage battled inside of him as he walked to the waiting limousine.

There was a small get-together at Debbie's house following the funeral. Parks had excused himself, saying he had to call his office in Phoenix and file a report on his investigation thus far. Weber did his best to run interference for Debbie when he saw that the constant loving pats and kind words of friends and community members were beginning to wear her down. Rachel seemed to hold up better, smiling bravely and moving about the house to make sure guests were fed and attended to.

Finally Weber convinced Debbie to go to her bedroom and rest. When the last visitor left, Rachel moved about the living room, picking up glasses, wiping off end tables, and trying to keep herself busy. Weber had shed his suit jacket and tie and leaned in the doorway watching her.

"You okay, Rachel?"

She smiled weakly at Weber and nodded her head.

"I'm okay, Jimmy. How are *you*?"

He shook his head. "I don't know. I'm just so damned *angry*. I want to find whoever did this and tear them to pieces!"

Rachel came closer and placed a gentle hand on his cheek. Her eyes were sad when she looked into his.

"I know, Jimmy. Me too. I try to be strong, but I...." her voice broke.

Weber nodded in understanding, and she looked up into his eyes a moment longer, then stepped into his arms. Weber pulled her tight against him as her body began to shake and the tears came. They stood together like that for a long time, taking comfort in each other's arms and seeking emotional support in the closeness. Eventually, Rachel pulled slightly away, then looked back into Weber's eyes. She tilted her head upward and kissed him.

Weber tasted her lipstick as their lips met, then her mouth opened slightly and her tongue slipped inside his. Weber ran his hands down her back and she pressed her body into his, moaning slightly. After a long moment, they reluctantly broke contact.

"This isn't a good idea," Weber said.

"It's okay, Jimmy," she reassured him. "It's *okay*."

Rachel Perkins and Weber had always had a friendly relationship, and he couldn't deny his attraction to the woman. Whenever she came to Big Lake to visit her brother, she and Weber had enjoyed harmless flirting, but it had never gone any further. Debbie and Mike had tried to fix them up on several occasions, but the logistics of time and distance had always seemed to get in the way. Now he felt like a traitor, coming on to Mike's sister just hours after the funeral.

"Jimmy.... I think you're a wonderful guy. I know you loved my brother. I know how much this hurts you too. But one doesn't have anything to do with the other."

"I know, Rachel.... I guess it's just the timing."

She kissed him again, this time with less passion, but a deeper tenderness.

"Give a girl a rain check?"

"Yeah," Weber breathed. "Count on it."

Parks was waiting in Weber's office when he arrived. He had commandeered a desk and was just finishing his paperwork. He looked up at his new friend. "How you doing, pal?"

Weber let out a long breath and ran his hands through his hair. "It's hard. Debbie's asleep. Thought I'd see what's going on here."

Robyn, the petite dark haired dispatcher, looked up from the radio console. "Town's quiet, Jimmy. It's like everyone took a day off from needing the police for the funeral."

"Yeah, well, we need the break. Tomorrow the skiers will hit town and it'll get crazy," Weber predicted.

"You up for a try at Ernie Miller?" Parks asked.

Weber shrugged his shoulders. "Can't hurt. I need to go by my place and change clothes first."

"It's almost five," Parks said, looking at his watch. "Think maybe he'll be in one of the local bars?"

"Could be," Weber said. "I don't think it's a good idea to show up at his brother's place when it's almost dark. But we'll cruise the local hangouts and see if we can spot him."

A half hour later, back in uniform, Weber parked the Bronco in front of the Tip-Top Saloon, and surveyed the parking lot.

"What does Miller drive?" asked Parks.

"Usually an old white over orange Scout. But that crowd has a bunch of old beaters. Hard to tell."

They walked into the bar. It was a rustic place, decorated with mounted deer and elk heads and the crowd was friendlier than the one at the Antler Inn. No one had seen either Ernie Miller or his brother Jesse.

From the Tip-Top, the lawmen drove to Buck's Tavern, another mountain bar that catered to locals. The bartender told them that Ernie had been in earlier in the day, but wasn't drinking hard, and seemed amicable. They avoided the tourist oriented nightspots and concentrated on the working class saloons. No one else reported seeing Miller, and they finally gave up after four or five stops.

Darkness comes early to the mountains in winter, and it had turned into a black night. Weber told Parks he had promised to stay at Debbie's that night, and the sheriff dropped him off at his cabin with a promise to pick him up in the morning.

Debbie, Rachel and Marsha had eaten an early dinner and were sitting around the living room reminiscing about Mike.

"You really don't have to spend the night," Debbie assured her brother. "I'm in good hands."

"I know. Maybe I just need the company," he admitted.

"You mean you left that good looking FBI guy all alone?" Marsha demanded to know. "If I hadn't promised my Mom I'd be home tonight, I'd go keep his back warm!"

"Still living at home?" Weber teased, knowing that Marsha shared a house with her elderly mother to care for the woman. "No wonder you're not barefoot and pregnant!"

"See here, Sheriff," Marsha said haughtily. "I'll have you know that I depend on my personality for birth control!"

Her friendly banter never failed to lighten any situation, even one as grim as this. Weber thought once again how lucky his sister was to have such a loyal friend.

The day had been long, and by nine o'clock, Marsha excused herself. "Mom's been pretty much alone the last couple of days. I'd better get going," she said. "But you call me if you need anything at all, I'll be right here," she promised Debbie.

Debbie had taken a sleeping pill and her eyelids were heavy. Shortly after Marsha left, Weber convinced her to go to bed. Rachel excused herself, saying she was going to take a long shower, and Weber turned off the lamps and sat in the darkened living room. He stared into the fireplace, his memories of Mike dancing in the flames. He grew weary and stretched out on the sofa, pulling a comforter over himself.

Weber was beginning to drowse when a slight noise caused him to open his eyes. Rachel stood over him in a terrycloth robe. Her long black hair, still damp from the shower, was pulled over one shoulder. Even without makeup, she was beautiful. She smiled down at Weber and bent to run a hand along his chin, his beard stubble rough under her gentle fingers.

"I'm thinking there's a rain check I really need to cash," she told him.

Weber pulled the comforter back and Rachel hesitated only a brief moment, then shrugged off the robe and snuggled down beside him.

A wicked snowstorm blew in overnight and the temperature plunged. Sometime during the night, Weber got up to throw another log on the fire and stepped to the window to peer out at the storm. The moaning of the wind echoed his own lonely feelings. He stood a long time staring out into the darkness before he shivered with the chill and returned to the warmth of the sofa and the woman who slept there. Rachel murmured softly in her sleep when Weber snuggled against her, then her deep breathing resumed.

By morning, heavy snow blanketed the trees, branches sagging under the added weight. When Weber and Parks drove out to Jesse Miller's compound, the sheriff had to use four wheel drive as soon as they turned off the paved road. They bumped nearly three miles down a gravel secondary road before turning off onto an even rougher track, a narrow one lane path that wound through the timber. The Bronco's big tires threw white plumes into the air as they churned a path through the fresh snow, the transfer case growling in low range four wheel drive. Finally they came to a stop in front of a locked gate.

"We there?" Parks asked. "I don't see a thing."

"You will," Weber said.

For several minutes, the only sound was the ticking of the engine as it cooled. Then a rumble broke the stillness and two four wheeled off-road vehicles came out of the trees.

"Keep your hands in plain sight," Weber warned the FBI agent as they climbed out of the Bronco. "These nuts are liable to shoot both of us if you give them a reason."

The quad-runners came to a skidding stop on the other side of the gate. Both drivers wore white military style snow parkas, gloves, and face masks. A black AR-15 semi-automatic assault rifle was mounted across the handle bars of each machine. The drivers cut their engines and climbed off their machines, dragging their rifles clear with them. Parks tensed beside him and Weber spoke softly.

"Easy. This is all show on their part. Keep your hands out in the open."

Pulling his face mask off, Jesse Miller cradled his weapon and stared levelly at the lawmen. "What do you want, Sheriff?"

"Jesse. You remember Agent Parks."

Jesse turned hard eyes on the agent. "Last time we met, you jammed a pistol in my nuts and acted like a big man. Had a lot of funny things to say. Got any jokes today, funny man?"

Parks grinned back at him. "What can I say, Jesse? I'm just a funny fellow. I always thought I missed my calling. Should have gone into standup comedy."

Unmoved by the humor, Jesse glared back at Parks.

"Jesse, we're looking for Ernie." Weber said, "Is he here?"

"You got a warrant, Sheriff? This is private property."

"No, no warrant. I just want to talk to him."

"Then I guess you're out of luck," Jesse said.

"I hear Ernie and Phil Johnson had a fight a while back. What was that all about?" Weber asked.

Jesse shifted the rifle in his arm and shook his head.

"Wasn't anything, Sheriff. Just a little roughhousing between friends who had a couple drinks. If you're thinking Ernie killed those guys, you're wrong."

"Maybe yes, maybe no," Weber replied. "We need to talk to him to hear his side of things. If he's innocent, he's got nothing to worry about."

The second driver had been waiting a few steps back, holding the AR-15 casually in both hands. Now the figure stormed forward.

"Ernie never killed no one! You just get the hell out of here. We're free citizens and this is our land. You got no right here!"

"That you Tina?" Weber asked. "How you doing?"

Tina Miller jerked her face mask up. Her features were contorted with rage. When she spoke again, her voice was shrill.

"You heard me, get the hell off our land!"

"Calm down, girl," Jesse told his sister. "They're not going to come in here. If they do, they know we'll defend ourselves, as is our right as free Americans."

"This isn't Waco," Parks said. "We just want to talk to Ernie."

Jesse shook his head. "Can't help you, funny man. Come back with a warrant."

"Look Miller, this doesn't have to be a big thing," Parks said, and took a step forward. Immediately both rifle barrels were trained on the lawmen. Parks froze. The AR-15 is the civilian version of the military's M-16, capable of spewing thirty 5.56mm rounds out of its magazine as fast as the trigger is pulled.

"Try it, you Nazi," hissed Tina. "Give me a reason!"

"Easy now, everybody," Weber said calmly, slowly raising his hands, palms forward. "Parks, back off."

Parks had his hands up too. "Okay, you win," he said. "I'm taking a step backward now. No problem."

The rifles stayed on them. "I think you boys best get out of here now," Jesse said.

"Okay, we're going," Weber told him. "But we're still going to need to talk to Ernie. You tell him that for me, Jesse."

"I told you, Ernie didn't kill anyone," Tina screamed at them. "Phil loved me and I loved him. Ernie didn't have nothing to do with those guys getting killed!"

"Tina, shut up," ordered Jesse sharply. Her jaw worked, but she bit off whatever she was going to say next. The barrel of the gun she held on them never wavered.

"Go on, Weber! Get the hell out of here," Jesse said. "If I talk to Ernie, I'll tell him you want to see him. But I want you off our land!"

The lawmen cautiously climbed into the Bronco. Weber started it, reversed and made a u-turn, heading back down the rutted path that served as a driveway.

"You okay?" the sheriff asked once they were clear of the compound.

"Yeah," Parks said, his voice echoing his relief. "Man, those people are crazy as a bunch of loons! I thought for sure that silly bitch was going to shoot me!"

"She would have," Weber assured him. "I imagine killing an FBI agent would rate right up there on the list of achievements with that bunch. She'd probably get a merit badge or something."

Parks shook his head in disbelief. "You know, you read about people like that all the time. I've heard the briefings on Waco and Ruby Ridge. But Jesus Christ! When you're looking down the barrel of one of those guns, it all becomes real."

Weber fought the wheel as they bounced over a rough spot and lurched onto the gravel road. Neither man spoke again until they were back on the paved road. Then Parks broke the silence.

"Let's play 'what if.'"

"Okay."

"It must take a lot of money to play soldier like that all day and pay for those toys of theirs. Where do the Millers get their money?"

"Good question. I know they cut some timber from time to time. But none of them holds regular jobs, that I know of."

"A lot of these militia and survivalist types have been connected to bank robberies, even armored car hijackings across the country," Parks said. "You don't suppose that bunch back there cozied up to Johnson to set him up, do you?"

"Anything's possible," Weber replied. "I think it's a scenario we need to look at real close."

A gust of cold wind rocked the Bronco and Parks shivered in spite of the heater.

"Well, when we look, let's look at a distance, okay? I don't want to get too close to those psychos again any time soon!"

From Jesse Miller's compound, Weber drove back to the Wilson house on Saddleback Mountain. This time Laura Wilson answered the door. Weber had never met a man who was immune to the combination of Laura's good looks and perfect figure. Parks didn't seem to be any exception. He obviously had trouble keeping his eyes off Laura's cleavage, generously displayed in a black silk blouse with the top three buttons open. There was no mistaking the fact that she wasn't wearing a bra. She wore matching black silk lounging pants, and was barefoot.

"Hello?" Laura said, looking puzzled as to why two law officers stood on her doorstep at mid-morning, with the snow falling around them.

"Sheriff Weber," Weber introduced himself, though he was sure the redhead knew who he was. "This is Agent Parks from the FBI office in Phoenix."

A slight smile replaced the look of uncertainty on her face. "You must be collecting for the Policemen's Association or something! Let me get my checkbook." She started to turn away.

"Laura? Mrs. Wilson?" She paused when Weber spoke. "We're not here to raise money. We need to talk to you. May we come in?"

She hesitated, puzzled again, then seemed to remember her manners.

"Of course! I'm sorry, please come in." She opened the door wider and stepped back to admit them.

The foyer of the Wilson home was as large as Weber's living room. Laura Wilson led them into a huge great room, where floor to ceiling windows greeted them with a panoramic view that Weber figured was worth a million dollars in itself. A fire crackled in a massive stone fireplace on one wall. To either side of the fireplace, glass fronted gun cabinets held well oiled and polished long guns. Weber recognized several Weatherby and Browning shotguns and high powered rifles. He wondered if Roger Wilson was a hunter, or if the expensive firearms collection was just another possession to be put on display by the wealthy developer.

"Does your husband hunt?" Weber asked.

"What? Oh, those," Laura dismissed the gun cabinets with a wave of her hand. "A couple of years ago we went to Alaska on some sort of safari thing. It was awful! Mosquitoes and flies everywhere. Roger decided as long as he was going to go there, he might as well have the best. Roger demands the best in everything," she explained.

Weber wasn't sure if the statement and the look that accompanied it were meant as a challenge, or a declaration of her own value. He stepped away from the gun cabinets. Laura gestured at a leather covered sofa, part of a five piece set that the sheriff imagined must have cost as much as he earned in several months. He sat down, while Parks seated himself on a matching recliner. Laura positioned herself between them, perching on a heavy oak coffee table.

"Is your husband home?" Weber asked.

Again the vague look of confusion. Weber wondered if Laura Wilson was under the influence of some type of drug that might explain her apparent state of mild confusion. The thought also crossed his mind that Laura might be playing the part of the beautiful but dumb leading lady in her own private drama. He remembered that she had been an actress, even if for only a brief time. She hadn't answered his question.

"Roger? Is he home today?"

Comprehension seemed to come into her eyes. "No. I'm sorry. He's been out of town all week. I expect him back sometime today, if the storm doesn't close the roads."

"Laura," Weber said. "You're the person we really needed to talk to. It's about you and Phil Johnson."

If she was alarmed to learn that the sheriff knew about her lover, Laura Wilson managed to cover it well. Weber thought that she might have had a good future in Hollywood if she hadn't decided to marry Roger Wilson. Laura favored him with a smile.

"What do you want to know about Phil?"

"You know he was murdered Monday?"

The actress was still in character. Again the vague look, a small wrinkling of her eyebrows.

"No, I hadn't heard. But I've been gone myself. I was down in Tucson, visiting my parents."

The news that her former lover was dead didn't seem to upset Laura Wilson. It appeared to have little effect on her at all. Weber could just as easily have been telling her about a famine in Africa, or a bake sale at the church.

"Laura.... we know you had a relationship with Johnson. We need to know about it."

"What do you need to know?" She blinked big green eyes at the sheriff innocently. Weber found himself growing impatient with her act. He reminded himself not to let his irritation show. Whenever an interrogator allowed a subject to gain any degree of control over him, the interview was lost.

"How did you get involved with Phil Johnson?"

Laura stretched languidly, her full breasts straining the thin silk of her blouse. Weber forced himself to keep his eyes on her face.

"Oh, it was just one of those silly things," she said casually. "I was bored, Roger was spending a lot of time out of town on some project or other. I bumped into Phil someplace and we started talking. One thing led to another." She didn't seem to be experiencing any great degree of regret over her infidelity.

"How long were you involved with him?"

"With Phil? I wouldn't really call it involvement." She seemed to become a little more alert. "It was just sex, that's all. You know... a diversion."

"A diversion?" Weber repeated.

Laura Wilson smiled and looked Weber in the eye. "I got lonely. It happens sometimes to a girl when she's left alone all the time." Her eyes narrowed slightly and Weber wondered if he saw a hint of invitation when she spoke again. "I get lonely a lot, Sheriff."

Weber was relieved when Parks spoke. "Mrs. Wilson, how long did you see Johnson?"

She shrugged her shoulders absently. "It only went on for a little while. We made it two or three times, I guess."

"Did it end when Candy Phillips walked in and caught you?" Weber asked.

"Candy Phillips? Oh...from the bakery!" She shook her head. "God, that was embarrassing! Phil got really mad."

"Was that when it ended?" Weber asked again.

"No." She tilted her head back to expose an ivory throat and shook her head, as if trying to remember what had ended the affair. When she looked back at him, a new Laura Wilson was in her place. Like an actress stepping into a new role, Laura had transformed in an instant into another woman, becoming animated and involved in the conversation.

"No, it ended when Roger came home early one weekend and caught us." She laughed gaily. "He wanted to surprise me. He was the one who got the surprise!"

"What happened then?" Parks asked.

"Oh, Roger went crazy. He started screaming and throwing things. Called me a slut and a whore. About what you'd expect under the circumstances, I suppose. Can you blame him?"

Weber decided he couldn't, but he remained silent. Laura waited for him to speak.

Again, Parks broke the silence. "What happened then, between your husband and Phil Johnson?"

Laura giggled. "Did you ever realize how ridiculously vulnerable a man looks when he's standing there naked in front of a cuckolded husband? Phil and I seemed to have a knack for getting caught. First Candy Phillips, and then Roger. Talk about bad luck!"

"Did they get into a fight?" Parks asked.

"Oh, you'd have thought they were going to go at it, but nothing happened. Roger likes to act macho once in a while, but he's basically a coward. He waited until Phil left, then took it out on me."

"How did he do that?" Parks asked.

"Oh, let's see...." she ticked off Roger Wilson's revenge on her fingers, as if recalling events from a recent vacation. "Typical Roger tantrum. He busted up some furniture, punched me around a little bit and threw me across the room a few times. Broke a rib and bruised me up some." She looked up. "Roger is always very careful when he bruises me. He always hits me on the body, never on the face or arms so nothing ever shows. Can't cause a scandal, you know."

"He beat you?" Weber asked. So much for the perfect marriage! The sheriff knew that spousal abuse happened in even the most stable appearing marriages, but Laura's revelation took him by surprise. He would never have thought of rich, successful Roger Wilson, Big Lake's own aristocrat, as a wife beater.

Laura shrugged it off. "What can I say, Sheriff? Like I said, I get bored sometimes. Then I have to pay the price."

"Why haven't you reported it? Or left him?"

"Oh, he's got enough to deal with already, Sheriff. His last couple of projects have gone sour on him and money is tight. And after all, I bring it on myself."

Weber couldn't comprehend the indifference she seemed to show to her marriage, her infidelity, or to the abuse she suffered.

"So, your husband and Johnson? They didn't fight?" Parks asked.

"No. Oh, Roger said he was going to kill Phil, but that's just Roger."

"Do you think he would be capable of killing someone?" Parks asked.

She shrugged again. "Who knows? When he gets home, you can ask him."

Driving away from the big house with its nasty little secrets, Weber pondered the question of whether or not Roger Wilson could be a killer. The picture didn't fit the public image of the man. But the conversation with Laura Wilson had taught him that things weren't always what they appeared to be.

"But don't forget," he reminded himself, *"She's an actress. How much of what we just saw and heard was real, and how much was just part of the act?"*

Chapter 9

The wind that had blown in the storm overnight had calmed, but the snowfall had increased steadily all day, big puffy white flakes that turned the landscape surreal and piled up a foot deep on the sidewalks of Big Lake. Shopkeepers were busy shoveling the fronts of their stores clear as Weber and Parks rode slowly down Main Street. Weber parked in front of the Frontier Cafe and they entered, taking a rear booth.

Annie Conners, a heavyset, cheerful woman with a mop of curly black hair, poured their coffee and placed plastic folders with the restaurant's typewritten menus in front of them. Both lawmen ordered the lunch special, chicken fried steak, and Weber leaned back against the vinyl booth. He started to say something when his expression darkened and he cursed under his breath.

The cause of the sheriff's sudden mood swing was a short, portly man in a blue nylon parka and ski cap who waddled up to the booth and scowled down at Weber through beady eyes. He was trailed by a conservatively dressed, pale, thin woman of about thirty-five, her dark hair pulled back in a severe bun and with the vaguest hint of a mustache.

"Sheriff, we need to talk!"

"Afternoon, Mayor. Say hello to Special Agent Larry Parks of the FBI. Parks, this is Chet Wingate, our Mayor." He didn't introduce the woman, which earned him a dark look from her.

Wingate nodded curtly to Parks and turned back to Weber, dismissing the FBI agent. "I am not happy about this incident with Ernie Miller the other day. Neither, I might add, is Councilwoman Smith-Abbott!"

Weber shrugged. "I see Jesse has been on the telephone."

"That's another thing," the mayor said, his voice rising. "Jesse Miller is a respectable citizen of this town, a taxpayer and a..."

"And a contributor to your election campaign, not to mention a steady customer of your hardware store," Weber interrupted.

"Now see here, I will not tolerate your insolence!" declared the mayor, in a voice loud enough to make heads turn at nearby tables. He realized he was drawing attention and lowered his voice, but the tone was still stern and disapproving.

"You went way too far over there at the Thriftway, Sheriff. You *do not* beat citizens of this town with a baseball bat! Just who do you think you are, anyway?"

"Should I have let Buz Carelton shoot him instead?" Weber asked.

"Of course not, you fool! But I can see no possible explanation for your actions except for the fact that you overreacted and lost control of yourself. We'll be lucky if Ernie Miller doesn't file a lawsuit against the Town!"

"Let him," Weber said. "He assaulted three people, two of them law officers, he destroyed a store, and was violating a court issued restraining order. He'll go away for this one."

"Well, that may be what *you* think," the mayor said primly.

Weber felt his skin prickle. He had a suspicion of what was coming. "Meaning what?"

"We had a meeting with Ernie and Jesse just now. The charges have been dropped!"

Weber had been trying to hide his irritation, but now it boiled over. "What the hell do you mean, *dropped*?"

The mayor's smile was sanctimonious. "We, Councilwoman Smith-Abbott and myself, have reached an out of court settlement with the Town's attorney and the Millers."

Weber could feel the rage building up in him, a stinging bile that crawled up from the pit of his stomach and burned its way through his system. He had to work to control himself when he spoke again.

"And just what was that agreement, Chet?"

The mayor frowned at the use of his first name, but didn't comment. Instead, he explained, with obvious delight at Weber's distress, the agreement that would allow Ernie Miller to escape punishment for his latest outrage.

"The Miller's have agreed not to file civil lawsuits against the Town of Big Lake or the Sheriff's Office for police brutality, violation of their civil rights, and denial of due process, in exchange for all charges being dropped against Ernie in this unfortunate incident."

Weber exploded. "What the hell have you done, you pompous ass? Drop the charges? He wrecks a store, beats hell out of his ex-wife and two of my deputies, and just walks free?"

Councilwoman Smith-Abbott spoke up for the first time. "Mr. Miller has agreed to reimburse the Thriftway for any damages. I think it's a fair settlement for everyone, considering his treatment at your hands, Sheriff."

"You do, do you?" Weber raged. "Well, that's just wonderful, Councilwoman! Why don't you go tell that to my two deputies? Or go tell Elaine Miller. See if they think it's a *fair* settlement!"

Most of the lunch crowd had put down their forks and coffee cups and were watching the drama being played out in public.

"Calm yourself, Sheriff," hissed the mayor. "You're causing a scene."

"Call a cop," Weber suggested. "Jesus Christ, you people make me sick!"

"No, it's *you* who makes *me* sick," Councilwoman Smith-Abbott retorted, her voice dripping venom. "You strut around town with your badge and gun, and act like some sort of Neanderthal, abusing citizens, and then act like a common ruffian in a public restaurant!"

Parks laid a restraining hand on Weber's arm as the sheriff started to rise. "Calm down, Jimmy," he cautioned.

"And you," said the mayor, turning on the FBI agent. "Just who do you think you are, coming into this town and pulling a pistol on one of our citizens? This isn't Russia, sir! I fully intend to make a report of this incident to your superiors in Phoenix."

Parks refrained from comment.

"Furthermore, Sheriff, I fail to see why you have devoted the better portion of the week investigating a case that did not happen in your jurisdiction. As I understand it, this murder case should be handled by the Gila County Sheriff's Office and the Federal Bureau of Investigation. I do not believe it is a prudent use of local tax dollars for you to involve yourself in a criminal matter that in no way concerns your office."

"The victims were citizens of Big Lake," Weber said. "Investigative leads that we have developed give us reason to believe that the solution to the hijacking and murders may very well be right here in Big Lake."

"Sheriff, I have called a special meeting of the Town Council for 7 p.m. tonight to discuss your involvement in the beating of Ernie Miller. At that meeting I also intend to raise the issue of your wasting taxpayer dollars on this matter. I expect you to be present." The mayor gave Weber a smug smile and turned to his companion. "Come along, Councilwoman. We'll be late for the tea at the Ladies Club Art Show."

The mayor turned away, and Councilwoman Smith-Abbott, like an obedient dog, followed his retreating form out of the restaurant.

"That old boy's about as windy as a bag full of farts. Just what in the hell was that all about?" Parks demanded to know.

"Small town politics at its best," Weber told him, his face still flushed. The waitress was approaching their booth, arms laden with plates, but the sheriff stood up and threw some bills on the table. "Sorry, Annie, I just lost my appetite! Come on, Parks."

Weber's foul mood wasn't helped any when he discovered Margo Prestwick waiting for him at the Sheriff's Office. Mary Caitlin sent a sympathetic look Weber's way when the heavyset barmaid pounced on him the moment he walked in.

"Listen you pig, you're going to get me killed!" she screeched. "I'm going to have my lawyer drag your ass into court! What the hell do you think you're doing, getting me messed up in all of this?"

"Margo, calm down," Weber said. "What's wrong now?"

"What's wrong? *What's wrong!* I'll tell you what's wrong, you stupid bastard. What's wrong is that you're going to get me killed, that's what's wrong!" She jabbed a fat finger into the sheriff's chest. "You and your Goddamn questions...."

Before Margo could say another word Mary Caitlin grabbed her wrist and pulled her hand away from Weber, strong fingers squeezing through the thick flesh to bring severe pressure to bear on the bones underneath. Margo yelped and took a step backward. Mary held her grip on the barmaid's wrist. As Margo tried to resist, Mary increased the pressure even more. Fire blazed in Mary's eyes, but when she spoke, she never raised her voice, though her words and her intentions were clear.

"Young lady, this is the Sheriff! You need to learn some manners and clean up your dirty mouth right now, or I'm going to personally throw your fat butt into a cell and leave it there until you do! Is that clear?"

Suddenly contrite, Margo nodded her head, her lips tight in a grimace of pain.

"There, I think we understand each other now," Mary said, releasing her arm.

To everyone's surprise, the tough outer shell evaporated and Margo burst into tears. Great sobs shook her as she bawled out loud. Weber and Mary Caitlin looked at each other in mild shock, not believing Margo could have such a low threshold of pain, for all her tough acting. But when she spoke, it was obvious it wasn't pain that brought the tears, but rather, fear. Terrifying fear. Paralyzing fear.

"They're gonna kill me! I know they are."

Mary quickly snatched a box of tissues off a nearby desk and gently patted the back of the woman whose wrist she had just been crushing.

"It's okay, Margo. No one's going to kill you," Mary said, handing her a wad of tissues. "You're just buying into all that crap the Millers have been spreading forever. Nothing's going to happen."

Margo blew her nose and shook her head. When she looked up, mascara ran down her cheeks in two black streams. "You just don't understand. None of you do. They *will* kill me! I know they will! They're like a bunch of wild animals, running all over with their guns and their knives and...." she broke down into another spasm of tears.

"Margo," Weber said gently, "I promise you, I won't let the Millers hurt you, okay? Have they been around? What happened?"

The woman's body trembled as she spoke. "I was in the cooler, getting some beer out when Tina walked in behind me. She was like a crazy woman! She told me that you had asked Jesse about the fight that Ernie got into with Phil, and they knew I was the one told you about it. She said if you came around asking any more questions, they were going to get me. Sheriff, I'm scared of those people! I can handle the drunks and wise guys at the Antler, but those Millers are crazy! You've got to help me!"

"I will," Weber said. He helped Margo into a chair, then turned to Mary Caitlin. "I want an officer assigned to watch Margo. Have them parked outside the Antler at all times when she's open. I want an escort when she goes home, and I want a car driving by her house every thirty minutes while she's there."

Mary nodded. Weber patted Margo's shoulder. "I have to go forward with this investigation, Margo. You need to understand that. Two men are dead, I can't just walk away from it. But I'll have an officer watching you at all times. The Millers aren't going to hurt you. I'll see to that."

Margo seemed to accept his words. Or maybe she was just resigned to her fate. In either case, she wiped her eyes again and nodded. "I need to get back. I left Henry watching the place and he'll drink up more than he sells if I'm gone long."

"Who's on duty?" Weber asked.

"Tommy's covering a fender bender out on the highway," Mary said. "Chad's out near the school someplace."

"Raise Chad on the radio." Weber ordered. "Tell him to come over and follow Margo back to work and to stay there until he's relieved."

Mary nodded and stepped to the radio console. The sheriff gave Margo a final pat on the shoulder and walked into his inner office.

A final unpleasant surprise awaited Weber when he sat down at his desk. A pink message form instructed him to call Raul Loraz as soon as possible. The Gila County detective must have been awaiting his call, he came on the line immediately.

"Sheriff, we've come across something here we need to talk about."

Weber could tell from the tone of Loraz's voice that he was excited.

"We've found out that Mike Perkins was having an affair. Do you know anything about that?"

The bottom seemed to drop out of Weber's world. His head began to spin, the room suddenly grew hot, and for a moment he thought he was going to vomit. He couldn't reply.

"Sheriff? Still there?"

Finally Weber managed to find his voice. "I'm here. I don't know where you came up with that crazy idea, but it's impossible!"

"I don't think so," Loraz said. "We had a call from a local motel owner who had been listening to the news stories about the hijacking. She claimed that Perkins had checked into her place on three different occasions. She said a woman showed up at the room within a few minutes each time, and they stayed a couple of hours."

"There has to be some mistake! Mike was as straight an arrow as they come."

"I've read the registration slips," Loraz said. "Mike Perkins, Big Lake Arizona. Each time, the room was paid for with your brother-in-law's Visa card. There's no mistake. It was him. She identified him from a photo in our local newspaper."

Everything Weber believed in began to disintegrate in front of his mind's eye. He couldn't function, he couldn't speak. He felt like he was mired in quicksand, sinking deeper and deeper into a bottomless pit of lies, murder and deceit.

"You understand where this leads us?" Loraz was asking, but Weber had to fight the thick fog clouding his mind to understand the detective's words. "Whoever this woman Perkins was seeing, she could be our killer. Or lead us to the killer."

"I can't talk right now," Weber said. "I... I can't talk. I'll call you back."

He hung up the phone and stared sightlessly at a spot on the far wall of his office.

"I know this has to be hard for you to accept." Parks said. "But from what Loraz told you, I don't see how there can be any mistake." They were sitting in Weber's living room. The sheriff, dumbfounded at the news Loraz had related, had walked out of his office without a word to his staff. Finally, Parks had taken his Bureau car and driven to the sheriff's house, finding his friend lost in a void inside his mind, unable to comprehend the implications of this newest direction the case had taken.

"Face it, Jimmy. Guys screw up, they mess around sometimes. They get in over their heads. It happens. Even to the good guys."

"Not with Mike," Weber shouted, finally giving vent to his anger. "I knew that kid! He was like my own brother, for Christ's sake. It just wasn't in his being to fool around. Not on Debbie!"

The FBI agent tried to reason with Weber. "Jimmy, nobody's perfect. Face it, he was riding around with Johnson all day, listening to all his stories about bedding down every woman in the county. Maybe he finally just fell into it. Maybe Johnson introduced him to a friend of one of his bimbos, and it just went from there."

"I'm not buying it," Weber said, shaking his head. "I tell you Parks, that kid loved my sister too much. He'd never have cheated on her."

"Then explain the credit card, explain the motel registry, explain the eyewitness," Parks argued. "Jimmy, I'm your friend, but I have to ask... do you think you might be too emotionally involved in this thing?"

Weber jumped to his feet so fast Parks thought for a second that he might strike him, but he only stormed across the room and smashed his hand into the knotty pine wall.

"No shit, Parks! My Goddamned brother-in-law was gunned down! I had to identify his body! Look at his brains inside what was left of his skull! My sister was left a widow when she should have been entering the best time of her life. I'm finding out people I thought I knew were sleeping with that sleaze ball, Johnson. And now I've got Loraz telling me that Mike Perkins, a kid I loved, was cheating on my sister and may have brought all of this down on himself! You're damned right I'm emotionally involved!"

Weber suddenly realized he was bent over, shouting in Parks' face, taking out his hurt and anger on his friend. He drew back and his shoulders slumped.

"I'm sorry, Parks. I just..." he waved a hand vacantly at the room around him.

"Hey Jimmy, it's *okay*!" Parks reassured him. "Let it out, man."

Weber arched his shoulders and looked toward the ceiling, shaking his head.

"I need some time alone to work this out, Parks. I'm sorry, I just need to get a handle on this and process it all."

"No problem," said Parks sympathetically. "Look, I need to make some calls anyway, let my Agent in Charge know your silly ass mayor may be filing a complaint. How about I go back to the office and get some calls made and paperwork done, and I'll catch you later?"

"Yeah.... later," Weber said. He was still staring upward, lost inside himself, when Parks closed the door behind him.

When Parks returned to the cabin three hours later, the sound of a high performance engine revving drew him into the kitchen, through a utility room with a matching white washer and dryer, and on into the cabin's garage. The upper half of Weber's body was under the hood of a gleaming fire engine red 1958 Chevrolet pickup. The sheriff worked the carburetor's throttle linkage by hand and the truck's motor raced again. Parks leaned into the engine compartment across from Weber and whistled appreciatively.

"Where did you get this? You've been holding out on me."

Weber grinned and straightened up, wiping his hands on a red shop towel, though there was no need. The truck's engine was spotless, offset with chrome valve covers, air cleaner and other accessories, all showroom perfect. There was not a drop of oil, or a smudge of grease anywhere. Weber leaned inside the cab and switched off the ignition. The garage went silent, except for the electric vent fan that drew the engine's exhaust outside.

"I used to drive this thing back when I was in high school. It was a beater even then. When I closed down the ranching operation, I found it sitting in the barn under a pile of junk. I've been restoring it ever since. I guess you could call it my therapy."

Parks inspected the truck from every angle. Wide Goodyear tires mounted on chromed mag wheels, a four speed racing transmission shifter, leather seat and headliner, six speaker stereo system.

"I love it!"

"I pulled the original six cylinder and dropped in the Corvette 350. Added an independent front suspension and disc brakes all around to stop it." Weber said proudly. "She'll do 130 on a straightaway."

The sheriff held out his hand to his friend. "Sorry about earlier. It's just all getting to me."

Parks shook his hand and smiled at the sheriff. "Jimmy, this case has so many angles and twists, we don't know what happened or how it's going to come out. But whatever did happen, we'll get to the bottom of it, okay?"

Weber nodded. "Here's how we're going to play it, Parks. We'll keep an open mind on Mike's supposed affair, but I want to see those credit card receipts myself. I want to hold them in my hand before I'll believe it. Meanwhile we keep working on every angle."

"Works for me," Parks agreed. He stepped back as Weber lowered the hood on the truck. "But one thing, Jimmy. You can't keep this from Debbie. Sooner or later it's going to come out. I think you need to talk to her before she hears it from someone else."

Weber nodded and stared at the truck a long time before he spoke. When he did, his voice was that of a man with the weight of the world on his shoulders. "Yeah, I know. I just don't know how much more she can handle."

"She might surprise you," Parks said. "She comes from good stock, Jimmy. I think she's got a lot more going for her than you realize."

"I hope so," Weber thought to himself as they walked out of the garage and he reached back inside to switch the light off. *"God, I hope so."*

"Sheriff, I have called this special meeting of the Town Council to review your recent behavior in regards to the beating of Ernie Miller," Mayor Wingate said, as he opened the meeting. Weber had changed out of his uniform and wore black jeans and a royal blue wool sweater under a brown leather bomber jacket. The only observers at the hastily called Town Council meeting were Parks, Mary and Pete Caitlin, and Weber's deputies, with the exception of Dolan Reed, who was on stakeout at the Antler Inn, guarding Margo Prestwick.

Kirby Templeton, a senior member of the Council, spoke next. Weber had always respected Templeton, the town's pharmacist, as a fair man who was willing to hear every side of an issue before making any decision. "Sheriff, Mayor Wingate has made some serious accusations against you. He states that you beat Ernie Miller with a baseball bat when you arrested him in the Thriftway the other day. He accuses you of brutality, and of waging a continual campaign of harassment against the entire Miller family. I'm sure you can understand our concern."

Weber stood up. "Councilman, I don't deny for a minute that I hit Miller with a baseball bat. A baseball bat, I might add, that he was using as a weapon against two of my men and his ex-wife."

"So that make's it acceptable, in your opinion?" the mayor asked.

"As I explained to you today, Mr. Mayor, my deputies would have been within their parameters to shoot Miller. He was drunk, he was out of control, he was using a deadly weapon. I thought my actions were the lesser of two evils. No one got killed, and Ernie is alive today to go crying on your shoulder."

Behind him, one of Weber's deputies chuckled, and the mayor rapped his gavel. "Order!"

Councilwoman Smith-Abbott spoke up. "I see no reason why three grown men couldn't arrest one person without resorting to beating him with a club!"

"With all due respect, Councilwoman, you have no clue what it's like to be in a situation like myself and my deputies faced inside that store," Weber replied. "Not to mention the fact that if we had all piled on him, you'd be asking us why three men ganged up on Ernie to arrest him. I wasn't about to let him brain one of my men with that bat."

"Sheriff, I don't want to try and second guess your actions, I wasn't there" said Councilman Frank Gauger, a retired postal worker. "But let me ask you this. Looking back, would you have done the same thing, now that you've had the opportunity to think it over?"

"To be perfectly honest with you, Frank, I haven't given it much thought. I've had a murder investigation to work on. But right now, I can tell you that I'd do the same thing all over again."

"That's exactly my point," Mayor Wingate shouted, pointing his gavel at the sheriff. "You think you can just go around beating on people, and it's okay! Doesn't even deserve a second thought!"

Weber felt his ears color, but he held his tongue.

"Didn't you also slap Mr. Miller after he was on the floor, in custody?"

"No sir, I didn't," Weber said. "I slapped him while he was still uncuffed. I wanted to be sure he wasn't going to continue resisting arrest."

"You were dealing out your own brand of vigilante justice," snapped Councilwoman Smith-Abbott. "You're an animal!"

"All right, let's all calm down," said Councilman Templeton said. "There's no need for personal attacks, Cynthia."

"What was the treatment Ernie Miller received, if not a personal attack?" she demanded.

"I'll ask you this, Sheriff. Understanding that you were in a dangerous, highly stressful situation, did you believe you were acting in the public's best interest in the way you handled Ernie Miller?"

"Yes, I did," Weber told Councilman Templeton. "I thought then, and I still believe, that the only other alternative would have been a shooting. I had two injured deputies, a woman on the floor, and he was totally out of control. Ernie Miller wasn't going to surrender and come along peacefully."

"I don't think it's fair of this Council to second guess Sheriff Weber," said Councilman Templeton. "None of us are trained police officers. None of us have had the experience he has in dealing with violent confrontations. I think we have to take him at his word on this, and trust his professional instincts."

"I totally disagree," said the mayor. "But let's leave that and move on for now. Sheriff, didn't I tell you today you were spending too much time on this murder investigation? An investigation of a crime that occurred outside your jurisdiction?"

"As I told *you* today," Weber explained, "We have reason to believe that the key to those murders is right here in Big Lake. And I'll remind you again that the victims were both citizens of this town. This is a multi-agency investigation."

"And would you give the same attention to the case if one of the victims wouldn't have been your brother-in-law?"

"I resent that!" said Pete Caitlin. "I was sheriff of this town for fifteen years. I trained Jim Weber myself, and no one has any right to question his professionalism! Least of all you, Chet Wingate!"

The mayor rapped his gavel. "Order! I will not tolerate another outburst!"

"Wait a minute, Mr. Mayor," Councilman Templeton objected. "You convened this meeting to talk about the Sheriff's alleged assault on Ernie Miller. Let's stick to the issue at hand and not get off on tangents." One or two other Council members nodded their heads in agreement with Templeton.

Mayor Wingate didn't appreciate the censure, but turned back to Weber. "Sheriff, isn't it true that you have been harassing the Miller family for a long time now? Didn't you go to Jesse Miller's place today to harass him further?"

"We're investigating a double murder," Weber repeated. "We have reason to believe that Ernie Miller may have information that would further that investigation."

"And just what information would that be? How does Ernie Miller figure into a crime that was committed almost 75 miles from Big Lake?"

"You know I can't divulge that information," Weber said. "It's an open investigation."

"More like another excuse to harass the Millers," offered Councilwoman Smith-Abbott snidely.

"Sheriff, I am going to make a motion to this Council that you be suspended without pay until we can bring in an outside investigator to look into your actions recently," said the mayor. "I don't think you deserve the title of Sheriff of Big Lake."

Before Weber could reply, his deputies stood up and approached the Council members seated at the dais. "What is this?" demanded the mayor. "Order!" He rapped his gavel sharply.

"If you're going to suspend Jimmy, you can have our badges now, too," said Chad Summers. "We don't work for this Council, we work for Jim Weber." He unpinned his badge and dropped it on the top of the dais in front of the mayor. Tommy Frost and Buz Carelton followed suit.

"Now wait just a minute," said the mayor. "There's no need for...."

Before he could say another word, Robyn burst into the Council Chambers from the Sheriff's Office next door, panting.

"Jimmy! Come quick, Dolan's on the radio. There's been a shooting at the Antler Inn!"

Chapter 10

Weber and Parks piled into the Bronco and tore away from the curb, followed by Tommy and Buz in a patrol car and Chad in his personal vehicle, a big 4x4 Ford pickup. Fishtailing around a corner, Weber pointed the Bronco toward the highway and the Antler Inn and grabbed his microphone. "Dolan, this is Jimmy, he said, ignoring established radio procedure. "What's going on out there?"

Immediately Dolan Reed's voice came over the speaker, his stress and fear clear even through the radio. "Jimmy, someone's got me pinned down out here! I need help now!"

"We're coming, "Weber assured him. "Are you okay?"

"Yeah, but my car isn't!"

"Can you see the shooter?"

Suddenly the sound of three rapid-fire shots came over the radio, followed by Dolan's voice, rising to a higher pitch. "I can't see anything! I think they're across the highway in the field. Dammit Jimmy, get me some help out here!"

"We're on our way, partner," Weber told him. "Keep your head down. Has anyone been hit?"

"I don't know! I can't tell."

Weber tried to picture the terrain around the Antler Inn. He seemed to recall an open field that sloped sharply uphill, topped by a thick grove of pines. Weber remembered there was a gravel road that crossed maybe 200 yards behind the trees and intersected with the highway a mile or so past the Antler.

"Tommy, I want you and Buz to go into the parking lot, but keep your heads down. Do you have a rifle in your car?"

"Negative," replied Buz, "just a shotgun and our handguns."

Weber knew their weapons would be useless against a sniper so far away. He keyed his mike again, knowing that while Chad couldn't reply, the police scanner he had mounted in his personal vehicle would allow him to monitor the radio traffic. Weber also knew Chad kept a bolt action hunting rifle in his truck.

"Chad, I can see your headlights behind Tommy. Blink if you copy."

In his rear view mirror, Weber saw Chad's lights flash from dim to high and back again.

"Okay, got your .270?"

Again the lights flashed.

"I'm betting the shooter is probably up in that grove of trees on the hill across from the bar. There's a road that goes along the hill and comes out to the highway over by Fred Baxter's place. I want you to go on ahead of us and cover that crossing. Got it?"

The headlights blinked again and the big Ford pickup pulled into the left lane and shot around Tommy's patrol car and Weber's Bronco.

"You up for this?" Weber asked Parks. The FBI agent pulled Weber's Ruger Mini-14 semi-automatic rifle from its rack on the dash and nodded, his jaw set firmly.

"How's it going to go down, Jimmy?"

"I'm going to stop just short of the field and let you out. Then I'm heading right across that son-of-a-bitch and up the hill. Hopefully whoever it is will either haul ass, or open up on me and give the guys in the parking lot time to get inside to cover. If you see a muzzle flash, let loose on him!"

"You're not going to make it in this snow," Parks said. "It must be a foot deep at least."

"I can try," Weber replied. "At least I think I can get him to stop shooting and make a run for it. Maybe Chad can nail him at the highway."

"You be damned careful," Parks warned him.

"I will," Weber said, then keyed his mike one more time. "I'm going across the field, guys. Parks is gonna cover me, so if you see shots coming from the side of the road down here, don't shoot him!"

Weber braked hard, the Bronco sliding on the snow packed road. "This is it. Keep your head down!"

"You too," Parks shouted back as he jumped out of the still rolling truck, but his words were lost in the night as Weber roared away.

Jamming the four wheel drive transfer case selector into low range, Weber felt the Bronco's big tires bite in as it bounced off the roadway and onto the field. The ground was frozen and offered a firm, though very rough, surface.

As soon as Weber started across the field, he saw a tiny flash of fire up on the hill and knew the shooter was still there. A second flash and the sheriff hunched down as far as he could in the seat, trying to make himself a smaller target.

The Bronco lurched and bumped violently as Weber floored the gas pedal and hung on to the steering wheel. He was bouncing too much to see a third flash, but a star appeared on the right side of his windshield. Weber cursed and urged the Bronco on, willing it to greater speed as the truck jostled across the frozen ground. Suddenly he felt the front of the vehicle start to incline and knew he was starting up the hill. Something struck the windshield again and he heard a bullet whap into the seat back beside him.

Weber had no way of knowing, but Parks had also spotted the muzzle flashes from up the hill and began to lay down a covering fire, squeezing off two quick shots, rolling sideways to keep from presenting a stationary target, then firing another pair of shots before he rolled and fired again.

Branches screeched against the side of the Bronco. The engine howled as the tires dug for traction in the snow, but miraculously, the sheriff's vehicle continued to bounce its way up the side of the hill. After what seemed forever to Weber, but was in all actuality only two or three minutes, he crested the hill and was in the trees. Slowing down to avoid bashing into the side of a pine, Weber saw a light come on ahead and begin to rapidly move away. He slammed on the brakes and brought the Bronco to a skidding stop, grabbing his radio microphone.

"He's moving, Chad! Get ready!"

But suddenly, with a sinking heart, Weber realized the shooter hadn't taken to a car or truck to flee down the road. The high pitched whine of a snowmobile engine floated across the night and the light diminished rapidly as the sniper fled off across the gravel road and through the forest, where the Sheriff's Bronco had no chance of catching him.

"Damn it!" shouted Weber, smashing his fist down on the dashboard in frustration. "Damn you to hell you back-shooting bastard!"

Flashing red and blue lights illuminated the cinder block front wall of the Antler Inn, and even in their distorted light, the pockmarks where the sniper's bullets had struck the building showed clearly. In a couple of places, the high velocity slugs had actually penetrated the wall, and Weber was relieved to learn that no one had been wounded in the attack.

"I don't think he was really trying to hit anyone," Parks theorized.

"He was sending a message. Look at the cars here in the parking lot. He shot hell out of them, but when he could have hit Dolan, he didn't."

Weber's deputy wasn't particularly comforted by Park's observations. "He could have killed me even if he wasn't trying," declared Dolan Reed. "Those bullets were just tearing hell out of everything!"

"Oh, no question about that," Parks agreed. "Whoever it was, he might not have been trying to kill anyone, but he damn sure wasn't worrying too much about the people in the bar either."

"What do you mean 'whoever it was?'" Weber demanded. "We both know that it was Ernie Miller or someone else in that crazy family of his! I'm going out there and I'm gonna tear that place of Jesse's apart!"

"Now, calm down, partner," Parks warned. "You don't have any proof it was one of the Millers. You go up there tonight and someone's liable to get killed for sure."

"Don't tell me how to run a case in my town!" Weber shouted. "The crazy son-of-a-bitch shoots up a building full of people, he shoots up one of my patrol cars with my deputy inside it, he shoots out the windshield of *my* truck and you tell me to calm down? I don't think so, Parks!"

Parks tried to grab the sheriff's arm as he turned away, but Weber pulled loose and stalked across the parking lot to where Chad stood looking at the bullet riddled patrol car.

"Where are Tommy and Buz?" he demanded.

"Up in that grove of trees where you sent them," Chad replied, motioning up the hill to where Weber could see flashlights bobbing in the darkness. "Looking for spent casings and to see if they can spot any blood. But I doubt that Parks could have hit him with all those trees for cover."

Weber surveyed the car and shook his head in disgust. "I can't get the damn Town Council to pay for new snow tires, let alone rebuilding what's left of this pile of junk!"

"I don't think they've got much choice now," Chad said.

Every piece of glass in the car was shot out, the fenders, hood, and trunk were perforated in several places and the tires were punctured. But it almost appeared the sniper had intentionally not shot into the doors behind which Dolan crouched for cover.

"Sheriff, here comes Margo," said a still shaken Dolan as the overweight barmaid approached. The tough talking persona was long gone, replaced by a terrified woman searching for refuge from a threat that was beyond her experience, or even comprehension. Margo was shaking uncontrollably as she stood in front of Weber.

"What am I gonna do?" she asked. "He's gonna kill me. You know he is!"

"No he's not, Margo," Weber assured her. "If he wanted you dead, you'd be dead by now. It would have been just as easy to wait up there until you closed the place up and shoot you, if that was what he wanted. He was just trying to scare you, and send us a message."

"Well, he scared me, all right," she said in a weak voice. "I'm getting out of here tonight! I called my brother down in Safford. He's coming up to get me right now."

Weber looked at the bar, empty now, the patrons off trading tales of their ordeal for free drinks at some other gin mill. "Maybe that's best for a little while, Margo. It'll give me a chance to run these clowns down."

Looking at her, Weber felt guilty for letting the barmaid down. He had forced her to talk to him, and when she had come to him for help after being threatened for doing so, he had promised her he would protect her. Obviously his protection hadn't been worth much, Weber reflected.

"Margo.... I'm sorry. I really didn't think they'd go this far. I didn't listen to you, I didn't take you seriously enough. I thought they had just gotten to you and you were running scared."

"We thought we'd take her to the Sheriff's Office to wait for her brother," said Pete Caitlin, who had shown up at the bar with Mary. Pete had strapped on his old Colt Python .357 magnum and pinned his old badge to his shirt, unofficially deputizing himself for the duration of the crisis.

"Good idea, Pete. Thanks. Keep an eye on her, okay?"

The old sheriff looked at Weber with his hard grey eyes and nodded. "Bastards will have to get through me to get to her, Jimmy."

Weber knew Margo was in competent hands and felt better for that, at least. Mary placed a gentle hand on her shoulder and turned her toward their waiting truck.

"You okay, hoss?" asked Parks, coming up alongside the sheriff.

"I seem to be yelling at you a lot today," Weber said. "I'm sorry. This isn't the usual caseload we deal with around here."

Parks slapped his shoulder good naturedly. "Hells bells, Jimmy! No need to apologize. Your little town here is just full of surprises. I ain't had so much fun since the hogs ate my brother!"

Weber grinned in spite of himself. "So now what, Mister FBI man?"

Parks looked across the field to where he could see the bobbing flashlights carried by Weber's deputies as they searched for clues up on the hill. "Well, I'm a lousy shot under the best of circumstances, so there's not much hope I hit the damned fool. Guess we can rule out checking the hospitals, assuming you have one in this one horse town. And I doubt even Ernie Miller would be fool enough to show himself around one of the local saloons tonight. I think we're stuck for now, Sheriff. What say we go inside and drink up some of old Margo's beer while she's gone?"

Weber shook his head at his crazy friend and allowed himself to chuckle.

"Seriously Jimmy, we're not going to accomplish anything tonight. You know that. If we're going to take on that wild bunch, we need to do it on our own terms, not theirs."

Weber nodded reluctant agreement. "They teach you that in FBI school, too?"

"Hell Jimmy, wait 'till I tell you about what they taught us about fixing parking tickets! You're gonna be amazed."

"One thing about it," he said to Parks, "I guess the Town Council won't be suspending me tonight."

Parks laughed and slapped his back again. "Damn straight, partner! They're afraid if they do, old Mayor Prissy and his frigid friend there will be the only thing standing between them and the thundering herd!"

Chapter 11

Weber's bone-weary deputies assembled in the Sheriff's Office at 9 a.m. the next morning, in preparation for the raid on Jesse Miller's compound. Each man was heavily armed, carrying a Mini-14 or shotgun, as well as their sidearms. Weber had ordered all of them to wear their Kevlar vests.

"Okay guys, here's the plan," Weber said, stepping up to a portable chalkboard he had set up in his office. "Parks and I are going right up the road to the gate. Buz, I want you on the right flank with your Ruger, just inside the tree line. Tommy, you'll be on the left, on this little hill about twenty yards away." He pointed to a circle he had drawn on the chalkboard. "Dolan, there's a back road from Jesse's place that goes across Raccoon Creek. I want you at the bridge across the creek. If they come that way, you stop them even if you have to shoot them. Got it?"

Dolan nodded, his jaw set. He still hadn't quite gotten over his experience of the night before. Weber didn't really expect the Millers to make a run for it, and had purposely placed Dolan in the least likely spot for a confrontation.

"What about me?" Chad asked.

Weber pointed to another hilltop on his map. "This hill has a clear view of the gate, and from the top I think you can see into the compound. You're my best shot, Chad. It's about 200 yards to the gate, another 100 or so to the house. Think you can hit anyone with your .270 at that distance if you have to?"

"Piece of cake," Chad assured him.

"Good. I expect you to cover our asses if things go bad out there."

"Do you think it will?" Buz asked.

Buz had earned his nickname back in high school, a result of his skinny neck and hawk-like nose. The kids used to say he was part buzzard. But Weber knew his deputy to be among the coolest heads in a crisis.

"I really don't know, Buz," he admitted. "It all depends on how Jesse reacts. He may realize that if he puts up a fight, we'll just call in more reinforcements. Maybe he'll be sensible."

"Or?"

Weber looked each of his men in the eye. "Or, he might want to make an issue of it. If he does, I expect somebody could die out there today."

Weber left his men to make their final equipment checks and drove over to the courthouse to pick up the search warrants that the judge had prepared. As he pulled out of the parking lot and headed back toward the Sheriff's Office, he was shocked to realize that Ernie Miller's old International Scout was ahead of him. Weber switched on his overhead lights and sped up, closing the distance between his Bronco and the orange 4x4. Miller's brake lights blinked and the Scout stopped. Weber stepped out of the Bronco and leveled his .45 over the door.

"Ernie! Both hands out the window, now! Let me see them!"

Miller's hands showed out the driver's window. The Scout appeared empty except for the driver.

"Reach down with one hand and open the door from the outside! Do it!" Weber ordered.

Miller fumbled the door open.

"Don't shoot, Sheriff! I'm not armed!"

"Out of the truck. Face away from me and keep your hands up where I can see them!"

Miller stepped outside. Traffic slowed to witness the unfolding drama.

"Down on your knees," Weber said, keeping his pistol on Miller, who quickly complied.

Weber stepped out from behind the Bronco's door and moved forward cautiously, keeping the Colt aimed at Miller, alert for any sudden movements.

"Okay, face down! I want to see those hands at all times!"

Miller stretched out in the snow alongside his Scout. Weber moved toward him, pulling his handcuffs free. He knelt over his prisoner and placed his knee in the small of Miller's back.

"Put your right hand on the back of your neck!"

Weber snapped a handcuff on the wrist, then ordered Miller to put his other hand behind him. Once the prisoner was secured, Weber patted him down expertly and then pulled him to his feet and spun him around.

"You damned idiot! You could have killed someone last night!"

"I didn't do anything!" Miller protested. "I just heard about the shooting and was coming to talk to you. I swear, Sheriff, I didn't shoot that place up!"

Weber cursed and hustled Miller back to the Bronco and shoved him into the passenger side.

"Don't move! Don't give me a reason to shoot your ignorant ass right here!" he warned.

Weber went back to the Scout and switched off the engine and took the keys. A quick search showed there was no weapon in the truck. He climbed back into the Bronco and sped toward the Sheriff's Office.

Conversation in the room stopped when Weber pushed open the door and shoved Ernie Miller inside. Weber pushed the prisoner into a chair and leaned into his face.

"Okay, let's hear it!"

"Look, I was over in Springerville." Miller declared. "I knew you were looking for me to ask me about Phil Johnson, so I went over there to my uncle's place. The storm came up and I just stayed over. I wasn't even in town last night! First I heard about the shooting was when Tina called me this morning. I headed right over here, because I knew you'd go up to Jesse's place looking for me, and I didn't want anybody to get killed!"

"If you knew I was looking for you, why did you run in the first place?" Weber demanded.

"I don't know! I was pissed because you beat me up and all. Why should I talk to you?"

"Because there's a murder investigation going on, you dumb shit!" Weber shouted in his face.

"I didn't kill them boys, Sheriff. I swear it!"

"I know you and Johnson got into a fight at the Antler Inn! What was that about?"

"Aw, Jesus Christ! He was messing around on my kid sister. What would you have done?"

"I wouldn't have let my sister get involved with the creep in the first place," Weber told him.

"Yeah? Well, I didn't have much say about that! And then it was too late."

"What do you mean, too late?" Weber demanded.

"Just too late. He'd already got her pregnant!" said the big man. "She wouldn't get a divorce!"

The office went silent at Miller's bombshell announcement. Finally Weber found his tongue.

"You're telling me that Tina and Phil Johnson were married?"

"Yeah. They went over to New Mexico and got hitched back in September."

"I don't believe you," Weber said. "Why wasn't Tina living with him then? Why didn't he tell Mike Perkins or anyone else?"

"I don't know why he didn't tell anyone," Miller told him. "He and Tina got into a big fight a couple of days after they got back from New Mexico, and they had an on and off thing ever since. I was against it right from the start."

"What did Jesse talk to Phil about after you two got into it at the Antler?" asked Weber.

"Jesse's always been the big protector. He was trying to talk some sense into Phil. Convince him he had a kid on the way and needed to take care of business. I guess Tina was silly enough to still want him back, even though she knew he was sleeping with everyone in town."

Weber looked over at Parks. "You buying any of this?"

"Easy enough to check on the marriage," Parks said. "One phone call will tell us if he's lying about that."

Weber paced across the office a couple of times and then went back to Miller, and when he spoke his voice was better controlled.

"Ernie, do you know who killed those two men, if it wasn't you? Did Jesse have anything to do with it?"

"No way!" Miller protested. "Jesse was the one that put Johnson and Tina together in the first place. I was against it, but he told me he had his reasons."

"And what reasons were those?" Weber asked.

"I don't know. You know how Jesse is, always getting ready for the big showdown. He's got Tina thinking just as crazy as he is these days." He looked up at Weber and his eyes were scared. "Sheriff, I'm not denying I've been in trouble a lot. I get to drinking and I just go nuts. I know that. But those two... they're something else! Always talking about the revolution that's coming and how the government is out to get them. Sometimes I think they're really gonna do something stupid some day! They're just waiting for the right time and the right place."

Weber looked at Parks and the unspoken thought was shared between them. $300,000 would buy a lot of revolution.

"His story checks out," Mary Caitlin told Weber an hour later. "I had to really put some pressure on the county recorder's office in Albuquerque, it being a weekend and all. But they sent someone down to look up the information." She read from a notepad in her hand. "Philip Arnold Johnson and Tina Marie Miller were married September 25 by a Justice of the Peace in Albuquerque. Home of residence for both of them was listed on the marriage license application as Big Lake, Arizona."

Parks whistled and shook his head in amazement. "Every time we turn around something new comes up! Where do we go from here?"

"That still doesn't let Ernie off the hook for last night," Weber said stubbornly. "I'd bet my badge he's our shooter."

"You'd lose your star, handsome," Mary told the sheriff, referring again to her notebook. "According to the Springerville Police Department, one of their officers called in a rolling NCIC check on Ernie last night about five minutes after the shooting ended, because he had had problems with him before and was hoping to find an outstanding warrant. The officer is sure it was Ernie driving the Scout, though he didn't stop him when the computer check showed no wants or warrants." She looked up from her notepad and smiled sympathetically at Weber. "Sorry to be the bearer of bad news. Ernie Miller's not our boy."

Faced with the fact that Miller had a reliable alibi that placed him over twenty miles away at the time of the shooting, Weber stood up and walked down the hall to the light green holding cells in the rear of the building. Ernie stood up when he saw Weber approaching.

"Come on, Sheriff, let me out of here! I've cooperated with you. I told you, I didn't shoot up the Antler last night."

"Keep your shirt on, Ernie," Weber told him. "You're clean on this one, you're getting out. But I want you to tell me everything you know about Phil Johnson and his relationship with your family first."

Armed with the knowledge that he was off the hook in the shooting, Miller began to revert to his old contrary self and shook his head. "Forget it, Sheriff. I don't talk against my family."

Weber leaned his head close to the bars of the cell. "You were damned sure willing to talk against them just a little bit ago when it was your ass on the line, Ernie. So stop with the self-righteous routine, okay? Talk to me."

Miller shook his head again. "All I wanted to do was keep anyone from getting killed. I'm not going to turn against my family. That's all there is to it."

"Did Jesse and Tina have anything to do with the hijacking?"

"I already told you no! Tina was in love with the no good cheating bastard, she wouldn't have done anything to him."

"Maybe she got fed up with him running around on her?" Weber suggested.

"It didn't happen that way," Miller declared. "Jesse and Tina saw Phil as being on their side, even if he and Tina were having their troubles. Besides, he was always bragging about his military shit, what a big time soldier he had been. I think they probably thought he'd be a big help when the shit hit the fan."

"Johnson was a rear echelon type," Weber said. "He was never in combat."

"So he lied! Go roust his dead ass," Miller said. "I never believed a word he said right from the start. It was Jesse and Tina thought he was so wonderful."

"Maybe they just thought he would come in handy and they were using him." Weber said. "Could that be what happened?"

"I don't know," Miller shouted, his face red with anger. "Now, I already told you, I'm not saying another word. Let me out of this damned cell!"

Weber knew the interview was going nowhere and reluctantly unlocked the cell door. He stepped back as Miller walked out, and when he spoke, his voice carried a warning that even Ernie Miller couldn't ignore.

"Ernie, I'm not letting go of this. If I find out that Jesse or Tina had anything to do with those killings, I'm coming after them. You got that?"

"Yeah, I got it," Miller replied. "But just so's you know, Sheriff.... if you do, I'll be right there with them with a rifle in my hands. I think they're crazy as hell with all this militia bullshit, but they're my family." He turned to Weber, and his face was sad as he continued. "I know they can't win, if it all goes to hell. But they're my family. I'll be there with them." He opened the door and walked down the hall toward the outer office, his shoulders slumped.

"So is the raid off, or what?" asked Dolan, after Ernie Miller had collected his wallet and truck keys and left the Sheriff's Office.

"Yeah," Weber said. "I don't see the point now. Ernie couldn't have been the shooter."

"But what about Jesse? Or even that crazy sister of theirs?"

It was obvious, and understandable, that Dolan wanted payback for the attack he had suffered the night before. But Weber knew they needed more to go on than suspicion.

"We'll get them sooner or later, Dolan. This isn't over. I promise you that."

"I can call the glass shop over in Springerville and have them send a truck up to replace the windshield in your truck," Mary told the sheriff. "Might make it a little more comfortable than riding around with that duct tape stuck over those bullet holes."

Weber nodded absently. "Yeah, go ahead. We'll use Parks' car if they can get to it today still."

As Mary picked up the telephone, Weber faced his deputies. "Go ahead and stand down, men. Get some rest. I'll cover the duty until you come on at four o'clock, Chad."

As his deputies stowed away their equipment, Weber walked into his inner office. The adrenalin rush from the anticipated confrontation with Jesse, combined with the arrest of Ernie, had left him drained and listless. He sat at his desk and began to doodle on a yellow lined notepad. Weber knew that somewhere in the intricate weavings of the canvas the case was drawn on was the solution he was seeking. But right then, his mind was stuck in neutral, and it was all too much to comprehend.

Weber was still sitting listlessly at his desk when Debbie and Rachel Perkins walked into his office. Both women's faces were strained.

"We just saw Dolan's squad car on the back of Ted Walker's wrecker," said Debbie. "Is he okay?"

"Yeah," Weber told them. He related the events of the night before.

Debbie perched on the corner of his desk, while Rachel took a seat across from Weber. Her eyes sent silent messages across the distance between them. He had been so wrapped up in the events unfolding around him that he hadn't had the opportunity to talk to her since they had made love the night of Mike's funeral. Weber felt guilty looking at her, but she seemed more concerned for his welfare than offended or upset.

"So now what?" Debbie asked.

"I don't know," Weber admitted, then decided that he was going to have to broach the subject of Mike's infidelity sooner or later, and no time was going to be good. He took a deep breath.

"There's something else, Debbie."

She looked at him with questioning eyes. Weber hated knowing that the news he had to share with her was going to kill a little more of the innocence in those eyes.

"According to Gila County, there's a possibility that Mike was involved in something."

"Involved in *what*?" Debbie asked, uncomprehending.

Weber couldn't look her in her eyes as he continued. "Debbie, they say Mike was meeting a woman down there in some motel. They have registration slips, credit card receipts, even an eyewitness."

It was the final straw for Debbie. Weber had been surprised at her strength during the days leading up to Mike's funeral. A strength he never knew she possessed. But at this latest assault on the world she had known, Debbie became hysterical, screaming at Weber, pounding his chest with her fists and knocking items off his desk.

"Stop it! You're lying!" she screamed. "Mike would never have cheated on me. He loved me! How can you say that? Stop it, Jimmy!"

Weber tried to enfold her in his arms, but Debbie fought him off and glared at him with a rage like he had never seen before. "Don't touch me! I hate you! I HATE YOU!"

Mary Caitlin and Rachel managed to get their arms around Debbie and walk her out of Weber's office, her sobs loud in the suddenly quiet room.

"You son-of-a-bitch!" Rachel hissed as she helped Debbie out of the room. "How could you be so cruel?" Her eyes blazed at him, and Weber felt naked and vulnerable under her stare. Mary Caitlin shot him a sympathetic look as she followed the women out and closed the door.

Chapter 12

The previous day's storm had been good for the ski business, which was bad timing for the Sheriff's Office. With only one vehicle operational, and all of his deputies exhausted from working the shooting investigation most of the night, and reporting in early in anticipation of the raid on Jesse Miller's compound, Weber was the only officer on duty during the day. He knew he needed to talk to Debbie, but a couple of minor traffic accidents and a few routine calls kept him busy until Robyn radioed him in the afternoon to tell him that Chad was reporting for duty. Weber drove the S-10 Blazer back to the office to discover the windshield of his Bronco had been replaced. Dolan Reed came in shortly after Weber arrived.

"I didn't think you were scheduled to come on 'til six," Weber said. Dolan looked to be in better spirits. Weber suspected, correctly, that his deputy had a better handle on the previous night's shooting.

"I figured we'd be short handed," he said. "And with it being a Saturday and all..." he looked at Weber, seeking understanding. "I needed to get back into uniform, boss. I guess it's like climbing back on a horse after you're thrown. I was afraid if I didn't, I might never be able to again. I've never been shot at before, Jimmy."

Weber nodded and put a hand on his deputy's arm. "I need you here, Dolan. I know it must have been pretty crazy out there last night. I'd have been scared to death in your place."

Gratitude showed in Dolan's face as Weber spoke. "Jimmy, I'm no coward. But I'll tell you, I was sure glad when you assigned me to the back entrance of Jesse's place this morning. I didn't know what I'd do if they would have pulled guns on us. Part of me was scared, and another part wanted the chance to get back at them for shooting at me."

"Where are you at now?" Weber asked.

"I'm okay. We don't know for sure if it was one of the Miller's up on that hill last night. But whoever it was, I can handle it professionally. I'm a cop. It's part of the job."

Dolan Reed was 40, a balding man who wore glasses and had just the beginning of a pot belly, though he worked hard to keep in shape. Weber knew he had three children at home and a wife he doted on. The sheriff understood that much of Dolan's reaction to the shooting was more concern for what would have become of his family if he had been killed than for his own personal safety.

The telephone rang and Robyn turned to the sheriff. "Jimmy, Kirby Templeton is on the phone."

Weber went to his desk and picked up the receiver. "Hi Kirby. What can I do for you?"

"Sounds like you folks had a rough night," Templeton said.

"Yeah. But at least no one got hurt, thankfully."

"I've had the Mayor screaming in my ear all day," Templeton told Weber. "Accusing you of everything from harassing the Millers to precipitating last night's shooting, to starting the Chicago fire. I just want you to know that the majority of the Council is behind you, Sheriff."

"I appreciate that," Weber replied. "Kirby, I don't know if the Millers are behind this or not, but they're strong suspects, I can tell you that."

"Well, don't worry about Chet Wingate. He'd love to see you gone, but he doesn't have enough of us behind him to get the job done. You do what you have to do."

"Thanks again. We're going to have to do something about some vehicles, Kirby. The Caprice is trashed, and the S-10 needs a lot of work. That just leaves the Bronco. The Council has been sitting on that purchase order for the new vehicles for weeks now."

"I know," the councilman told him. "We never got a chance to get that far last night before everything went nuts, but I've got authorization for your office to buy three new vehicles. Maybe that'll cheer your guys up a little bit."

"We can use them," Weber said, gratefully. "It's going to help a lot. I need to call Mike at Hall Automotive. I know he's got the Bronco and Crown Victoria in stock. Shouldn't take more than a few days to get the pickup. If I call him right now, maybe they can put a rush on things and have them set up and ready to roll by the end of next week."

Councilman Templeton laughed. "I'm ahead of you, Jimmy. I called Mike yesterday morning as soon as we took the vote. He got his guys busy installing the heavy duty electric harnesses and emergency lights yesterday. I'd say by Monday he'll have your decals on and the radios installed. You've got yourself a new fleet, Sheriff. Try not to get it shot to pieces any time soon."

"Great!" The good news lifted the sheriff's sagging spirits.

"That'll put each deputy in a vehicle. You get to decide who gets stuck with the old S-10."

Weber grinned. "We'll work it out. Thanks, Kirby."

"Jimmy, don't worry too much about Chet and the Councilwoman," advised Templeton. "The Council knows you're doing a good job. The way this area has grown, you and your deputies have had to take on a lot of new problems. We're aware of that, and appreciative."

"Thanks, Kirby. That means a lot."

Templeton paused a moment, then dropped the other shoe. "But there's good news and bad news Jimmy."

"Okay, what's the bad news?" Weber asked warily.

"You also got that new deputy you've been asking for."

"Don't tell me," Weber warned.

"It was the only way I could get Chet to go along with the purchase order. Archer goes on the job next week. Sorry, Jimmy, but that's small town politics at work."

"It's nepotism!" Weber stormed. "Jesus Christ, Kirby, he's useless and you know it! I won't have him."

"Give it a try," the councilman urged. "Knowing Archer, he'll get underfoot for a couple of months and then get bored and wander off on his own. I'm sorry, Jimmy. It was the only way."

Archer Wingate was Mayor Chet Wingate's only child, a flatulent, pudgy young man who had been the butt of jokes all through school, and carried his unpopularity into adult life with him. His father had bankrolled Archer in several small business ventures, all of which had failed, falling victim to Archer's laziness and slovenly manner, as well as his petulant treatment of the public. A year earlier, Archer had decided he wanted to become a deputy, and the mayor had urged Weber to hire him. As short handed as the sheriff was, he had refused to put him in uniform, even after Archer completed a semester of law enforcement courses at a college in Tucson and his father had connived him into a state certification class. Archer may have completed the basic requirements to work as a police officer, but Weber knew his personality and lack of ambition would prohibit him from ever succeeding in the job. The sheriff's steadfast refusal to hire his son had strained an already tense relationship between his office and the mayor.

"Before I let you go," the councilman said, "I want to ask you something. Off the record."

"Go ahead."

"What did it feel like to thump that loud mouth with that baseball bat?"

In spite of his dismay at the appointment of his new deputy, Weber chuckled and hung up the telephone.

"Great news, guys," he told his deputies when he returned to the outer office. "Kirby Templeton came through for us. By Monday, we should have at least two of our new vehicles!" Weber didn't spoil their delight by telling them about Archer. Bad news could always wait.

Chad whooped with glee. "About time, Slugger! I was afraid we'd be riding horses any day now."

"You know me, Chad, I don't ride nothing I can't put gas in," the sheriff replied.

"Yeah, you're a real western lawman," said Parks.

Weber thumbed his nose at the FBI agent and headed for the door. "I need to go talk to my sister, if she hasn't disowned me by now."

Rachel Perkins met Weber at the door and told him in a frosty voice that Debbie had gone for a drive alone. "She's got a lot to sort out."

When she didn't invite him in, Weber stepped past her, conscious of his shoulder brushing against her in the hallway. Rachel didn't try to hide her lack of enthusiasm for his visit. Weber wanted to explain that he didn't believe the allegations against Mike Perkins any more than she or Debbie did, but Rachel cut him off when he started to speak.

"I don't want to hear any of this! That man loved Debbie, Jimmy. Hell, he even loved *you*! I just don't see how you could entertain the thought that he was being unfaithful."

"Dammit, Rachel, I didn't say I believed it. I *don't*! But how can I get to the bottom of this unless I look at every angle, follow up on every clue?"

Weber took off his Stetson and threw it on the sofa.

"Now, the Sheriff's Office in Gila County has those receipts. They have an eyewitness that swears that Mike was in that motel with a woman. I didn't say I believed it, but I need to follow up on this!"

"By hurting your sister, at a time like this?" shouted Rachel. "By dragging Mike's memory through the mud, based on someone's word you don't even know?"

Jimmy reached for her hand, but she jerked away and stood her ground, trembling. Tears ran down her face. "Jimmy, I knew my brother, even if you didn't. He would never have cheated on Debbie!"

"Okay, Rachel, we both agree on that," Weber reasoned. "So what's the explanation? That's what we need to find out."

"I don't know," she snapped. "You're the cop here! You go figure it out!"

Weber's temper began to boil over. "That's right, I'm the cop! But I'm also Mike's brother-in-law! And I'm hurting too, you know? But I can't let that show, can I? Because I'm the cop! I'm the one who has to take care of everyone. I can't let my hurt show, I've got a job to do! But I'm hurting, and I'm pissed off, and I want to get whoever did this. And the only way I can do that is to dig under every rock, look in every corner, and chase down every lead. Now, if Mike wasn't shacked up in a motel room with some woman, *someone* was! And they were using his name to do it. I've got to find out who that was, and who the woman was, too!"

Rachel was silent for a long moment and when she spoke, her voice was tired and sad. "I don't know what the answer is. This is all so crazy! I just want it all to go away!"

"Me too, Rachel. Me too." His pain and anger seemed to soften her own, and Rachel stepped forward and hugged him. Weber drew her to him in a tight embrace, wanting something solid to hold on to as much as the physical comfort of her body close to his.

It was late when Weber left his sister's house, but Debbie still hadn't returned. Weber thought she might have stopped at Marsha's house, or to visit another friend, and though the temptation to linger longer with Rachel was strong, he didn't want Debbie to walk in and surprise all three of them. He kissed Rachel goodbye at the door and promised to see her the next day, before she started back to her home in Phoenix.

Weber was restless and not ready to call it a night, so he cruised around town for a while, finally ending up on Wapiti Road, which paralleled the lake. He was nearly at the Game and Fish Department boat ramp on the south end of the lake when something suspicious caught his eye. A pickup was stopped several yards down a fire road, and Weber would have missed it except its brake lights were on.

"*Probably some damned fool flatlander who got himself lost and then stuck*," the sheriff thought to himself, as he backed up and swung into the fire road. When Weber's headlights illuminated the truck, it appeared empty at first, then the shape of a head popped up, a hand wiped the fog from the truck's rear window, and someone peered out, then disappeared again. Weber trained his spotlight on the truck, a primer gray old Dodge Power Wagon, and stepped out of his Bronco.

"Okay, whoever you are, step out of the truck," he ordered.

After several long seconds, the driver's door opened hesitantly, no more than a few inches.

"Come on, it's cold out here," Weber called. "Out of the truck!"

The door opened further and a teenaged boy climbed out and faced Weber, his hands held up at shoulder height. The boy was tall and lanky, with a shock of curly dishwater blonde hair and acne. Weber sighed and shook his head.

"Billy Carelton, what the hell are you doing out here in the middle of the night?"

"Nothing, Sheriff! I swear it!" The voice was high pitched and frightened. Billy wasn't wearing a coat and Weber noted that his shirttail was pulled out.

The sheriff put his hands on his hips and looked at the cab of the pickup.

"All right, young lady. Come on out!"

Nothing happened for half a minute.

"Come on," Weber ordered.

"I can't!"

Billy darted a glance inside the cab. "She's... ummmm..... she's not exactly dressed, Sheriff."

"Well, she'd better damn sure get dressed before she freezes off whatever you've been playing with, Billy!"

After several moments of bobbing and fumbling inside the pickup, another young figure stepped out. This time, a teenage girl with short brown hair and a tear stained face. Her makeup was smeared and she had forgotten to zip her jeans. Weber squinted at the girl, then walked up to the couple.

"Why, Gina Reed!" the sheriff exclaimed in wonder. "Does your Daddy know you're out here?"

The girl shook her head, her eyes downcast.

"Look, Sheriff, if our parents find out we're out here, they'll kill us," Billy pleaded.

"Well, Dolan's got the duty tonight," he told Billy. "You're lucky it was me who caught you. If he'd have found you half naked with his little girl, he might have just shot you right here."

A scent drifted to Weber from the direction of the Dodge and he frowned at Billy.

"All right, kid. Let's have it."

Billy's eyes grew even larger and Gina looked up, panic stricken.

"Don't play games with me," Weber said, cutting off Billy's denial. "Give me the pot."

"Honest, Sheriff, we just had two joints," Billy said. "We only smoked one."

Weber wasn't sure if the frightened boy was more likely to burst into tears or start running off into the forest. "Okay, Billy. I hear you. Where's the other joint?"

Billy leaned into the pickup and turned, handing Weber the marijuana.

"Where'd you get the grass?"

"My cousin Danny gave it to me when he came up from Scottsdale last month," Billy told him. "Honest, Sheriff, it's the first time we ever tried it. To tell you the truth, we like beer better!"

Weber shook his head and stared hard at the teenagers for a long time, watching them fidget.

"At least tell me you're practicing safe sex," he asked hopefully.

"Oh, yes sir!" Billy assured him, digging in his pocket and pulling out a foil wrapped condom.

"Billy!" shouted the girl in embarrassment.

Weber had to stifle a chuckle. "So, I've got two of my deputies' kids smoking pot and making out in the middle of the forest. How am I going to handle this?"

Neither teenager replied, both trying to avoid his eyes. Weber let them stew a couple of minutes longer, then spoke again, his voice stern.

"Okay, I want you to get dressed and go home. Each to your *own* homes! I'm not gonna tell your parents *this* time. But I'm gonna be watching you two. Don't let me catch you again, hear me?"

"Oh, don't worry, Sheriff, you won't catch us again!" promised Billy.

Gina shot him a shocked look.

"Billy!"

"That's not what I meant!" stammered Billy. "I just meant to say..."

Weber cut him off. "Billy?"

"Yes, Sheriff?"

"Go home, Billy."

"Yes, sir!"

A hundred yards down the road, Weber broke into a hearty laugh and rolled down the window of the Bronco. With one hand he shredded the joint and dropped it into the night, his laughter whipped out of the window to mingle with the marijuana in the night air behind him.

It was almost midnight when Weber drove past Pete and Mary Caitlin's big old two story home, but the lights were on in the living room. Pete was a night owl and Weber knew he'd be up.

"Come on in out of the cold," the old sheriff told him when he opened the door. "Cup of coffee?"

"No thanks, Pete. I was just going home and I saw your lights on. Mary still up?"

"Naaa… she's been asleep a couple of hours. I got to watching a documentary on Pancho Villa on PBS. I think I'd have liked that old bandit, to tell you the truth!"

"That's because you're an old bandit yourself, at heart," Weber told him.

Pete laughed and motioned Weber to a chair while he sat back down in his leather recliner.

"Town quiet tonight?"

"Pretty much." Weber laughed. "I caught Buz's boy, Billy, and Dolan's girl making out and smoking pot."

"Well, I'm not all that convinced that wacky tabaccy is all bad for you," observed Pete. "Hell, I saw a thing on *Sixty Minutes* said they're giving it to cancer patients. I got myself up to two packs of Camels a day, just out of curiosity!"

Weber couldn't help but grin.

Pete's laugh was almost a cackle. "You remember the time I caught you and Clarissa Jackson bumping bellies in the back of your old pickup, behind the Forest Service office? Christ, you were scared!"

In spite of himself, Weber's face flushed at the memory from long ago. "Shit yes! What was I, sixteen?"

"Yup. You got that old drunk, Terry Cook, to buy you a bottle of redeye and you took advantage of that little gal."

"Me take advantage of Clarissa?" Weber protested. "Hell, Pete, I seem to recall that little girl taught me more about human anatomy than I ever learned in a classroom!"

Pete wiped tears of laughter from his eyes. "You was in the back of that old Chevy, trying to buckle your britches and climb out in your delicate condition. I was afraid you'd do yourself permanent injury getting over that tailgate, boy!"

Weber roared at the memory, the laughter a catharsis for all the emotions he had been holding in check. He laughed so hard he thought his heart might stop beating, and by the time he gained control of himself, his ribs ached.

"Whatever happened to old Clarissa?" Pete asked.

"She married the guy who drives the Frito Lay delivery truck, "Weber replied. "She's got five kids and weighs 200 pounds. Clarissa always did have those breeder hips, you know."

They laughed again.

"I got myself a new deputy," Weber said.

"It's about time," declared Pete. "You boys are stretched way too thin. Another hand will sure help."

"Don't bet on it," Weber told him. "It's Archer Wingate."

Pete hooted in wonder. "Archer? That's boy's just about as useless as his Daddy. Who you gonna assign to dress him every morning?"

"I don't know," Weber said. "Kirby Templeton said it was the only way he could get my new fleet approved. It really pisses me off!"

"Well hell, Jimmy. Worst comes to worst, you can always use him for target practice!"

"He'd be awfully hard to miss," Weber admitted.

Pete Caitlin smiled fondly across the room at his protégée.

"I know you're going through a rough time, Jimmy. But you've been there before, and you've always come out on top. Just keep plugging away at it, son."

"It's just so damned hard," Weber said, solemn now. "Pete, Larry Parks says maybe I'm too close to all this. I don't see how I can't be. How do I handle it, and still keep doing my job?'

The old man leaned toward his former deputy. His hair and handlebar mustache were grey, his eyes reflected too many years of police work, too many horrible memories for one man to carry. But when he spoke, his words were gentle, and full of love for the only son he had ever known.

"You do it just the way you are, Jimmy. One day at a time."

Chapter 13

As so often happens in the high country of the Southwest, Friday's fast moving winter storm was followed by a warm front, and when Weber and Parks left the sheriff's cabin Sunday morning, the temperature had climbed to the mid-40s. They drove to the Frontier Cafe for breakfast, huge stacks of buttermilk pancakes, thick slabs of sizzling bacon, and seasoned hash brown potatoes. Parks dug in with glee. Weber was amazed that a man could maintain Parks' fitness level while devouring such great quantities of cholesterol.

"Man, I swear, Jimmy. I'm going to go back to the Valley, resign, and come back up here and go to work for you! Forget my retirement plan, I can't leave this good mountain cooking!"

Weber chuckled and watched Parks spoon strawberry jam onto buttered toast. "Come on, Parks, you can't tell me they don't have *any* good restaurants in Phoenix?"

Parks wiped his mouth with a napkin and reached for a second serving of bacon. "There was a place down on Alma School Road that used to serve up a pretty good meal, but that was back in the old days, Jimmy. I'm talking back when cabdrivers *and* convenience store clerks spoke English. But the last time I stopped in, they had switched to 2% milk! Can you believe it?"

Weber shook his head at the news of his friend's misfortune. "It sure sucks to be you, pal."

"You got it...."

Parks stopped in mid-sentence and nodded over Weber's shoulder. "You've got company."

Weber turned to see a handsome, well built, tanned man in his late 30s. When he smiled, Weber thought to himself that there was enough money invested in Roger Wilson's teeth to put a new deputy on the town's payroll.

"Hello, Roger."

Wilson wore one of those insincere "we're best pals" smiles that Weber hated. He realized that there was much about Roger Wilson he disliked, and he wasn't sure if it was all based upon Wilson's shallowness and the new knowledge that he was a wife beater, or partly on his envy of the man's money, big house, expensive cars, and beautiful wife.

"Sheriff, may I join you?"

Wilson was used to getting his way, so he didn't wait for acknowledgment, but slid into the booth, next to Weber.

"You must be the FBI agent that's helping out in this murder case. Terrible thing for the town. And for Sheriff Weber's family too, of course. I'm Roger Wilson." He stuck a hand out toward Parks, who shook it and grinned his best aw shucks, good old boy grin at the wealthy developer.

Wilson directed another smile at Weber and said "So."

"So?" Weber asked.

"So.... I'm sorry I missed you the other day. Laura said you had visited. I think it's terrible, Sheriff. I mean, we went to high school together, didn't we? We live in the same town, but we never seem to get together or see much of one another."

"Actually, I think we were in different classes," Weber said, realizing he was telling Wilson about more than just high school. He found himself having a hard time being civil when he replied. "And you know, ever since my old hound dog chewed up my tennis racket, I haven't been back to the club."

For just the briefest second, Weber thought Wilson might lose his practiced smile, but it didn't happen. In fact, the developer laughed out loud.

"Is this guy funny, or what?" he asked Parks. "You had me going there for a second, Sheriff!"

"Oh, he's just a hoot," simpered Parks.

"What can I do for you, Roger?"

Wilson's transformation from happy go lucky buddy to Mr. Serious was instantaneous, and Weber wondered who was the better actor, Wilson or his wife.

"Actually, Sheriff, I wanted to talk to you about the ah.... unfortunate incident between Laura and this Johnson person."

"Johnson person? You mean Phil Johnson, the guard who was murdered with Mike Perkins?"

"Was that the other gentleman's name? He must have been the one that was your brother-in-law?"

"So, what about your wife and Johnson?"

"Well, I know Laura told you about her indiscretion. Actually, I suppose I'm the one to blame. I've been very busy lately and I guess Laura just needed some reassurance that she was still an attractive woman."

"She's a very attractive woman," Weber said.

"Yes, she is. It's sad that she had to choose a man like Johnson to get involved with."

"As opposed to a man like who?" Weber asked, wondering if Wilson would have felt better if his wife's lover came from a higher social caste.

If Wilson caught Weber's sarcasm, he ignored it.

"Laura's not a bad woman, really. It's just that she seems to be rather shallow, I'm afraid. Her entire being is tied up in her perception of her beauty and desirability."

"Oh, I just *hate* shallow people, don't you?" asked Parks.

Again, either Wilson didn't notice the jibe, or chose to ignore it.

"So what's your point, Roger?" Weber asked, watching Parks stir sugar into his coffee.

When he replied, Wilson was all business. "My point, Sheriff, is that my wife had absolutely nothing to do with this murder. I have no idea why you'd even be bothering her about it."

"We're talking to anyone who had any connection to the victims," Weber said. "That doesn't mean we think any particular person is involved in the murders."

"Well, I should think we've settled that by now," said Wilson. "Laura made a little mistake. It's over, and we've put it behind us. But she certainly had nothing to do with those men getting killed."

Weber thought to himself that both Roger Wilson and his wife seemed to consider her affair as an inconsequential thing. He wondered if that was because it was a frequent occurrence.

"I don't think she did, either," Weber said. "But I have to ask myself about you, Roger."

The pasted-on grin was back. "Me?"

"Well, look at it from my point of view," Weber explained, knowing that a man like Roger Wilson could never consider anything from his perspective. "You come in and find your wife in bed with another man. You get upset, you throw your wife around a little bit. You threaten to kill Phil Johnson. Then he comes up dead."

Weber decided that Wilson was an even more accomplished actor than his wife. The man never displayed a hint of emotion or concern when learning he was a suspect in a double murder case.

Mr. Serious stepped back on stage. "That's ridiculous, Sheriff. I had nothing to do with this crime. I'll be honest with you, it wasn't the first time I'd caught Laura in a 'compromising position,' shall we say? But I'm not your killer."

"You threatened to kill Phil Johnson." Weber reminded him.

"In the heat of the moment, Sheriff! That's all it was. I never meant it. We've all said stupid things from time to time, won't you agree?"

"Where were you Monday morning?" Weber asked.

Wilson thought for a moment. "I'd have to check my Day Timer for exact times throughout the day, but I was over on the coast."

"California?"

"Yes. We've got a project coming together up near Big Sur. I was meeting with various county officials, trying to get some zoning snarls worked out. All very boring stuff, actually."

"And if I were to check with these "various county officials" over in California, they could verify you were there Monday?"

Wilson looked at the sheriff levelly. "Are you asking if I have an alibi, Sheriff?"

"I guess I am."

"Well, I'm sure they could tell you where I was. However, you must understand, if they thought I was involved in some sort of a crime, even having to speak to a policeman, it might cast a bad reflection on my project over there. It certainly would with my investors. I wouldn't appreciate that, Sheriff. In fact, I'd hold your office, and you personally, responsible for any setbacks I experienced as a result."

"From what your wife tells me, you've experienced a *few* "setbacks" recently," Weber replied.

For the first time, Wilson seemed taken aback. "What do you imply by that, Sheriff?"

"Well, Laura said your last couple of projects went bad on you, and money was tight. To my way of thinking, $300,000 could dig a man out of a pretty deep hole."

Wilson stared at the sheriff a long time, then burst out laughing. "Oh, you tiny little man, you! Yes, Sheriff, I can see how that would seem like a lot of money to a man in your line of work. But let me assure you, I deal in millions, even billions of dollars. To put it in terms you can understand, $300,000 is chickenfeed."

"You feed your chickens a lot better than I do," Weber told him.

Wilson laughed again, but his eyes weren't laughing with him. "Look, I don't let Laura get too involved with my work, for obvious reasons. Yes, I had a deal or two fall through and lost some money. But only a couple of mil, okay? No big deal. I don't expect I'll be applying for welfare anytime soon."

"Well, if it was just a couple of mil..." Parks said.

Wilson stood up to leave, and Weber asked him a final question.

"How do you handle it, Roger?"

"Handle what?"

"A beautiful wife like yours, and you catch her in bed with another man. I'd blow my brains out. And hers too."

Wilson showed off that dazzling smile again.

"That, Sheriff, is just one of the differences between you and me."

He was laughing over his shoulder as he left the cafe.

Parks suggested he have his office run a complete background check on Roger Wilson, and when they left the café, Weber dropped him off at his cabin to pick up his Bureau car, then drove to Debbie's house. His sister seemed to have forgiven him for yesterday's revelation. She greeted him at the door wearing a brightly colored ski sweater over black jeans and gave Weber a hug.

"I'm sorry I got so mad at you, Jimmy. I just can't accept the fact that Mike would cheat on me. I know I overreacted. I drove around a long time last night, thinking. I refuse to accept this nonsense that Mike was doing anything wrong behind my back, but I know you're just doing your job." She squeezed him again.

Weber kissed her cheek and smiled down at her. "Thanks, Princess. I'm sorry to have been the one to bring it up. But we have to see what it's all about. I don't believe it any more than you do, okay?"

Debbie nodded and took Weber's hand, leading him into the living room. Rachel came into the room in her terrycloth bathrobe, drying her hair with a towel. Weber thought again how beautiful she was. She greeted him with a warm smile.

"Okay, let's get this over with," Debbie said. "Tell me exactly what they said about Mike and this so called affair."

Weber shifted in his seat and began to run down what they had learned. "A woman who runs a motel in Globe reported that Mike had rented a room there three times. Each time he was with a woman, the same one every time. They've got his credit card slips, his signature on the motel registration. They're sending them up for me to take a look at. And the motel operator identified Mike from photos in their local newspaper."

"Did she describe the woman?" Rachel asked.

"Only as young and pretty." Weber said. "Apparently the woman never came into the office, she always showed up in a separate vehicle and went right into the room, so the witness never got a close look at her."

"I still don't believe it," Debbie said. "It just wasn't something Mike would do."

"Debbie, do you have your Visa bills handy," Weber asked.

"Some place. Let me look," Debbie said, getting up and going to a bureau, where she pulled out a drawer and began sorting through a pile of paperwork. "Mike always handled the bills and all, but they have to be here."

"According to the motel, the last time they showed up was the Saturday before the hijacking."

Debbie paused and turned to Weber. "That was the day I was over in Flagstaff. I called Mike two or three times, but he didn't answer. He said he was with you, working on your pickup."

Weber thought back and shook his head. "Debbie, I was on duty all that day. Chad had a root canal the day before and was still feeling pretty bad. I covered for him."

"There must be some mistake," Debbie said, dismissing the evidence. "Maybe you got your days wrong, Jimmy. You work so much, I don't know how you could remember when you take a day off."

She pulled a rubber banded bundle of envelopes loose and walked back to the sofa. "Here we go, our Visa bills for the entire year. Mike never threw anything away."

Weber began sorting through the invoices, checking the charge dates against the information Loraz had supplied him. What he discovered didn't make him happy.

"Here they are, kid, two dates in October, the 22nd and 29th, both Saturdays."

When Debbie looked at him, tears glistened in her eyes.

"Every Saturday in October I was in Flag, studying and doing research at the University library, Jimmy."

Rachel snatched the credit card invoice from Weber's hand. "I can't believe this! There has to be some explanation that makes sense out of all this."

Weber looked at Debbie and felt the hollow feeling inside him grew even larger. "Debbie, I have to ask... were there any problems between you two?"

"You mean something that would drive Mike into another woman's arms?" Debbie asked. "I don't think so, Jimmy. I mean, I was putting in a lot of time with my classes and all, but Mike seemed to be behind me all the way." She paused for a moment to reflect. "Now I have to wonder if it was because he wanted me to make it, or just because it gave him time to screw around behind my back!"

Rachel burst into tears and threw the invoice down on the coffee table, then fled from the room and down the hallway toward the guest bedroom. Weber wanted to go after her, but forced himself to turn back to Debbie instead.

"I know this is personal, kid, but.... were things normal between you and Mike, intimately?"

"You're asking how our sex life was?" Debbie said, her face coloring. "God, Jimmy!"

"I have to ask, Debbie. Sometimes when a person is having an affair, things at home taper off or change. Sometimes they even get better, like they're trying to overcompensate."

Debbie sighed and tried to get past her embarrassment at revealing the secrets she and her husband had shared in bed. "It was okay, I guess. I mean, if anything, I was the one who had slowed down, what with school and all. There just didn't seem to be a lot of time." She paused reflectively a moment, then went on, "But when we did make love, it was good."

Weber finally left her and walked down the hall to knock on Rachel's door. When there was no answer, he turned the knob and opened the door slightly. Rachel was sitting on the bed, facing away from him. She had changed into a blue pantsuit and her suitcases were packed and on the bed.

"Rachel?"

Her back stiffened.

"Go away, Jimmy!"

"Rachel, we need to talk. This whole thing...."

She turned to him, deep lines of grief and anger etched into her face, tears streaming down her cheeks.

"I don't want to talk to you, Jimmy! Not now, not ever again. I don't want to talk to you, I don't want to talk to Debbie. I never want to see

Big Lake again. I just want to take what good memories I still have of my brother and leave. Just go away, Jimmy. Please, just go away and leave me alone."

Weber stared at her a long time, his heart aching, searching for any words that might bring them back to where they had been. He couldn't find any. Finally he nodded and pulled the door closed.

Chapter 14

When Weber walked into the Sheriff's Office, Robyn was on the telephone, and she was obviously relieved to see him. "Talk about timing, Sheriff!" she said, her hand over the mouthpiece. "I've got Lucy Washburn on the line, and she's, to quote her, mad as hell!"

Hell being about the most profane thing Weber had ever heard Robyn say, he knew Miss Lucy must be on a roll. Robyn managed to interrupt her caller after several attempts.

"Miss Washburn, Sheriff Weber just walked in. Can you hold just one more minute?"

Obviously not, if the noise coming from the receiver Robyn held away from her ear was any indication.

"Yes ma'am," Robyn said, "Here's the Sheriff now." But it was obvious Miss Lucy didn't hear her.

Weber scooped up an extension, punched the illuminated button and said "Good morning, Miss Lucy. How are you today?"

"First of all, it's not morning any longer, Jim Weber! Morning has been over for 55 minutes. Doesn't the town pay you enough to afford a wristwatch? If you already own one, I might suggest you look at it on occasion. And in answer to your question, I'm mad as hell!"

Weber smiled at the old woman's tirade.

"I'm sorry to hear that, Miss Lucy. What's got you so upset?"

"I'm not 'upset' you danged fool! I told you, I'm mad as hell!"

"All right," Weber said. "And just why are you mad as hell?"

"Because I do not appreciate my cabin being searched over and over again. With Phil Johnson dead, I need to get that place rented again. Vacant properties do not produce a positive cash flow. When are you people going to release it to me so I can have Mr. Johnson's belongings removed?"

"I'm sorry, Miss Lucy," Weber apologized. "I should have returned your key to you last week. I don't think Johnson left anything behind that's going to do us any good in our investigation. We've been done with the cabin for days now."

There was silence for several minutes, then Miss Lucy spoke again, her voice concerned.

"Sheriff, are you telling me that you weren't in the cabin yesterday?"

"No ma'am," Weber said. "I wasn't anywhere near the place."

"Maybe it was one of your deputies, then?"

"It couldn't have been, Miss Lucy. I've had the key in my pocket all week." Weber felt his pulse quicken. "Was someone in there, Miss Lucy?"

"About dark, I happened to look out and spotted a light moving around inside the cabin. I just assumed that it was you or one of your people."

"Did you see a vehicle," Weber asked.

"No, just the light moving around from room to room. A flashlight, I think."

"I'm going to drive out there right now, Miss Lucy," Weber said. "I'll be back in touch."

He hung up the telephone and motioned with his head to Parks. "Let's take a ride."

From the end of the driveway, the cabin looked the same as it had when Weber had searched it Monday afternoon. They left the Bronco at the entrance to the driveway and walked toward the cabin, keeping to the edge of the driveway.

"Someone's been here," Parks observed, nodding to tire tracks in the melting snow.

Weber looked at the tread pattern. "A truck or sport utility vehicle. Those tracks were made by all terrain tires."

When they neared the cabin, Weber withdrew the key from the pocket of his Levis and started to unlock the door, when he noticed it was slightly ajar. Weber looked at Parks, and both men drew their guns.

"Police officers," Weber called out. "If you're in there, come out right now and keep your hands up where we can see them!"

Nothing. Weber thumbed back the hammer on his Colt and looked toward the FBI agent. Parks held his pistol in both hands and nodded. Weber pushed the door open and stepped inside, crouched over, the .45 in front of him. Parks, standing erect, covered the sheriff. The living room was empty, and the lawmen quickly swept the cabin, finding it unoccupied.

"Well, whoever it was, they're gone," Weber said, slipping the pistol into his belt behind his right hip.

"Kids maybe?" Parks asked.

"I don't think so," Weber said. "Kids would have trashed the place."

At first glance the cabin looked undisturbed, but Weber noticed little clues that someone had indeed been inside, and had been looking for something. Dresser drawers weren't fully closed, the bathroom door he remembered leaving open when he had searched the cabin was now closed, and several papers from Johnson's dresser were now on the bed. On a hunch he pulled a night stand drawer open. Weber's heart sank when he discovered Johnson's .38 Smith & Wesson was gone.

"Whoever it was, they took a Chief's Special that was in here," Weber said.

"Hell, Jimmy, the way you hillbillies shoot at each other around here with machine guns and all, one more little piss ant .38 isn't going to make much difference one way or the other."

Weber concentrated, trying to remember how the cabin had appeared the last time he was here. He was pushing the night stand drawer closed when something else caught his attention. Weber bent and picked up a small wicker wastebasket from the floor next to the bed.

"What you got, partner?" Parks asked.

"It's what I don't have," Weber told him. "There was a condom package in here. I threw it in myself."

"Well hell, Jimmy! I'm a warrior in the war on AIDS. We'll stop at the drugstore on the way back to the office and I'll buy you a whole box of Trojans. The ribbed ones. How about that?"

"No, Parks, not a condom. A condom package. An empty one."

Parks shrugged. "You're telling me someone broke in, searched the place, and all they took was a .38 and an empty condom wrapper? You people are way too inbred up here, Sheriff."

"No," Weber shook his head. "Whoever was in here, they had a specific reason to take that wrapper with them. Why would someone do that, Parks?"

The FBI agent shrugged. "Hell, Jimmy. I don't know. At first I was thinking it was just your regular burglary. You know, someone knows Johnson's dead and the place is empty and they decide to rip it off. This changes all that."

"Yeah it does," Weber replied. "The question is, why?"

"So where's the condom itself?"

Now it was Weber's turn to shrug. "Flushed?"

They both jumped when the telephone rang, then looked at one another with chagrin.

Weber picked up the receiver.

"Is that you, Sheriff? What's going on down there? Has someone vandalized my place?"

"No, Miss Lucy," Weber told her. "The cabin is fine. But there's been a new development in our investigation. I'm afraid I'll need to keep the key a while longer."

The string of expletives that exploded out of the telephone made it clear Miss Lucy Washburn had inherited more than land from her long deceased father.

Weber had thrown a load of laundry into his washing machine earlier, and was transferring the pile of damp uniforms to the electric dryer. "Parks, would you do me a favor?" Weber asked, discovering the box of fabric softener sheets was empty. "On the shelf there in the garage there should be another box of Downy sheets. Grab them for me, would you?"

"Sure thing," Parks said, opening the door he leaned against and stepping into the garage. He found the softener sheets and paused to admire Weber's Chevy pickup. Suddenly a frown crossed the FBI man's face.

"Jimmy?"

"Can't find them?" Weber asked over his shoulder, cleaning the dryer's lint trap.

He turned and saw the box in Parks' hand, the pensive look on his face. "What is it, Parks?"

"Where's Phil Johnson's truck?" Parks asked.

"His truck?"

"Yeah, his truck. Didn't that woman at the bakery say Johnson had a truck or a Jeep or something? Where is it?"

A picture of Johnson's white Jeep Wagoneer flashed through Weber's mind. He mentally kicked himself for not realizing the Jeep was missing earlier.

"He had a white Wagoneer," Weber recalled. "I never even gave it a thought. Damn!"

"Where did they park the armored car?" Parks asked.

"In a garage over by the bank," Weber said. "Let's check it out."

Five minutes later they were standing in an alley in front of the sliding door of the garage that normally housed the Copperstate armored car. Parks tugged at the heavy padlock. He looked around the garage, noting that it had no windows.

"Now what?"

Weber thought a moment, then went back to the Bronco and retrieved his cellular telephone from the glove compartment. He punched in a number and waited while the phone on the other end rang three times.

"Debbie?"

"Hi, Jimmy."

"Who had the keys to the garage on Lincoln Street?" Weber asked her.

"The garage? Copperstate's garage? Mike and Phil both had keys. Why?"

"We don't know where Phil Johnson's Jeep is. Could it be in the garage?"

"I don't know, Jimmy. Is that important?"

"Yeah, it might be."

"I've got Mike's key ring here. Want me to come down?" she offered.

"Would you, kitten? It'd save me a trip."

"I'm on my way."

Parks was regaling Weber with the story of a sting operation he had participated in against an auto chop shop when Debbie's Toyota 4Runner pulled in beside the Bronco. She climbed out and held up a key ring, jiggling it at Weber.

"Thanks, kid," he said, taking the key ring from her hand. The sheriff unlocked the door and slid it open, revealing an empty bay.

"So where's the Jeep?" asked Parks again.

"I don't know, but we'd better find out," Weber said, walking back to the Bronco. He scooped up the microphone and radioed his office.

"I want an APB on a white Jeep Wagoneer, I think it's a '95 model," Weber ordered Robyn. "I don't know the license plate, but it's registered to Phil Johnson out of Big Lake. Get on the computer and find it for me!"

He slapped the hood of the Bronco in frustration at his own negligence for not realizing the Jeep was missing sooner.

By the time the sun went down Sunday evening, most of the snow that had fallen two days earlier had melted away. Weber, Debbie, Marsha and Parks were sitting in a booth at Mario's Pizzeria, a pitcher of beer and a large pepperoni and sausage pizza in front of them. Debbie hadn't wanted to come, but Weber had insisted, telling her that she needed to eat, and to get out of the house. For his own part, Weber was still fuming at himself over the Jeep.

"Cheer up, cowboy," Parks consoled him. "With everything going on, you just never even thought about it. We'll find it."

"He's not bummed out about the Jeep," Marsha said, pulling a thick slab of pizza free, cheese dripping back to the platter in long strings. "He's heartbroken because Rachel went back to the Valley. I can tell when someone's been doing the deed." She leered at Weber.

"Not funny, Marsha," said Debbie. "Rachel is so mad, I don't know if she'll ever get over it."

Weber tried not to show how much the conversation affected him. He took a sip of his beer, and Marsha used a plump finger to wipe foam off his upper lip. "Get over it, Jimmy. You know you and me are meant for each other. Face it, it's fate. What say we go try out those air shocks in your police car?"

"Marsha!" Debbie kicked her friend under the table. Marsha yelped, but the wicked grin never left her face.

"The question I want to know," Parks said, changing the subject, "is how an old fart like Phil Johnson managed to lure so many women into his bed? Here we've got a good looking fellow like yours truly sleeping alone, and Johnson has them standing in line. It just isn't fair!"

"Going through a dry spell?" Marsha asked, folding her arms on the table in front of her and giving Parks an exaggerated wink.

"*Dry spell*? Darling, the Oklahoma Dust Bowl was a dry spell. My love life is the Sahara Desert of human sexual relations!"

"Well, drink up," Marsha ordered. "I see a monsoon coming your way, big boy." She sent another wink in Parks' direction.

"Marsha!" Debbie cried again, in response to her friend's outspokenness. "Have you no shame at all?"

"Hey, I'm just trying to bring some relief and comfort to my fellow man," Marsha protested. "Is that so bad?"

Debbie giggled in spite of herself and shook her head at the chubby woman beside her.

"Hey Jimmy, I just thought of something," Parks said, suddenly alert and all business. "What did we do with the slugs from the Antler? We may need them for ballistics checks down the road."

"Most of them were too beat up to do us any good," Weber told him. "But the one we dug out of my truck's seat was just like new. It's bagged and tagged."

"Your boys up on that hill collected a bunch of 5.56 shell casings. We know the Millers had AR-15s that day we were up there. Can we get a court order to test fire their rifles for a comparison?"

"We might, but it'd be a stretch," Weber said. "The judge wasn't too thrilled about issuing the warrants on Ernie, said I didn't have enough probable cause. Not to mention, I think if we went up there to seize their guns, Jess would try to turn it into a Second Amendment thing and we might actually start World War III, right then and there."

"So now what?"

"I think we need to concentrate on the allegations about Mike and an affair and put that all behind us first." Debbie's face colored and Weber patted her hand before he continued.

"It just doesn't make any sense," Marsha said. "Mike was as true as any man ever was to his wife. I think someone made a mistake. I don't know how, but they did. It's the only explanation."

Debbie smiled gratefully at her friend's support of her dead husband.

"Well, Mike never reported the card stolen, according to the bank" Weber said. "He never mentioned it was missing to you, did he, Debbie? Could he have loaned it to someone?"

"No," Debbie said. "Mike wasn't much for credit cards anyway. Especially as tight as money has been since I started school. I used mine a lot, for books and when I was on the road and all. But Mike hardly ever used his. In fact, I doubt he would have even known if it was missing."

"So," Marsha concluded, "If we find the missing credit card, or the missing Jeep, we may find out who did all this."

"*We?*" Parks asked. "When did you pin on a badge, little lady?"

"I thought every handsome detective needed a sexy sidekick," she replied, and ran the tip of her tongue seductively across her upper lip. "I'm sticking to you like glue, you big stud, you! Or at least like velcro handcuffs."

"My handcuffs are solid, good old American steel," Parks told her.

Marsha dropped her voice to a theatrical sultriness. "Just thinking about you and your handcuffs gives me an ovarian twinge," she said, and blew Parks a big wet kiss.

"Shit, Marsha," Weber teased. "If anyone ever took you up on it, you'd run home with your tail between your legs!"

She gave Weber a hurt look. "Jimmy, never say the word tail or mention anything between the legs to a woman as horny as I am, okay?"

"Marsha!" Debbie said, and the group at the table giggled, in spite of the tension and heartbreak of the past week.

Chapter 15

Weber's deputies reminded him of eager children on Christmas morning when he arrived at the Sheriff's Office early Monday. The entire force was on hand and squirming in anticipation of receiving the new police vehicles. They hadn't started bickering over who would get which unit yet, so Weber decided to address the issue first.

"Okay guys, here's the situation. We've got four officers and only three new cars coming. Someone's going to be stuck with the old S-10 for a while longer."

Tommy Frost raised his hand like a timid student on his first day in a classroom. "Jimmy?"

"Yes, the freckle-faced little boy in the front row," Jimmy said, and the deputies guffawed, while Tommy's face turned pink.

"Jimmy, I've been thinking about this...."

"Watch it, the kid's been thinking," warned Chad. "He could burst into flames any minute now!"

"Up yours," Tommy shot back, grinning, then continued his original thought. "Since I'm the newest deputy, it stands to reason that I should get the S-10. Hell, I've been driving it all along anyway, and I'm used to it. I think if we could come up with some money somewhere for a new carburetor and battery, I could fix it myself and get it running pretty good for now."

"I told you he was a great kid," Chad said, nudging Buz in the rib cage. "I trained him myself. Sharp as a tack."

"That's good of you, Tommy," Weber said, appreciating the young deputy's selflessness. "You get me an estimate on what you're going to need and I'll find the money somewhere."

"While we're on that train of thought," Dolan said, "I don't see why we should scrap the old Caprice either."

"The Caprice *is* scrap," Chad said. "Damn, Dolan, you were in it when that shooter opened up on you. There's not much left of it."

"Not really," Dolan insisted. "I mean, with some Bondo we can patch the body up and paint it ourselves. It'd be a good office project. I know we can never get it back to anything worth much, but in a pinch, it could come in handy. If nothing more than a backup vehicle for working the school crossings and such."

"A lot of the towns are using older cars for decoys," said Buz, getting into the spirit. "They put an old marked car out on the highway to slow traffic down, gives the tourists something to think about when they come barreling through town."

"I like it," Mary put in. "Hell, Jimmy, if nothing else, I can use it when I run errands and we can save paying me mileage on my pickup."

"Maybe so," Weber said, not completely convinced that the old police cruiser was worth salvaging, but willing to consider the idea. "I guess it would give us an extra presence around town. We'll park it out back and see how we feel about it this spring when the weather warms up."

"So who gets what?" Buz asked.

"Well, I thought the fairest way was to draw straws, shortest gets first pick, then on down the line," Weber suggested. "That okay with you fellows?"

"Works for me," Chad said, and scooped a box of wooden matches from off his desk next to his pipe. Dolan won the first round, and chose the pickup, with Chad coming out on top the next time around and claiming the Crown Victoria. Buz, finishing last, was just as happy to take the new Explorer. "But you're the sheriff, Jimmy," he said. "By all rights, you should have the new rig and I'll take your old Bronco."

Weber shook his head. "No Buz, you take it. I've been keeping the maintenance up on mine and I know it like the back of my hand. I'd just as soon stay in it for now."

Buz nodded and grinned, grateful that his boss wasn't the type to pull rank or act like a prima donna.

When the dealership opened for business at 9 a.m., the deputies were waiting. Mike Hall, a tall, gaunt man with a disposition better suited to a funeral director than an automobile salesman, led Weber and his men into the service garage.

"There you go, Sheriff. I've had my mechanics on overtime for three days now, getting them ready. I hope next time the Town Council gives us more notice."

"I'm sorry about the rush, Mike," Weber said. "With the shooting at the Antler Inn and all, we're pretty hard up for wheels. We sure do appreciate your helping us out on this."

Weber's explanation and words of gratitude did nothing to improve the morose man's attitude. "Well, here you are," said Hall, nodding at the new police fleet. "They're ready to go."

Dolan whistled in appreciation of the three new police vehicles. The new Explorer and four wheel drive F-150 pickup both sported all terrain tires, running boards, brush guards, and the truck had an electric winch mounted on its front bumper. All three vehicles were black, with gold stars on the doors, along with the words 'Sheriff's Office, Big Lake, Arizona' in gold. Red and blue police light bars were mounted on the roofs.

"Have at 'em," Weber told his men, and the deputies headed for their respective vehicles. "And behave going back to the office or home, you bunch of juvenile delinquents," he warned. "If I catch you hot rodding them, I'll write each one of you up myself!"

Weber turned back to Mike Hall and offered his hand.

"Thanks again, Mike. You really came through for us."

The walking cadaver just shrugged his shoulders listlessly and went off in search of gloomier company.

"I'm only going to be able to stay another day or two at the most," Parks told Weber. "My boss is screaming at me to get back to Phoenix if nothing new develops up here."

They were driving down Black Bear Road, near the high school. Weber glanced across the Bronco to Parks. "So where do we go from here? I'll admit it, I'm way out of my league on this one."

"Well, we should have something back today on Roger Wilson," Parks said. "I think he's a genuine jerk. But does that make him a killer?"

"I don't know. I don't like the man," Weber admitted. "But I don't know if he's got what it takes to kill someone."

"Then we have the Twisted Twins, Jesse and his little sister Tina," Parks offered. "I'm liking them for this, a lot. I keep thinking it wouldn't be much of a stretch of the imagination for Jesse to set his sister up with Johnson just to get close to him and arrange to rip off the cash shipment."

"Yeah, that's a damned good possibility," Weber agreed. "But, just for the sake of argument, we also have to consider any one of Johnson's conquests. He seems to have enjoyed using women and then dumping them. I can see where that could get a man killed."

"Well, even though she certainly had reason enough to want Johnson dead, I can't imagine the Zalenski woman doing it."

Weber shook his head. "Me either."

"Of course, there are two other avenues we still have to consider," Parks reminded the sheriff. "It could have been just your garden variety ripoff, but I don't think so. Pros wouldn't have had any reason to kill those boys. And amateurs would have left more clues. Whoever did this knew what they were doing, and they had good reason not to leave any witnesses. That means it was someone who at least one of them knew."

"Or?"

"Or?"

"You said there were two avenues we have to consider. What's the other?" Weber asked, knowing the answer.

"The other," Parks told him, "and it sucks, is that Mike Perkins really *was* having an affair, and that had something to do with it."

Weber didn't reply, just stared through the windshield and steered the Bronco down the road.

The FBI report on Roger Wilson, a long stream of fax paper, awaited Parks when they returned to the Sheriff's Office. Parks cut the fax into individual pages and collated them, then found an unoccupied desk and began to pore over the information.

Weber spent an hour whittling down the backlog of paperwork piled up on his desk; signing requisition forms, approving vacation schedules and overtime vouchers, and reviewing his deputies' activity reports. He was deep into a handwritten report explaining how Deputy Tommy Frost had managed to break a window in the upstairs bedroom of one Nellie Smith, an octogenarian spinster, while trying to retrieve her cat from the roof of her ancient two story house. Weber couldn't believe that even Tommy would have thought shooting at the cat with a slingshot might have frightened it back down to ground level.

"Knock, knock."

Weber looked up to see Debbie leaning into his office door. Her long blonde hair was piled up on top of her head, and she wore a soft pink sweater over a gray wool skirt.

"Come on in, Princess. What's up?"

Debbie took a seat across from Weber, pausing to allow him to kiss her cheek on the way.

"I'm off to Show Low. School, you know?"

"Are you sure you're up to that so soon?" Weber asked her.

Debbie took a deep breath and looked toward the ceiling for a moment, then sent her brother a brave smile. "No, I'm not sure, Jimmy. But I got to thinking... Mike and I both worked hard and put a lot into me getting my degree. I talked to my faculty advisor, and they've said that because of the circumstances, I can make up the finals I missed and still graduate on schedule. I think Mike would have wanted me to, Jimmy."

Her eyes seemed to be seeking his approval, and Weber smiled kindly at her. "I think so too, Debbie. You go show them how it's done, kid."

Debbie grinned and rose, bending over to hug her brother. "I love you so much, Jimmy!"

"I love you too, Princess. I'm here if you need me."

Debbie placed loving hands on either side of his face and looked deep into his eyes. "Yes, Jimmy, you always are. You always have been. I love you for that most of all." She kissed his forehead and went out the door to face the world.

Parks was still busy with his report on Roger Wilson, and Weber was restless inside the office. He craved fresh air and decided to take a ride. Without consciously planning it, he found himself on the road to Jesse Miller's place. At the turnoff, Weber hesitated, then said to himself "*This is nuts*" and pulled the Bronco onto the secondary road to turn around and head back to town. The sheriff knew facing down Jesse alone could only lead to trouble, as much as he wanted to drive right up to the compound, seize every firearm on the place, and run them through ballistics to see if he could come up with a match to any of the bullets involved in the investigation. Weber was just shifting into reverse to back onto the highway when a rusty old green Chevy 4x4 pickup skidded to a stop behind him, blocking his path. "*Now what?*" Weber thought.

The driver's door of the pickup shot open and Tina Miller stormed up to Weber's Bronco. Wearing baggy fatigue pants, a worn denim jacket over a dingy blue sweatshirt, with a red stocking cap pulled down over her head, Tina could have passed for a street person in any urban area of the country. Weber rolled down the window and nodded to the woman. "Hello, Tina."

"What are you doing here?" she demanded. "Why are you spying on us! We haven't done anything wrong, Sheriff! You're violating our right to privacy and I want it stopped!"

"Tina," Weber said calmly, "I'm just turning around, okay? I'm not spying on you."

Ignoring his reply, she shook a finger in Weber's face and shouted "If you think you can get away with harassing us like this, you'd better think again! The day of accounting will come, Sheriff! You just better back off!"

"Look Tina, I said I wasn't coming to your place," Weber said. "I just went for a ride and found myself here, okay? I'm leaving, if you'll be so kind as to move your truck so I can get out."

"You really think you know it all, don't you?" Tina sneered. "But you're going to find out one of these days. And it won't be long!"

"Goddamn it, Tina, will you just quit the shit and move your damned truck before I run over it?" Weber shouted back, losing his temper. "Jesus Christ, woman! It was your husband that was killed. If you and your crazy assed brother didn't have anything to do with it, I'd think you'd want to help me find out whoever *did*! But no! You're so busy running around here like a centerfold for *Soldier of Fortune* magazine that you haven't even noticed that two men are dead!"

Weber caught his breath, angry at himself for losing control, and started to apologize to Tina, when he realized the woman was crying. Fat tears rolled down her cheeks and she fought to catch her breath. For a moment Weber thought she was going to pass out. He climbed out of the Bronco and put a steadying hand on her arm.

"I know Phil's dead, Sheriff," she told him between gasps. "I know, and it's killing me. You just don't know how much it's tearing me to pieces. No one does."

She broke down and leaned against his chest, sobbing violently. Shocked by her reaction, Weber patted her back awkwardly.

"Its okay, Tina," he told her. "Let it out."

Weber held her as a new wave of sobs shuddered through her. He realized for the first time that, as crazy as she might be, Tina Miller was also a grieving wife, caught between her pain and her need to maintain the strong front her older brother demanded of her. The thought struck Weber that he and Tina had a lot in common just then, both wanting to give in to their grief, but feeling the need to keep up the bold front others expected of them. Sheriff and rebel stood along the side of the road together as he held her, while she allowed herself to grieve.

"I'm sorry," she finally managed to say, then broke away to dig into the snow with the toe of her boot.

"I know Phil was running around on me all over the place," Tina said without looking up. "But that didn't matter. I *loved* him! He's the only good thing that had ever happened to me in my whole goddamned life, Sheriff. I just know that once this baby I've got inside me was born, Phil would have settled down. I know he would have!"

Weber wanted to tell her that it was doubtful Phil Johnson would have ever allowed anything, including a child and wife, to change his ways, but he didn't want to hurt her any more than she was already hurting. And he knew, deep inside, Tina would have never believed him. She needed her fantasy of Phil Johnson, knight in shining armor, to face the rest of her life with. No matter what ever happened to her, until the day she died, Tina could always tell herself life would have been perfect if only Phil hadn't been taken away from her.

"I think he would have, too," lied Weber, and Tina looked gratefully into his eyes, silently thanking him for helping her believe.

"Yes, he would have," she said and leaned back into him as she burst into tears again. Finally, Tina's tears ran out and she stepped back from her natural enemy. But Weber knew that from this day forward, there was a new dimension, a common thread between them.

"Sheriff, I didn't have anything to do with Phil's murder."

"I believe you," Weber said, and he did. "What about Jesse, Tina?"

She shook her head. "Jesse would never do anything to hurt me. He knew how much I loved Phil. He couldn't have. He wouldn't have! Jesse was the one who introduced me to Phil! No way, Sheriff. Jesse didn't have nothing to do with Phil getting killed!"

Weber looked at her, but this time he couldn't bring himself to lie to support her belief. Tina held his eyes a long time, then walked back to her old pickup and moved it out of Weber's way.

"You're not going to believe this!" Parks said, as Weber walked back into the office. He scooped up his stack of fax paper and followed Weber into his inner office.

"What have you got, Parks?" Weber asked, hanging his hat on a hook and shedding his jacket while he sorted through a stack of telephone message slips.

"Well, it seems our high roller may be in some serious financial trouble," said Parks. "According to this, Roger Wilson lost a real bundle on his last two projects, a condominium complex in Sedona and an office tower in Denver. Jimmy, we're talking over ten million dollars! In both cases, the development companies filed for bankruptcy. It looks like that $300,000 worth of 'chicken feed' could have come in pretty handy!

Weber nodded and thought for a minute, his mind working over the possibilities. "We already know Wilson had one motive - revenge for Johnson sleeping with his wife. Throw in the chance to score some quick cash, and old Roger could just be our boy."

"Yeah," Parks said, then grinned like the Cheshire Cat. "But there's more. Hang onto your boots, cowboy, because this one is gonna knock your socks off!"

"Let me have it," Weber said, sticking a cigar between his teeth.

Parks referred to his report and read aloud. "In 1991, Laura Ann Carter, now known as Laura Ann Wilson, was charged with murder in Hollywood, California."

Weber's jaw dropped open and the cigar threatened to tip out of his mouth before he clamped back down on it.

"No way!"

"I've got it right here, in black and white," Parks assured him. "The *Reader's Digest* condensed version is this - Laura was charged with shooting to death a guy named Ronnie Sutton, in January of 1991. Sutton was a movie producer, fairly small potatoes. He put together some grade B movies. Laura had small parts in three of them."

"What happened?" Weber asked, rolling the cigar around in his mouth.

"From what I can gather from all this, Sutton was well known for his casting couch techniques. An actress didn't need much in the way of talent if she had a great set of jugs, as far as old Ronnie was concerned. People close to the case said he assigned starring roles based on how good the actress was at the horizontal hula. The word was that Ronnie had promised Laura the lead in his next movie, in exchange for giving up the goods. She came through, but by the time he was choosing the cast for his next project, some other cutie had caught his eye and Laura was stuck in another walk-through role. Apparently, the lady didn't take well to that."

"And she killed him?"

"Well, her story was that the victim tried to force himself on her one night in his office when she went to discuss a problem with the script." said Parks. "Laura claimed Sutton tried to rape her, there was a struggle, and somehow she got her hands on a .38 he kept in his desk and shot him in self defense."

"What happened then?" Weber asked, intrigued.

"Well, a psychiatrist Laura's rich daddy hired to help her defense team reported that she had a severe personality disorder, some sort of bipolar thing. I guess they were laying the groundwork for a temporary insanity plea if the self-defense thing didn't hold up. The DA didn't buy any of it, but you know how people are when it comes to a shot at their fifteen minutes of fame. Suddenly, women who couldn't make it in the business were coming out of the woodwork claiming that Ronnie had raped them, too. According to people in the know, all of them were girls Sutton had banged and promised to turn into stars, then didn't come through. But since the victim wasn't around to tell his side of things, and with all those poor abused women backing up Laura's story and giving the press a field day, the DA finally dropped the charges."

"So Laura got a walk?"

"That's about it," Parks said. "But, it ended whatever shot at a career she might have had. I guess the other directors in town decided it was easier to bed down someone newer and less lethal. Partner, we're in the wrong line of work."

Weber ran his fingers through his hair and considered this newest twist to the case. "If Laura killed once and got away with it, does that mean she'd do it again?"

"Who knows? They say the first time is the hardest." Parks said. "Maybe she just assumed she could get away with it a second time. Let's say Johnson dropped her after hubby came in and caught them. Would that be enough reason to kill the man?"

"I don't know," Weber replied. "It wouldn't be for a rational person, but according to her shrink, Laura may not be playing with a full deck to start with. You never know what a crazy person is going to do. Personally, I don't think it meant all that much to her. I doubt that a woman like Laura Wilson has to look far for lovers."

"No doubt about that," Parks agreed. "She's got legs to make you cry for, and an ass to die for. The question is, did Johnson die for it?"

"Or," Weber added, "Maybe the pair of them were in it together. Laura said something about 'having to pay the price' for getting caught cheating. Was helping Roger rip off the armored car part of that price?"

Parks tossed the report on Weber's desk and sat back in his chair, locking his fingers behind his head. "One thing's for sure," he told Weber. "We need to see more of those two. With all this, I think one or both of them could be as likely to be our killers as Jesse Miller and his sister."

"I think we can rule out Tina," Weber said. "I don't think she killed Johnson."

"Why not?"

"I ran into her today," Weber said and filled Parks in on his encounter with Tina Miller out on the highway.

"Hell, Jimmy, just because she claimed she loved the guy and cried a few crocodile tears doesn't mean she wasn't lying through her teeth," Parks argued. "Another thing they taught us in FBI school was that everyone lies when they talk to a cop."

"You could be right," the sheriff agreed, "But I don't think so. That girl is really hurting. I know a little bit about that myself. She wasn't faking it."

The FBI agent arched his eyebrows at Weber and nodded. "Yeah partner, I guess when it comes to hurting, you've done more than your share. I'll trust your gut on this one."

Weber didn't tell his friend he wasn't sure if it was his gut or his heart telling him Tina Miller was innocent.

A disturbance in the outer office caught Weber's attention and he went out to see what was going on. "No way," declared Buz Carelton. "I don't know where you're getting your information, junior, but you are *not* coming to work at this office!"

The object of Buz's derision was a flabby young man wearing glasses with smudged lenses and thick black frames, and a stained shirt stretched tightly over his belly that was a walking testament to what he'd had for breakfast and lunch that day. His hair was uncombed and Weber noticed that his fly was open.

"Archer, around here our day begins at 8 a.m.," the sheriff said. "What happened to you, did you get yourself dragged behind a produce wagon or what?"

"Hi, Sheriff," said Archer. "I'm reporting for duty!"

"Don't tell me this!" Buz pleaded. "Jimmy, what the hell have you *done*?"

"I didn't do it," Weber told him. "This is the tradeoff we got for our new fleet. Sucks, doesn't it?"

If Archer Wingate was uncomfortable in learning that his new position was a direct result of his father's influence, he managed to hide it very well. He stood in front of the sheriff and Buz awaiting instructions.

"I'm not working with him." Buz told Weber. "You can team him up with Chad or Dolan for his orientation, but I *am not* working with this useless slob!"

"You're just still mad about your television," Archer said, scowling at Buz. "It's not my fault the stupid thing fell off the cart!"

The television Archer referred to was Buz's beloved big screen RCA, a birthday gift from his wife that he cherished, especially during football and baseball season. A year earlier, at the height of the World Series, the television had developed a slight lessening in picture quality. Janice Carelton, wanting to surprise her husband, called Archer to adjust it. This was during Archer's short-lived stint as a television repairman.

No one will ever know if he was competent enough to repair Buz's television - while wheeling it out to his van, the flimsy cart Archer was using collapsed and the RCA burst into a hundred parts, on impact with the sidewalk. Archer claimed the incident was an 'act of God' and refused to compensate Buz. A week later Archer was out of the television business and pushing discount long distance telephone service.

"Calm down, Buz," Weber said. "I'll find someone to run him through his probation period. Not that I think he'll make it."

"My father said you'd better not try to run me off," Archer warned. "He's going to be watching you, Sheriff!"

Weber moved so close he bumped into Archer's protruding gut and bent down to stare him in the face. "You listen to me, and you listen to me damn close, Archer! I *am not* worried about your daddy. I *am not* intimidated by him! And I *am not* impressed with his one failed attempt to conceive a child! Do you understand me?"

Archer blinked and pushed his glasses up onto the bridge of his nose.

"Your old man may be the Mayor," Weber continued, his voice rising. "But I am the Sheriff! You work for me. We both know that the only reason you're standing here right now is because your dad forced you on us. Now, I'm giving you fair warning, if you screw up around here, if you don't carry your weight, if you so much as drop a cigarette butt on the floor, you're out of here! Do you understand me?"

Archer snapped to a semblance of attention and said "Yes sir! Sir?"

"What is it, Archer?"

"I don't smoke, Sheriff?"

"What?"

"I don't smoke. You said if I so much as dropped a cigarette butt on the floor. I don't think that's going to be a problem, since I don't smoke."

Weber would have thought his new deputy was baiting him, but the way Archer stood there blinking innocently at him, he decided he was sincere. Or at least as sincere as Archer Wingate was capable of being.

"Fine, Archer. Now, you get yourself over to the uniform supply in Show Low and you pick up your uniforms and equipment and report back here no later than 6 p.m. for duty."

"6 p.m.? Tonight?" asked Archer in dismay.

"Is that a problem, Deputy?"

"Well, no, I guess not. But I had plans for tonight," explained Archer.

"Well, you're just going to have to do your nails some other time," Weber said. "Now move it!"

"I tell you, Jimmy, law enforcement is going to hell," said Parks, watching Archer's retreating posterior. Archer almost managed to make it out the door without mishap, but at the last minute, he somehow stumbled over a loose shoelace and grabbed the closest thing for support. Unfortunately for both parties involved, the closest thing at hand was Robyn. Archer's flailing hand closed on the neck of her blouse and the material gave way with a loud rip, leaving Archer face down with a handful of blue printed cotton and Robyn covering herself with her hands and what was left of the blouse.

"You clumsy ass!" screamed the mortified woman, and as Weber snatched someone's uniform jacket off the coat rack to cover her, he couldn't help thinking that this was the second time in days he had heard Robyn curse. Obviously the harsh world of police work was taking its toll on her.

"Jimmy, you've got to do something! We can't have that idiot running around in a uniform," complained Chad Summers. As soon as word got out that Archer was joining the force, Weber's deputies descended on him en masse to protest.

"I'm no happier about it than you are, guys," the sheriff assured them. "But it was the only way the Council would spring for the new vehicles. I didn't know about until it was a done deal. Let's just try to make the best of it, okay?"

"The best we can hope for is that he won't shoot himself in the foot... or anyone else," said Buz.

"Come on, fellows," said Tommy, always the peacemaker. "Maybe we should give the poor guy a chance."

"Oh, shut up, Tommy," snapped Buz. "You're just glad to have him around so you won't be low man on the totem pole any more."

Tommy started to reply, but one look in Buz's eye convinced him to remain silent.

"I'm telling you," said Parks, "I've seen some sorry excuses for lawmen in my time, but that boy's in a league of his own!"

"Shut up, Parks. I don't need any help from the peanut gallery," Weber told him.

"You boys see what happens when you use those cheap bargain brand condoms?" Parks went on, ignoring Jimmy with a grin. "Enough seeps through to create life, just not intelligent life."

"Shut up, Parks," Weber said again, then held up his hand to cut off any more protest. "Guys, I'm stuck, okay? We all know Archer's a loser. We all know he won't cut it. So let's just try to minimize the damage until he gets bored with it or hurts himself enough to go on disability and is out of our hair, all right?"

"That's easy for you to say," said Robyn from her place at the radio console. "It wasn't you that he stripped naked!"

"By the way, I meant to tell you, you've got great boobs for a skinny girl, even if they're not all that big," teased the FBI man.

"Shut up, Parks!" Robyn shot back.

Chapter 16

It was just after 3 p.m. when Weber turned into Roger Wilson's driveway and almost collided with his white Ford Expedition. Weber slammed on his brakes to avoid a head on collision and looked through the windshield at an obviously unhappy Roger Wilson.

"What do you want, Sheriff? I'm on my way to Albuquerque."

Weber got out of his Bronco and walked up to Wilson's door.

"Business trip, Roger?"

"Yes," said Wilson, impatiently. "I've got a plane to catch and I don't have any time to waste. What was it you wanted?"

"Roger, you lied to me," said Weber. "We ran a check on you. Those last two projects of yours that went belly up lost a lot of money."

"I already told you they did," Wilson replied. "So how did I lie to you, Sheriff? I really don't have time for this." He looked pointedly at the Rolex on his wrist as he spoke.

"Well, maybe you didn't flat out lie. Let's say that you didn't tell the whole truth about them. Like the fact that you filed bankruptcy on both projects."

The developer laughed at Weber's ignorance of the world of high finance. "Sheriff," he explained patiently. "I really don't have the time to give you an education in the methods and wherefores of real estate development. But let me try to explain something to you to put your tiny little mind at ease.

"What I do is called *business*. Sometimes in business you succeed in a project, and sometimes things go wrong. It's all a crapshoot, and the whole idea is to have more winners than losers. Whenever I begin a new project, I form a corporation solely for that project. Investors put in their money hoping for a good return, which they usually receive. But if things go wrong, as they sometimes can, we have to bail out. The corporation files for protection under the bankruptcy laws, the investors lose a little bit, they show a loss on their income taxes, and they make it up the next time around. That's the risk they take. In these last two projects, it was the *corporations* that filed bankruptcy, not me. I didn't lose a cent. Just my time and effort. That's the risk *I* take."

"So who were the big losers?" Weber asked. "If it wasn't you and your rich buddies, who was it? The small contractors that invested everything they had in materials and labor and were left holding the bag when you walked away?"

Wilson snorted, an uncharacteristic sound for a man of his refinement. He shook his head at the sheriff. "Unfortunately, that's the risk *they* take. If they can't play in the big leagues, maybe they'd be better off sticking to remodeling garages and such. Now, I really do have to leave."

Weber didn't move, and Wilson fidgeted in his seat for a moment.

"Did you kill those boys, Roger?"

"Are you crazy?" said Wilson, his veneer of control cracking momentarily. "I told you, I was on the coast! Since you were so busy playing detective, I'd have thought you would have checked that out."

"Oh, maybe you didn't pull the trigger," Weber told him. "Personally, I don't think you've got the balls for that. But I'm about half convinced you had a hand in it, somehow. All I need is one little break and your ass is mine, Roger."

Wilson stared straight ahead through the windshield. "Sheriff, if you're ready to arrest me, go ahead. I'll have the best legal representation in the Southwest here in two hours, and by the time I'm done with you, you'll be catching dogs somewhere for a living. If you're *not* going to arrest me, please move your truck. I've got a plane to catch."

Weber looked at Wilson's profile for a silent moment, then stood up and started back to his Bronco. "You have a nice trip, Roger."

Laura Wilson seemed more animated than the last time he had seen her when she opened the door. "Sheriff! Back so soon?"

"Can I come in, Laura?" Weber asked.

She smiled and stepped back. "Of course! I always seem to leave you standing out there, don't I?"

Weber stepped past her, aware of her perfume, something that vaguely reminded him of lilacs and roses. This day, Laura was wearing a white silk lounging outfit, much like the one he had last seen her in, except for the color. The white top did even less to hide her nipples than the black one had.

Laura took his hand and led him into the great room and sat cross-legged on one of the leather sofas next to him. "Can I get you a drink, Sheriff?"

"No thanks, "Weber told her. "I'm on duty."

She pouted for a second. "You and Roger, always working. What's a girl to do?"

"Laura, tell me about Ronnie Sutton," Weber said.

For just a second he saw something move behind her eyes, but no other reaction.

"What's to tell? I had bit parts in a couple of his movies. He promised to make me a star and I was young enough, and naive enough, to believe him. He lied."

"Tell me about the night you shot him," Weber prompted.

Laura pouted again. "Oh, Sheriff, I don't want to go into all that again. Can't we just have a nice little visit and forget all that ugliness for a while?"

She placed a manicured hand on the sheriff's arm and Weber felt jolts of electricity run down his spine. "*Watch yourself*," he said silently. "*She's an actress, remember? And a killer.*"

"I really need you to tell me about it, Laura."

She sighed and leaned forward, and this time Weber couldn't keep himself from a long look at her cleavage. Laura ran a finger across his lips and shook her head. "Come on, Sheriff. Later, maybe. Not now."

Weber wanted her. He wanted her more than he had ever wanted a woman in his life, and Laura could read that in his eyes. Everything inside him, every inch of his professionalism, told him this was stupid. He knew he was setting himself up for a big fall. But he still wanted her. Laura's eyes closed and she leaned forward, her lips on his, her tongue darting out to brush his teeth. She sighed again and moved his hand to her breast. Weber felt the nipple harden under his palm and Laura thrust her tongue deeper into his mouth, demanding. God, he wanted her!

"Sorry," the sheriff said, putting his hands on her forearms and pushing her gently away.

"It's okay," Laura said, trying to reassure him, her voice husky. "Roger just left. He won't be home until Wednesday. No one will ever know."

Weber shook his head, trying to clear the fog of lust inside. "I'd know, Laura."

She smiled slightly and leaned back against the sofa. "You're too noble. Do you know that, Sheriff?"

"I'll probably kick myself in the morning," Weber told her.

"Oh, you will," she assured him. "You have no idea what you're missing. I'm very, *very* good!"

"What about Sutton, Laura?"

She shook her head and closed her eyes. "What do you want me to say? That I killed him because he used me and then didn't cast me in the lead role?"

"Is that how it happened?" Weber asked.

Laura Wilson gave Weber a look not unlike the one her husband had given him outside.

"Sheriff, I may look and act like the typical rich man's toy, but even I'm not *that* stupid! No, Ronnie tried to rape me and I shot him in self-defense. That's how it happened. It's all there in the records."

"How about Phil Johnson and Mike Perkins, Laura? Did you have anything to do with their deaths?"

She shook her head. "Sheriff, you're becoming boring. And I *hate* boring men! No, I *did not* kill them. I don't know anything about it."

"But like you just said, even if you did, you're not stupid," Weber said.

She smirked at him.

Weber stood up, and Laura grabbed his hand. "Stay! I really don't want to be alone, Sheriff. You don't know what it's like for me. I don't have any friends, I'm all alone. Please stay!"

When Weber looked down, her eyes were pleading. Laura drew his hand to her lips and kissed the palm. He felt her warm tongue on his flesh and his knees began to tremble. Lust and pity battled inside him. He drew his hand away. "I'll be in touch, Laura."

When he walked out, she was still there on the sofa, her eyes beseeching him to stay.

Weber was trying to make headway through the ever-growing pile of paperwork that seemed to be intent on covering his desktop. The sheriff was convinced that some day he would walk into his office and find the mountain of forms, disposition records, arrest reports and other papers had spilled off his desk, covered his floor, and begun working its way out the door and toward freedom, like some giant Blob from a bad 1950s movie. He was signing his way through a stack of arrest reports when Mary Caitlin knocked on his door and poked her head inside.

"Your new deputy is reporting for duty."

Weber pushed the papers away, grateful for any excuse to get away from the dreaded paperwork, even if it meant another encounter with Archer Wingate. Weber had accepted the fact that he was stuck with Archer and decided to make the best of it, but he suspected Archer's best would leave a lot to be desired.

Mary gave him an evil grin and said "Smile, Sheriff! It could be worse. He could always have a twin!"

"No he couldn't," Weber told her. "Archer is the kind of phenomena that only comes our way every hundred years or so. Mother Nature has her own system of checks and balances."

"Well, let's thank heaven for small favors," Mary said, stepping aside so Weber could get into the outer office.

Archer Wingate didn't look any more impressive in a Sheriff's Department uniform than he did in civilian clothes. The buttons of his sky blue uniform shirt threatened to pop if he took a deep breath, one shoelace was untied, and his slouching posture presented less than an authoritative figure. But at least the perpetual scowl was gone from his face. In fact, Archer was positively beaming, proud of himself now that he was officially a deputy.

"You're going to be assigned to Chad as your field training officer," Weber told him. "Every new deputy has a sixty day probationary period. I have to be honest with you, Archer, this isn't going to be easy for you. The deputies aren't too happy with the way you got on the force. I'm willing to keep an open mind, as long as you play by the rules. But goof up and you're gone, daddy or no daddy, got it?"

Archer nodded, still grinning.

"Chad, see what you can do with him," Weber said and Chad stepped forward to inspect the rookie.

"What are you carrying?" he asked, indicating Archer's holster.

Archer unsnapped the safety strap and drew his pistol, a chrome plated Colt Python with a six inch barrel. Weber was relieved to see that Archer at least had sense enough not to point the weapon at anyone.

"Jesus, Archer!" said Chad, throwing a hand in front of his eyes in mock distress. "At least you'll never have to shoot anyone with that thing. As big and shiny as it is, you'll just blind them!"

Tommy Frost giggled, but even the teasing couldn't get to Archer.

"Okay, put it away," Chad said. "Let's go see if we can't keep the world safe for democracy, at least until midnight. But first, tie your shoelace. You've done enough tripping around here for one day."

As they walked past the radio console, Robyn instinctively held a protective hand over her chest, but Archer managed to get out of the office without another attack on either her wardrobe or her dignity.

"You've been pretty quiet all day," Weber said to Parks, who was hanging up the telephone on the desk he had commandeered.

"I've been trying to run down anything else on Roger Wilson and his financial dealings," Parks replied. "He's a busy man."

"What have you come up with so far?"

"Aside from a couple of traffic tickets, he's never had any trouble with the law. It seems like what he told you about forming those short term corporations is the way it's done in real estate speculation. If they make money, great. If not, they file bankruptcy and walk away from it. It doesn't look like Wilson has taken any real hits from the failed projects. But he's got so much of his personal finances tied up in some corporation, trust, or another, that it's hard to get a clear picture of just where he stands financially."

"What do you mean?" Weber asked.

"Well, for example, his house here is actually owned by a trust that he set up. His cars are all owned by a leasing company. But he's one of the officers of *that* company! He's got a big condo in San Diego, but it's deeded to yet another company, one that Laura's father is a major shareholder in. It looks like it's all set up that way for tax purposes, but also to make it harder for anyone to find anything he actually owns if they were ever to get some kind of a judgment against him." Parks stretched and shook his head. "Who was it that said the rich are very different? Let's get some food, partner. I'm about starved to death here!"

As they were heading out the door, Parks glanced toward Robyn and said "Keep your shirt on, kid. We're outta here."

Robyn surprised Weber yet again when she gave the FBI man the finger.

"I think she loves me," he told the sheriff, and closed the door just in time to avoid a notepad that Robyn had flung in his direction.

"So now that you've got Howdy Doody on the payroll, you think you can get by without me for a while?" Parks asked, as he worked his way through a massive cut of prime rib at a corner table in the Roundup.

"They really going to make you go back to the big city?" Weber asked.

"Hey, nothing good lasts forever," Parks said philosophically. "I guess

I've got to earn my keep and all. I've got to be at a hearing in federal court Wednesday morning. Then I thought I'd see if I can make any headway from down there, just to reassure my AIC that the real investigation is up here. I'm as convinced as you are that our killer is up on this mountain somewhere, or at least it all started here, and this is where we're going to find the answer."

Weber realized that he was going to be sorry to see Parks leave. He had come to appreciate the FBI agent's wisdom and common sense, as well as his companionship and good humor.

"I'm going to miss you, Parks. You're almost useful around here. We make a good team."

"Hey, don't worry, hoss! You've got Archer working for you now. I can leave here with a clear conscience, knowing at least you've got adult supervision, don't you know?"

For the second time within an hour, a representative of the Big Lake Sheriff's Office made an obscene gesture toward the FBI's representative.

Chapter 17

Weber's telephone woke him early Tuesday morning and he fumbled for the receiver, dropping it once before he got it up to his ear.

"Hello?"

"Jimmy? We've got a break on the shooting at the Antler," said Dolan, obviously excited.

Weber sat up in bed, instantly wide awake.

"What time is it?"

"A little after six."

"What have you got?"

"I stopped Norman Calloway for a busted taillight just now, and he said he was heading out for Yuma to see his mother Friday night, just as the storm was letting up. Norman lives just across the top of Pine Mountain from the Antler, on Bluebird Road."

Weber pictured the area in his mind. Bluebird Road was a lonely little path that was more trail than road, unpaved and unplowed most of the winter. Only two full time residents lived year round on the road, Norman Calloway at the dead end, and a young man who had recently moved to Big Lake from somewhere in Utah and was on a mission for the Mormon church. Only someone with a reliable four wheel drive vehicle could depend on getting home during the winter if they lived on Bluebird Road.

"What did Norman know?"

"He just got back in town late last night and heard about the shooting. He said he was loading his truck to head out of town when a snowmobiler came flying out of the woods and past him. He said the rider had a rifle strapped over his shoulder," Dolan said.

"Could he identify who it was?" asked Weber hopefully.

"No, the rider was wearing a face mask. But a half hour later when Norman was leaving town, he spotted a pickup truck with a snowmobile on the back turning onto the highway. He swears that Tina Miller was driving it!"

Weber stomped on the brake pedal in front of Jesse Miller's gate and climbed out in the early morning air. Across from him Parks climbed out, Weber's Mini-14 in his hand. Doors slammed behind Weber, and Dolan and Buz joined them from their patrol vehicles, armed with assault rifles. Behind them, Tommy and Archer pulled up in another vehicle. Weber grabbed the chain securing the gate and jerked on the lock, which didn't budge.

"Cut it!"

Archer stepped forward with a set of bolt cutters and was just closing the jaws on the lock's hasp when the sound of an ATV split the morning and Jesse Miller roared into sight from around a bend.

"How does he do that?" Parks asked.

"Shit, he's got every kind of monitor and electronic surveillance you can think of," Weber said. "This place is as secure as a bank vault."

Miller skidded to a stop on the other side of the gate and jumped off his four wheeler, his hand on a pistol riding in a holster on his belt.

"If he draws that gun, shoot him dead!" Weber ordered and three rifle muzzles centered on Jesse's chest.

"You're trespassing, Sheriff!" Jesse shouted. "This is private property. As a free citizen, I demand that you leave immediately!" Weber noticed that Jesse's hand had moved away from the butt of his gun.

"Jesse, we've got a warrant for Tina's arrest," Weber said. "And a search warrant for a rifle that might have been used in the shooting at the Antler Inn, as well as for a black and red snowmobile. Now, we're coming in, and we're doing it right over your dead body if that's what it comes to!"

"You can't do that!" Jesse shouted back. "This is my property. I have rights!"

"Either you unlock this gate or we're cutting the lock," Weber told him. "It's up to you!"

"I refuse to surrender my sovereignty to your authority," Jesse said and turned back toward his ATV, where an AR-15 was mounted to the handlebars.

Weber held his portable radio to his lips and said "Send him a message."

There was a sharp crack, and a bullet slammed into one of the front tires of the Honda, which exploded with a hiss of air. Jesse froze and threw up his hands. Weber prayed a silent thank you to whatever gods of marksmanship had given Chad such a steady aim.

"Cut the lock!" Weber ordered again.

Archer clamped the cutter's jaws down on the lock again, and stared at Jesse. "You call it, Jesse."

"You can't do this!" Jesse complained, like a broken record.

"Keep your eyes open and be careful," Weber warned his men. "You can bet your ass Tina is up on a hill somewhere."

"Sheriff, I'm going to sue you!" Jesse screamed. "I'll own this whole goddamned town!"

"Call her out, Jesse, or we're coming in," Weber told him. "And if she fires one shot at us, Chad's going to kill her. I mean it, Jesse!

Miller put his hands down and shouted up toward a pile of logs on a nearby hill that Weber suddenly realized was actually a carefully camouflaged bunker. "Tina! Come on out, girl! Keep your hands where they can see them!

There was no response, and Weber called out to her. "Tina, we know you shot up that bar. Now, come on out before anyone gets hurt here. You've got a baby inside you that isn't any part of this. Come out for its sake!"

"How do I know you won't gun me down?" came a voice from the bunker.

"Tina, if we wanted to kill anyone, Jesse would be dead by now," Weber shouted back. "Now, come on out! Sling your gun and keep your hands where we can see them!"

After another pause, Tina climbed over the top of the bunker, careful to keep her hands in full view. A rifle dangled over one shoulder. She stalked down the hill defiantly.

"Tina, we've got a warrant for your arrest for assault with a deadly weapon," Weber told her. "We also have search warrants for your rifle and snowmobile."

"Goddamned Nazis!" said Tina shrilly. "I hate you all!"

Weber found it hard to believe that this Tina Miller, heavily armed and ready to shoot it out with lawmen, was the same woman he had held as she cried over her dead husband just the day before.

"Take their rifles," Weber said, but Tina shook her head.

"This is the one I used, Sheriff. You leave Jesse's property alone."

"Shut up, girl," Jesse ordered. "Not a word until we get a lawyer here."

"Jesse, all you're going to do is make it harder on her," Weber said.

Tina handed her rifle over the fence, and Weber released the magazine, then pulled back the charging handle to eject the chambered round, which popped out into the mud at his feet. He bent and picked up the bullet, noting from the head stamp that it matched the spent shell casings found at the shooting scene. "Come on out, Tina."

She fumbled a key out of her pocket and opened the lock, stepping through the gate.

"Give me your rifle, Jesse." Weber ordered.

"I told you, I used that one!" Tina protested, pointing at the AR-15 in Weber's hand.

"Fine, then he'll get his back," Weber told her. "Where's the snowmobile?"

"Back at the house."

Weber snapped handcuffs on her wrists and Tommy led her to his S-10.

The sheriff slapped the magazine back into Tina's AR-15 and chambered a round. "Step back, Jesse," Weber ordered, the tone of his voice warning the big man that further argument would be futile. "We're coming in!"

"Jesus H. Christ! This place is a fortress!" exclaimed Parks with one of his characteristic whistles as the lawmen searched Jesse Miller's property. The compound consisted of six dilapidated mobile homes spread out over ten muddy acres, along with several outbuildings. Several rusty 4x4 trucks in various states of disrepair were scattered about, and a mongrel dog seemed to live under every one. Five concrete and timber bunkers were situated strategically around the acreage. Every structure held firearms, paramilitary equipment, and ammunition. It was a gun nut's heaven.

"These guys have got better equipment than we do!" Chad complained, holding up a pair of night vision binoculars.

Weber thumbed through a stack of anti-government pamphlets and held up one entitled *Jew Criminals of the Modern World*. "Great family reading, don't you think?"

Jesse's wife, an obese, surly woman whom Weber suspected was probably slow mentally, chain smoked cigarettes and swatted at a pack of unruly children, ranging in age from three years to a pimply faced adolescent boy, who looked like he would have loved to get his hands on one of the many firearms close at hand and take on the lawmen. An older teenage boy, Jesse's sixteen year old son, had to be handcuffed after he swung at Buz when the deputy started to search his trailer.

The snowmobile was in a metal lean-to, and Weber ordered Buz to photograph it from every angle, especially its runners, to compare with photos taken in the snow at the scene of the shooting.

"We'll leave it here for now, but it's impounded," Weber told Jesse, slapping a bright orange Sheriff's Seizure sticker on the machine. "If I come back here and it's been moved one foot, you go to jail for tampering with evidence. Got it?" Weber knew that with Tina's admission, he didn't really need the snow machine to make his case stand up in court, but he wanted to keep his options open for a return visit to the compound.

Though the search warrant was very specific, Weber had instructed his men earlier to be alert for any evidence that would tie Jesse or one of his siblings with the murders of Phil Johnson and Mike Perkins. The deputies seized nine 5.56mm rifles, all AR-15s or Mini-14s, except for one .223 Remington varmint rifle with a target scope, a civilian firearm in the same caliber as the assault rifles. Weber would have loved to take all of Jesse's large arsenal, but knew he was limited by the scope of the warrant.

It was nearly noon when the search was over, and Weber walked to where Jesse stood next to the Bronco, his hands cuffed in front of him.

"You got no right to do this!" Jesse said. His tirade hadn't run down in the three hours the lawmen were searching the compound. "If I'm not under arrest, you can't handcuff me!"

"Sure I can, Jesse," Weber said. "It's for my officers' safety as well as your own."

"You can't take my weapons neither!" Jesse said, still belligerent.

"Jesse, I've explained all this to you about a dozen times," Weber said. "We're looking for the gun that was used at the Antler. Once we determine which one it was, you can come down to the Sheriff's office and get the others back."

"But Tina already told you which one she used," Jesse argued. "You don't need to take the rest! You're just harassing us."

"Call the ACLU," Weber suggested, knowing Jesse and his ilk blamed the American Civil Liberties Union for many of the nation's ills, for its support of minorities and Liberal causes. Racism seemed to be one of the primary tenets of the militia movement.

Jesse was still cursing Weber when the lawmen finally withdrew from the compound.

Tina Miller made no better a prisoner than her brother Ernie had a few days earlier, cursing at Weber when he walked back to her cell.

"Let me out of here! I want my lawyer!"

"Shut up, Tina!" Weber said, shutting the door to the hallway and pulling a chair up to the cell door. "You lied to me. I believed you the other day when you said you weren't involved in all this. Now, here's the way it's going to go, so you listen real carefully to me!"

Weber held up his hand and ticked off his points on his fingers as he spoke.

"Number one, you're under arrest for attempted murder and assault with a deadly weapon. Number two, I'm going to have the judge swear out more warrants for armed robbery and two counts of murder. Number three, you're going to jail forever, if they don't give you the death penalty. Number four, you're never going to get to be a mother to your baby, Tina. Is that what you want?"

The thought of losing her unborn child seemed to affect Tina more than the threat of imprisonment, or even being put to death. Tears welled up in her eyes and she shook her head.

"No, Sheriff! I already told you, I didn't kill Phil. I loved him!"

"You also said you didn't have anything to do with the shooting at the Antler," Weber reminded her. "Why should I believe anything you tell me?"

"I never said I didn't shoot up that bar," Tina said. "*You never asked me that!*"

Weber realized that she was right, he had never asked her about Friday's shooting, and Tina had never volunteered any information on the incident. He was angry at himself for the oversight. He had allowed Tina's breakdown out on the highway to distract him from asking about the bar shooting.

"Don't play games with me, Tina," he said, trying to cover up his error. "Would you have told me if I had asked you?"

She shook her head, tears running down her face. "Please, Sheriff. This baby is all I've got. Don't take that away from me, too! Please!"

In spite of himself, Weber felt sympathy for the woman, floundering in a situation that seemed to get worse every day. "You come clean with me, Tina. Tell me everything you know about the hijacking, about the Antler, all of it. You talk, and we'll see what happens. But you keep playing games with me, holding out, and you're gone!"

Tina wiped her eyes with the back of a hand, and Weber got up to draw a Styrofoam cup of water from the sink and handed it to her, then sat back down.

"Okay, I shot up that bar. And your police car, and your truck when you came across the field at me! But I wasn't trying to hurt you, or anyone else! I just wanted to scare that fat bitch Margo so she'd shut up about Ernie."

"Some of those bullets went right through the block wall," Weber told her. "You could have killed a lot of people, Tina."

"I'm sorry," she blubbered, shaking her head. "I never gave any thought that they'd do that. I just wanted to shut her up. And.... I was mad because she had taken Phil to bed."

Weber wanted to tell her that she was going to go through a lot of ammunition if she shot at every woman her husband had slept with, but held his tongue.

"I know it was wrong," Tina said. "But I was careful not to hit you or your deputy, Sheriff! Believe me, I could have if I had wanted to!"

Weber knew she was right, but didn't acknowledge the admission. "What about the hijacking and the murders?"

"I swear to you, Sheriff! I didn't have a thing to do with any of that! I loved Phil!"

"What about Jesse or Ernie?"

"No, they didn't do it! I know they didn't!"

"Ernie said Jesse thought Phil was going to be useful to him. What did he mean?"

Tina shook her head. "I don't know! Jesse is real smart, he's read up on all the things the government's up to, and he and Phil talked about it a lot. I guess with Phil's Army training and all, Jesse thought he'd help us when the attack comes."

"What attack, Tina?"

"When the government comes after us! We're the last of the free Americans, Sheriff! Us and those like us! We're on their list!"

Weber wished she was lying to him again, but he knew Tina and her brother really believed the Big Conspiracy Theory, with all it's predictions of doom and gloom.

"No sign of Johnson's Jeep, or the money from the hijacking. There wasn't a .38 on the place," Parks said. "Every handgun was a .45 or high capacity 9mm. Strictly heavy duty stuff. I guess that bunch would figure a little old .38 isn't enough gun for their kind of work."

"What happens with Tina now?" Mary asked.

"She'll be arraigned this afternoon. We'll see what happens." Weber replied. "I imagine Jesse will post her bail. He always seems to be able to when one of them gets popped."

The door flew open and a very red-faced Chet Wingate marched into the office and planted himself in front of Weber. His ever faithful follower, Councilwoman Smith-Abbott, trudged along two steps behind. When the mayor spoke, he was so angry he was trembling, and bits of spittle struck the sheriff's face.

"Sheriff, you just won't learn, will you? I want Tina Miller out of that cell, and I want her out right now!"

"Chet, let's talk about this in my office," Weber suggested, but the mayor wouldn't move.

"I'll talk to you *where* I want, *when* I want, Sheriff! Did I not tell you to leave the Millers alone? Yet you went right back up there and invaded their property, and seized a bunch of firearms and arrested that poor pregnant girl!"

Weber wiped his face and waved a hand toward his office door. "I really don't think we need to get into this out here, Mr. Mayor. Let's go..."

"I will *not* go anywhere!" Wingate shrilled. "I want an explanation, and I want it now or I'll have your badge!"

The irritation Weber had been trying to hold in check in front of his staff exploded out of him in a great burst that caused the mayor to step backward in alarm, and the councilwoman to dodge behind the mayor's pudgy form for protection.

"All right, we'll do this right here!" Weber shouted. "That 'poor pregnant girl' has admitted to shooting an assault rifle at a building full of people! She's admitted shooting two occupied police cars! The firearms we seized are material evidence, and everything we did was on the basis of bonafide warrants from the judge! Now, either you trot your chubby ass right out that door, or I'm going to arrest you for obstructing justice, and I'll throw Mary Poppins here right in the cell with you!"

The mayor started to sputter a reply, but when Weber took a step toward him he retreated, nearly bowling Councilwoman Smith-Abbott over as he backpedaled.

"Archer!"

The rookie had been sitting at a desk, as awestruck by Weber's outburst as anyone in the office, and trying to make himself look inconspicuous.

"Yes, Sheriff?" he asked in a weak voice, somehow knowing what was coming.

"Deputy, escort these people out of this office right now. If they don't go, arrest them!"

Archer turned big, pleading eyes toward the sheriff.

"Uh, Sheriff? It's my..."

"Do you want to be a deputy or not?" Weber demanded. "If you do, get them out of here. Otherwise, throw your badge on a desk and get out!"

Archer looked panic stricken for a moment, then he braced himself and stepped forward, placing a tentative hand on his father's arm. "Come on, Poppa....."

The mayor shook his son's hand off and pointed a finger at Weber. "I'm leaving, Sheriff! But you mark my words, your days are numbered in this town!" He stormed out the door, the councilwoman fretting as she followed in his wake.

The office was silent for a full minute after they left, then Parks spoke up. "I'm sure going to miss all this small town life, Jimmy. You suppose you could put in a good word for me if he does fire you? I could use the job. I've always wanted to be Sheriff of Dogpatch."

"Shut up, Parks," Weber said and slammed the door behind him as he went into his office.

Tina's arraignment that afternoon was pretty much what Weber had expected. Judge Ryman set bail at $75,000 and Jesse put up the deed to his property as collateral to have her released pending trial. Weber thought that the deed must spend as much time at the courthouse as it did in Jesse's safe deposit box.

"I want my guns back, too" Jesse told the judge, but the magistrate shook his head.

"Sorry, Jesse. They're evidence. I will instruct the Sheriff to expedite the ballistics tests on them as much as possible, but until we can ascertain which, if any, were used in the shooting, they're in police custody."

Jesse grumbled, but ushered his sister out of the courtroom.

"How's Debbie doing?" Judge Ryman asked Weber, when the courtroom was empty.

"Good, Judge. She's back in school. She said she thought it was what Mike would have wanted. I have to agree with her."

The judge nodded and looked at the sheriff. "Off the record, what do you think about Tina?"

Weber scratched his neck and shrugged. "I don't know, Judge. I think she's a borderline psycho, but hell, so are half the people in this town. I'd hate to think she's going to get a long prison term out of this, but if you'd have asked me that Friday night, when my windshield was being shot out, I'd have told you something else! I have no doubt that if she'd have wanted to kill someone, she would have. She was just trying to scare Margo off. You've got to remember, those people play with guns like you and I do with our television remote controls."

The judge nodded. "I'm like you, Jimmy. I believe every citizen has the right to own a gun, but there sure are a lot of them out there that shouldn't have them!"

Weber rubbed at a spot on the back of a courtroom bench. "I still don't believe Tina had anything to do with the murders, even after all this. She was too much in love with Phil Johnson."

"What about Jesse or Ernie?" the judge asked.

Weber shook his head "I don't think Ernie did it, either. For all his bullying, he's basically a coward. Jesse's another story, he's so full of all this militia crap, I wouldn't put a thing past him. But... I have a couple other people I'm looking at pretty closely, too."

"Well, you keep after them, Sheriff. And Jimmy...?

"Yes?"

"Don't worry a lot about Chet Wingate, okay? He was in here today after you threw him out of your office, trying to get me to order Tina's release. I told him to get out too, though in less harsh terms than you did, I imagine. You are still the law in Big Lake, Sheriff."

Weber nodded in appreciation of the support, picked up his hat, and left the courtroom.

Parks stopped by the Sheriff's Office to drop off the spare key to Weber's cabin on his way out of town

"Back to the real world?" Chad asked.

"Yeah, well, you know how it goes." Parks said. "I've got to be in court tomorrow, and then I'm going to try and see what I can run down from that end. I'm hoping to be back up here by the end of the week."

"Why don't you hang onto the key," Weber suggested. "You'll need it when you get back anyway."

"Okay," Parks shook the sheriff's hand. "We're not backing off this thing, Jimmy. Our guys down in the Valley have been following up every loose end they can find down there. The armored car company is cooperating, but there doesn't seem to be much we can do from that end. Let me just get my AIC mellowed out a little bit, and I'll be back and we'll run down whoever did this. That's a promise."

Weber nodded and watched his friend walk out of the office.

"Sheriff?"

Weber turned to Robyn, who was sitting at the radio console. "What's up?"

"It's Archer, Sheriff. He's been in an accident."

Weber looked toward the ceiling. "Please tell me this accident didn't involve a firearm, Robyn. It's only Tuesday, and it's been a very bad week already."

She smiled sympathetically. "No, Sheriff. He ran into someone with Chad's squad car."

Weber pulled up behind the new Crown Victoria and a Dodge minivan on the highway, a mile outside of town. Chad walked back to the sheriff, his shoulders slumped in defeat. Archer stood by the front of the police car, his eyes downcast.

"I give up, Jimmy. I can't turn this clown into a deputy. Hell, it's all I can do to keep him awake through a whole shift!"

"What happened?" Weber asked, walking to the front of the police car. The headlights were broken, the grill smashed. The minivan had fared even worse, its tailgate caved in and tail lights shattered. An obviously agitated woman in her late 30s stood with her hands on her hips, surveying the damage. Archer didn't say a word, just nudged a piece of broken glass with his toe.

"Will you look at this!" she demanded. "Will you just look at this mess! Who's going to pay for this?"

"What happened?" Weber asked again.

"I let Archer drive and we stopped her for going ten over the speed limit." Chad explained. "When we got out of the car to talk to her, he forgot to put it in Park."

Weber looked toward Archer, who finally looked up. "It wasn't my fault, Sheriff, I just forgot! It was my first traffic stop and I was kinda excited, I guess."

"Well, that explains it," Weber said sarcastically, and turned to the minivan's owner. "Ma'am, I'm very sorry for all this. Were you injured?"

She shook her head. "No, just pissed off."

"I can't blame you," said Weber. "Are you from Big Lake?"

"No, I'm from Holbrook. I just came down to visit my sister, Joyce Taylor."

"From the bank? I know Joyce. She's a real nice lady."

The woman seemed a little calmer now, but still upset.

"Look, Miss....?"

"Clark. Sharon Clark. And it's Mrs."

"Mrs. Clark, I'm Sheriff Weber. Again, I apologize for all this. Are you sure you're not injured at all?" When she shook her head, Weber continued, "How about this? I'll follow you to your sister's place and then have a deputy drop your car off at the auto repair shop. We can get the tail and brake lights fixed tonight, and then when you get back home, you go to your body shop or the dealer where you bought the van and get this thing fixed, okay? Tell them to call me, and we'll handle the bill."

"Please, Sheriff, tell me *he* won't be the one driving my van!" she said, pointing at Archer.

"No ma'am, I promise. I'm not sure we'll even let him ride in the front seat of a police car for a week or two."

Sharon Clark nodded and took another deep breath. "My husband's not going to believe this!"

When she got behind the wheel of the minivan, Archer spoke up. "Aren't we going to give her a ticket for speeding?"

"Shut up, Archer," Chad snapped. "We'll be lucky if she doesn't claim whiplash and sue us!"

Weber looked at the two day old police car and shook his head in dismay. "Chad, you can't drive it without lights tonight. Drop it off at the dealership and I'll have Buz bring you his Explorer. And, Chad?"

"Yeah, Jimmy?"

"Don't let Archer drive it, okay? He'll tear up our fleet quicker than Tina Miller did with her rifle."

Weber walked back to his Bronco and followed the minivan toward town.

It was near midnight, but Weber couldn't sleep and was making another attempt at the paperwork on his desk. Robyn peeked into his office. "You want a cup of coffee, Sheriff?"

"What? Oh, sure. Thanks."

She disappeared for a moment and then was back, placing a coffee mug on Weber's desk.

"What's going on out there?" he asked her, taking a sip.

Robyn shrugged. "It's a Tuesday night in Big Lake. Not much. Chad and Archer just signed off and Buz came on duty. He's cruising out toward the campgrounds." There had been several instances lately of vandalism at the four Forest Service campgrounds in the area, graffiti and broken bottles, mostly. Weber suspected a group of high school boys, and had instructed his deputies to keep an eye out for suspicious activity.

Robyn had been working as a part time dispatcher since July, and Weber had been impressed with her dedication to duty and common sense. He intended to petition the Town Council to put her on full time at his next budget meeting with them. Robyn was a petite woman with big almond shaped brown eyes, a tan that she somehow managed to maintain even during the winter, and wore her dark brown hair in a feathered shag cut. She stifled a yawn and said "Excuse me," drinking from her own coffee cup.

"You look tired," Weber told her. "If you want to go home, I'll answer the phones until Buz comes in." After 2 a.m. on weeknights in the winter, the on-duty deputy manned the Sheriff's Office, forwarding the telephones to a cellular telephone for the twenty minutes every hour when he took a quick drive around town to be sure everything was quiet. Like the local bears, crime in Big Lake had always gone into hibernation during the winter months.

Robyn smiled gratefully, but shook her head. "I'll be okay. I never got the chance to thank you for covering me up so quick after Archer ripped my blouse yesterday." She blushed at the memory.

"Well, it was either grab a jacket or pull my gun and fight off those animals before they got to you, once they saw bare flesh." Weber teased.

Robyn blushed again. "Well, Sheriff, there wasn't all that much to see," she admitted ruefully.

Weber grinned at her. "Well, what I saw wasn't bad at all. Of course, it was just that quick glance."

The sheriff got yet another surprise from his pixie faced dispatcher when Robyn looked him in the eyes, leaned slightly forward, and said "Call me sometime, if you want a longer look." She gave him an impish grin and retreated to the radio console, leaving Weber to his coffee.

Chapter 18

Weber met Debbie for breakfast at the Frontier Cafe Wednesday morning. His sister was wearing a brown suede leather jacket over a ribbed white turtleneck sweater and tan jeans. Her hair hung loose over her shoulders and just a touch of makeup highlighted her eyes.

"So how's school going?" Weber asked.

"Good," Debbie told him, smiling. "If I pass this test today and the last one on Friday, I'll graduate right on schedule."

"Mike would have been so proud," Weber told her. "Mom and Dad, too."

Debbie smiled wistfully and reached her hand across the table to take Weber's. "At least I've still got you, big guy."

"Always," Weber told her and gave her hand an affectionate squeeze.

"I've been thinking," Debbie said, hesitantly. "I might be leaving Big Lake, Jimmy."

"What?" Weber felt his heart flutter. The idea of Debbie leaving took him totally by surprise.

Debbie's eyes misted slightly and she smiled sadly. "Oh, Jimmy! So much has happened here. First Mom and Dad dying. Now Mike. I don't know, there are just so many bad memories for me here."

"Yeah, but there are a lot of *good* memories too, kid." Weber argued. "This is our home!"

"It's *your* home, Jimmy!" she said, trying to make him understand. "Listen to me, Jimmy. Mike and I were going to wait to tell you this, but we had planned to move after I got my teaching certificate."

"Where to, Debbie?"

She shook her head. "I don't know. Maybe Tucson or Phoenix. Somewhere where I could get a job in a school system. Someplace where they have real restaurants, real stores. Somewhere where they don't roll the sidewalks up at nine o'clock. Oh Jimmy, I know you love this place! But you got to get away, once. You got to join the Army and go places.

All I've ever known is Big Lake! I need to see the rest of the world. too!"

Weber was hurt, but he had to admit the truth of what his sister was saying. He *had* left Big Lake at the first opportunity after high school, heading for the Army. He wanted to remind Debbie that he had only returned to Big Lake to look after her when their parents had been killed, but he didn't want to argue. One part of Weber's mind understood her need to spread her wings, and he could hardly blame her for wanting the chance to experience more of life.

"Hey, Jimmy! It's not like I'm going to Africa or anything," Debbie said, squeezing his hand again and looking at him with those gorgeous blue eyes that had always been able to melt his heart. She smiled fondly at him. "I need to see if I can make it on my own, Jimmy. All my life someone's taken care of me. First Mom and Dad, then you, and then Mike. It's time to let me grow up a little bit, Jimmy."

Weber experienced some of what a parent must feel when their first child leaves the nest. He managed a weak smile for Debbie and pulled her hand to his lips and kissed it. "Promise me I can swing in for a home cooked meal now and then?"

"You'd better, or I'll drive back up that hill and kick your butt!" Debbie threatened.

Weber was parked across from the high school at noon, a visible police presence to keep the students from killing themselves or other drivers, as they piled into cars and pickups and headed for Big Lake's two popular teenage hangouts for lunch.

Billy Carelton pulled out of the parking lot in his old Power Wagon and gave Weber a sheepish grin as he passed. Gina Reed, sitting beside him, slumped down in her seat and looked like she wanted to disappear when the sheriff nodded at the young couple. Weber was thinking about young love, and recalling bittersweet memories of his own time in high school, when a red Corvette shot past him in a blur.

The sheriff jerked out of his reverie and started the Bronco, cutting off a carload of squealing sophomore girls in a blue Nissan Sentra as he took off in pursuit of the speeding sports car. The Corvette, by now two blocks ahead, turned onto Lake Road and disappeared before Weber could get to the intersection. He made the turn and spotted the sports car far ahead, just leaving town. Siren wailing, Weber accelerated after the red car. He knew his Bronco was no match for the Corvette, and was just reaching for his microphone when the car pulled to the side of the road and waited for him.

Weber rolled to a stop behind the Corvette and climbed out, walking up to the driver's door. He bent over to peer inside, and Laura Wilson greeted him with a dazzling smile. "Why, Sheriff Weber, are you following me?" she asked in her best Scarlet O'Hara imitation.

"License and registration, Laura. Where are you going so fast?"

"Oh, nowhere," she said with a shrug. "Just out for a ride. It's such a nice day, isn't it? I can't believe it's only five weeks until Christmas!"

"License and registration," Weber repeated. Laura pouted and dug into her bag, finally locating her driver's license and automobile registration. When she handed them to Weber, she held on just a second longer than was necessary, before letting go of the documents.

Weber walked back to his Bronco and wrote out a ticket for speeding in a school zone and took it back to the Corvette.

"It's going to cost you $100," he told Laura.

She grinned conspiratorially at Weber and ran the tip of her tongue across her upper lip sensuously. "Sure we can't work something out, Sheriff? Roger's going to be *so* mad. I just got a ticket in Tucson last week."

Weber shook his head and stood up. "Just what is it you want from me, Laura?"

The redhead stuck a delicate hand out the window and traced a red lacquered fingernail along Weber's zipper. "Oh, I think you're smart enough to figure that one out all by yourself, Sheriff."

Weber felt himself stir and stepped back.

Laura laughed wickedly. "Scare you, cowboy? Come home with me and let Mama make it all better!"

"I don't think so," Weber told her.

"Why not, Sheriff? We both know you want me. And I want you. So what's the problem? It'll be fun!"

"Oh, I want you," Weber admitted. "But there's more to life than fun. Somehow, I just don't think I'd ever feel clean again, Laura."

"Well, we *do* have that big old sunken bathtub for afterward, if you ever change your mind," she said, and ran seductive fingers across her breast.

"It'd take more than soap, Laura," Weber told her and walked back to the Bronco. As he got behind the wheel, Laura shifted the Corvette into gear and laid rubber as she peeled out, throwing a fine spray of gravel over the front of the Bronco.

It seemed that women were going to be a thorn in Weber's side all day. When he returned to his office, he had two messages to call Miss Lucy Washburn. Before he could make it to his desk, Mary informed him that Margo Prestwick was back in town.

"She said since you had arrested Tina, she thought it was safe to come back," Mary told him.

Weber had hoped the Antler Inn would stay closed a while longer. His deputies' workloads had decreased markedly since the night of the shooting.

The sheriff dialed Miss Lucy's number and she answered on the first ring. "When can I have my cabin back?" she demanded. "I need to get Johnson's junk packed up and out of there so I can rent it again!"

"Miss Lucy, I just keep hoping that whoever was there the other day will come back again and we can catch them." he told her, "I think it has something to do with this investigation. Can you let me hang onto the key just through the weekend?" Weber's deputies had been checking the cabin, but hadn't seen any activity around it, or any evidence of a return visit by the mysterious intruder.

"Do you promise you'll be finished by then?" she pressed.

"I hope so. If not, I'll see if I can't maybe get the Town to pay you something for your trouble, okay?" Weber knew there was little chance of the Council authorizing any more money, but hoped she would give him a little more time.

Miss Lucy rang off with the warning that she would be calling again Monday morning if Weber hadn't returned the key to the cabin by then.

Archer slouched into Weber's office and took a seat. He stared at the sheriff with porcine eyes. Weber stared back, his eyes riveted on a spot that looked like dried egg on the deputy's shirt. When it became evident the rookie wasn't going to speak first, Weber finally broke the silence. "What can I do for you, Archer?"

"I want a car, Sheriff."

"A what?"

"A car. A police car. Everyone has one except me."

"I already explained to you," Weber said. "You're on probation your first sixty days."

"I know," Archer argued. "But I know that Tommy was out in a car while he was still on probation. Why can't I have one, too?"

"Look, Archer, we only have four cars. Each deputy has one."

"Except me."

"That's right, Archer, except you. Do you really expect me to take one of the more experienced deputies out of a car and give it to you when you've only been on the job two days?"

"I need a car." Archer said simply, as if that settled the matter. Weber understood that, in Archer's mind, it did.

"You know, you're right, Archer. You do need a car. Your shift starts at six, right? When you come on duty, you'll have a car."

Archer beamed, the spoiled child who had gotten his way yet again. Without so much as a thank you, he walked out of Weber's office.

"Mary!" Weber called, and when his assistant stuck her head in his door, he said, "Call the guys for me. I've got a plan!"

At six o'clock, when Archer reported for duty, the entire force was on hand. Every deputy was working hard to hide the grins on their faces, with little success.

"Archer, you wanted a car, you got it!" Weber told the rookie. "You have to remember, every deputy starts out low man on the totem pole and moves up from there. And every deputy has to take care of his own vehicle. Come on, let's go see your police car!"

Weber, followed by a beaming Archer, led everyone out into the alley behind the Sheriff's Office. The deputies had scrambled after Mary's phone calls, and they had gleefully joined in the fun of Weber's heinous plot. The Chevy Caprice that Tina Miller had shot into scrap metal a few days earlier, awaited their attention and final delivery to Archer Wingate, Deputy Sheriff.

The old police car had new tires and a windshield, but that was the only major repair to the cruiser. The plexiglass of the shattered light bar had been taped together with silver duct tape, and the same tape bandaged the many bullet holes in the car's fenders, hood, and trunk. The side and rear windows had been replaced with heavy plastic. The police radio antenna, clipped off halfway up the shaft by one lucky bullet, had a length of coat hanger spliced to it and a yellow rubber duck was perched on the end of the makeshift aerial.

Archer stood staring at the police car for several moments, then turned to the assembled deputies. "What's my radio call sign?"

No distress over the sad state of his assigned vehicle, no complaints that it was a rolling eyesore. Weber realized that it didn't faze Archer, who was a *walking* eyesore! All Archer Wingate wanted to know was his radio call sign. His response broke up the deputies even more than the tantrum they had expected. Weber was sure their howls and shrieks could be heard three blocks away, disturbing diners at the Frontier Cafe.

It was Dolan's night to pull the late shift, and when Chad and Archer signed off at midnight, he stopped at the office before making his first circuit through town. Robyn had been subdued around Weber, keeping to herself and not leaving the radio console through most of her shift. Weber suspected she was uncomfortable in his presence after their encounter of the night before. Robyn was slipping into her jacket.

"You want me to switch the phones over?" she asked Dolan, not meeting Weber's eyes.

"Yeah, forward them to my cell phone," the deputy said.

Robyn punched in the appropriate code, then turned to Weber after Dolan went back out. "About last night, Sheriff...."

"Hey, Robyn, it's no problem!" he assured her. "I didn't take it seriously. If we can't all tease and have fun around here, it'll get to us sooner or later."

"I wasn't joking," she said quietly, and looked into his eyes challengingly.

Weber stared back at her, and neither broke eye contact or said a word for several seconds that seemed to last for hours. Finally Weber broke the standoff. "Need a ride home?"

Robyn broke into a smile and took his hand as they walked out to his Bronco.

"I think the management experts would say this isn't a good idea."

Early morning sunlight was streaming through Weber's window, bathing the bed where he and Robyn snuggled under a down comforter, in its golden light.

"What isn't a good idea?" she asked.

"Oh, sheriff and dispatcher spending the night together. Boss and employee fraternizing. Fishing off the company pier."

Robyn was lying in the crook of Weber's arm, her head on his shoulder. She tilted her face to look at him. "What do we have here? Post-coital guilt, Sheriff?"

Weber smiled. "No guilt at all. It's just that I've never..."

"Judging from last night's performance, I hope you don't expect me to believe that it was your first time," Robyn teased.

Weber shook his head. "I just meant, I've never gotten involved with anyone from the office before."

"Well.... let's see," Robyn said, feigning concentration, "Buz definitely isn't your type, Chad's too old for you, and Tommy's too young. And with Mary, it'd be almost incestuous. I guess if you were going to sleep with one of the help, I was the best choice." She gave him her impish smile and wrinkled her nose at him.

Weber laughed and kissed the tip of her nose. "You're nuts, do you know that?"

She snuggled back into his shoulder. "Just for you, big guy."

Robyn sat up in bed and turned to face him, showing no hint of self-consciousness as the comforter fell away from her breasts. Her face was serious.

"Look, Jimmy. I'm not the type to sleep around, okay? It has to mean something to me. With you, it did. But where it goes to from here is up to you. I just want you to know that."

Weber propped himself up on an elbow and nodded. "Okay."

"I don't want this to change things at work between us, okay?"

"Now who's experiencing post-coital guilt?" he teased.

Robyn shook her head. "I care about you, Jimmy. I have for a long time now. But I care about you as a person too, as my boss, and someone I look up to. As good as this was, I don't want anything to interfere with the way things have always been, okay?"

"It's a small town, Robyn. It's a small office. No matter how we act, word will get around, sooner or later. Can you handle that?"

She leaned forward and kissed him. "I'm not ashamed. I'm a big girl, Jimmy."

Weber pulled her on top of him and kissed her again, the kiss turning more passionate. Somewhere along the line, the comforter was pushed off the foot of the bed, but they didn't notice until much later.

Chapter 19

Weber was drowsing when the telephone rang. He grappled for the receiver, hoping to get it before the ringing woke Robyn, but she opened her eyes and smiled dreamily at him.

"Jimmy?"

"Yeah. What is it, Mary?"

"Lucy Washburn has called twice for you."

"Jesus, I told her yesterday I'd be done with her cabin by the first of the week!"

"I don't know about that. She just said she wanted to see you today."

"Okay. She's probably planning a yard sale to get rid of Johnson's stuff and wants me to nail up the signs for her," he sighed and rubbed sleep out of his eyes.

"Jimmy?"

"Yes?"

"Can you drop Robyn off at the office on your way? I need her to help me clean up the old files in the storeroom."

"Robyn?"

He could hear the smirk in Mary's voice as she said "It's a small town, Sheriff," and rang off.

Half an hour later Weber was turning onto Pine Cone Road, en route to Miss Lucy's house when his radio crackled. "All units, we've got a 962 at Three Points, at least three injuries. Report in, please."

At the code for a traffic accident with injuries, Weber slammed on his brakes and made a quick U-turn and headed in the direction of Three Points, a notorious blind intersection where the highway, Lake Road and Pioneer Trail converged. A steep downgrade, tall trees, and a hairpin turn combined to make the crossing extremely dangerous. Weber had investigated more than one fatal accident at the site. Roof lights flashing and siren wailing, he sped toward the accident.

Weber's stomach lurched when he brought the Bronco to a stop on the shoulder of the highway. A red Toyota pickup lay in the ditch on its roof, a trail of twisted sheet metal, broken glass and other debris marking its slide from the highway into the ditch. A big Chevy diesel dually pickup truck sat in the intersection, its grill smashed in, radiator hemorrhaging green antifreeze.

Two blanket covered figures lay in the roadway, while Dolan and a paramedic worked over another form nearby. Weber heard a scream and looked to where Tommy was trying to comfort a hysterical high school girl, blood smearing her face and jacket. A grim faced Buz Carelton walked over to Weber.

"What the hell happened, Buz?"

"From what I've got so far, the red pickup was coming down Pioneer with a bunch of kids in it. They ran the stop sign and got T-boned by the dually. We've got two dead, both high school kids, and the boy they're working on over there," he indicated Dolan and the volunteer paramedic.

"What about her?" Weber asked, nodding at the girl Tommy was holding and talking to in soothing tones.

"Cuts and bruises," Buz said. "One of the DOAs is her brother,"

"What about the people in the dually?"

"The driver was Jeremy Judd. He's okay, just shook up."

Judd was a local rancher and heavy equipment operator. Weber knew him to be a solid citizen, a hard working man who devoted what spare time he could find to hunting, fishing, and rodeo.

"Was Judd speeding?"

"It doesn't look like it, Jimmy. He was doing 55 or so, but the kids never gave him a chance to stop. They were flying, according to Jeremy and the people in the car behind them. They said the Toyota passed them, doing about 70."

Weber shook his head and turned as Buz popped the top on a flare and lit it, laying it down on the highway. He made his way to the injured boy. "How is he?"

The paramedic shook his head. "He'll make it, but it looks like he's got some busted ribs and maybe a ruptured spleen." He was interrupted when an ambulance slid to a stop and the crew jumped out. Weber stepped back and walked to where a white faced Jeremy Judd leaned against his truck.

"I swear, Sheriff, I never saw them until it was too late!" Tears rolled down the rancher's face. "God, why did this have to happen? I've never had an accident in my life! Those poor kids!"

Weber patted his back, feeling the big man's body convulsing under his heavy flannel shirt. Suddenly Judd jerked away and stumbled to the side of the roadway, where he dropped to his hands and knees and heaved. Weber gave him a moment, then walked over and helped him to his feet.

"It's okay, Jeremy. From what I can see, it wasn't your fault. I know it's terrible, but you're not to blame. You were just in the wrong place at the wrong time."

Weber opened the door of the dually and helped the rancher inside.

"Sit here for now, okay Jeremy? It's going to be all right."

The big man wiped his mouth with the back of a calloused hand and nodded, unable to look the Sheriff in the face. Weber turned away to help deal with the carnage around him.

The one duty of police work Weber hated above all others was notifying families when a loved one had been killed or seriously injured. In a community as small as Big Lake, everyone knew everyone else in one way or the other, which made the task even harder.

He had just left the home of Charlie and Freda Beaumont, whose son Bobby was the driver of the Toyota, and had been killed instantly when the big Chevy pickup had smashed into his door. The other fatality was Misty Cooper, Bobby's pretty blond haired girlfriend. Both students were seniors, scheduled to graduate in just a few months. Gordon Marshal, sitting on the passenger side of the Toyota when the accident occurred, would live, but was facing a long recuperation. His girlfriend, Amber, who happened to be Bobby Beaumont's sister, had been sitting on Gordon's lap, and miraculously escaped the accident with only a broken nose and various minor cuts and bruises.

Weber was physically and emotionally drained when he finally walked into the Sheriff's Office. The human psyche can handle only so much bloodshed in a given period of time, and Weber's had been exposed to more than its fair share in the last eleven days. Robyn looked at him with dismay when he dropped into the nearest chair, and started to go to him, but Mary beat her to it.

"Here, you look like you can use this," she said, handing him a mug of strong black coffee. Weber drank gratefully, not seeming to notice when the hot liquid scalded his tongue.

"You get the notifications done?" Dolan asked, looking as worn out as the sheriff.

"Yeah. God, I hate that! You feel so impotent!"

Dolan nodded. "We didn't cite Jeremy. He didn't have a chance. Tough break, and he's such a nice guy, too."

"Yeah," Weber agreed. "I think he's got a real heavy load to deal with right now. I wouldn't want to be in his shoes."

"Oh, Larry Parks is back in town." Robyn told the sheriff. "He got in while you were over at the Cooper place."

"Back so soon? I didn't expect him until tomorrow."

Robyn shrugged. "He said there was nothing he could do down in Phoenix, and that he had convinced his supervisor that he could get a lot more accomplished up here.

"Where is he now?"

"Oh, Miss Lucy kept calling for you. Finally he said he'd go over and see what had her so riled up. No one else was around. He said he had some information for you, and that he'd be back as soon as he was finished with her. He seemed pretty excited.

Weber nodded and drained his coffee, trying to ignore the visions inside his head of young bodies lying torn and broken on the highway.

A major accident, especially one with fatalities, generates a tremendous amount of paperwork, and Weber was occupied with accident reports, checking to be sure that the photographs his deputies had shot at the scene were dropped off for processing, and fielding calls from the out of town news media. Big Lake had received more than its share of media coverage in the last few days, none of it positive. The sheriff imagined the folks over at the Chamber of Commerce were biting their nails a lot lately.

It was late in the afternoon before he realized he hadn't eaten all day, and his stomach was growling. Thoughts of food reminded Weber that Parks had never returned from his visit with Miss Lucy.

"He never came back or called," said Mary in response to Weber's inquiry. "He wouldn't still be up there, would he? That's been *hours* ago."

"Maybe he and Miss Lucy eloped," suggested Chad.

"He probably figured we were all busy here and went over to your cabin," said Mary. "Do you want me to call your place and see if he's there?"

"Yeah, and try Miss Lucy's if he's not there," Weber said. "Who knows, maybe the old bat is holding him hostage until I give her back the key to Johnson's cabin!"

A few minutes later Mary shook her head. "That's strange! No answer either place. I've never known Lucy Washburn not to answer her phone."

"I'll drive up there," Weber said. "The way this day has been, someone probably knocked over a telephone pole and the lines are down."

For the second time that day, Weber found himself on Pine Cone Road. He passed Phil Johnson's cabin, looking lonely and deserted, and turned into the driveway of Miss Lucy's big old two story house. Larry Parks' gray government issue sedan was parked next to the house.

Weber climbed out of the Bronco and walked up the ramp to the porch. The place seemed strangely silent, and it took him a moment to realize that Charlie, Miss Lucy's friendly old dog, hadn't come out to greet him. Weber couldn't remember a visit to Miss Lucy in the last decade when Charlie hadn't met him in the driveway for a pat on the head and the requisite stick throwing, followed by praise over the dog's fetching skills.

Weber pressed the doorbell, waited a moment, and then knocked. "Miss Lucy?"

Only silence came back to him, and he rapped harder on the door. "Miss Lucy? Parks?"

Weber tried the door handle and it turned. He pushed the door open and stepped inside. The house was silent. Worried now, Weber called out again. "Miss Lucy! It's Jim Weber! Where are you?"

Weber peered to the left into the kitchen and across the entry hall into the sitting room. Both were empty. The sheriff felt the skin on the back of his neck tingle. Something was wrong here! Weber drew his pistol, thumbing back the hammer. "Is anyone here?"

A faint sound reached his ears, a low whine, like an animal in pain. The Colt held ahead of him in both hands, Weber followed the sound down the long hallway through the house to Miss Lucy's bedroom in the rear. The bedroom door was standing ajar, and Weber cautiously pushed it the rest of the way open. Charlie looked up at him with mournful eyes and whined again. The big dog was lying next to the body of Miss Lucy Washburn, sprawled in front of her overturned wheelchair. Charlie looked up at the sheriff with soulful eyes.

"Miss Lucy!" Weber holstered the .45 and rushed to bend over her inert form, laying two fingers alongside her neck. Frantically searching for a pulse, Weber found none. Only then did Weber see the pool of dark blood behind the old woman, a congealed mass that had soaked through her green house dress and collected on the floor between her body and the wheelchair. At the same time, Weber spotted the round hole in the center of the backrest of Miss Lucy's wheelchair.

The sheriff scrambled to his feet and drew his automatic again, though the dried blood told him her attacker had probably fled a long time ago.

He found Parks just inside the back door of the house, in the mud room.

In a state of shock, Weber stepped to where Larry Parks lay on his back, one arm flung over his head. The pool of blood that had drained out of the FBI agent's body was even larger than that which Miss Lucy had shed. Two obscene dark holes were centered in Parks' chest, the edges of the bullet holes in the blue cotton scorched.

Weber crouched over Parks and checked for signs of life

"Oh God!" Weber cried, "Oh Parks! Noooo!"

Weber stumbled back into the kitchen and picked up the phone, managing to dial his office on the second try.

"Robyn? Get me some help out here! I need an ambulance! Now! Oh God!"

Weber sat at the kitchen table, his head in his hands. The house was filled with the sounds of police radios, men talking in subdued tones and bright flashes from Chad's camera, recording the crime scene. Weber was aware of all the activity, yet strangely removed.

Mary Caitlin stood behind the sheriff, her hands on his shoulders.

"Are you all right, Jimmy?"

Weber didn't answer, just stared vacantly into space. Some part of his mind was telling him that he was in shock, but his mental processes couldn't seem to make the connection necessary to allow him to function normally. He realized Mary was bending over him, her face inches from his. Weber saw her lips moving, heard the sound of her voice, but couldn't translate it all into words. All he could picture in his mind was an endless line of corpses, stretching into infinity.

"Jimmy! Come on, Jimmy. Snap out of it!"

Mary shook him firmly by the shoulders, finally managing to make a connection inside Weber's short circuited synapses and bring him back to the present. He became aware of the concern on her face and the words she was speaking finally fell into some manageable format and reached through the funk he was lost in.

"What?"

"Are you okay, Jimmy? Here, drink this." Mary placed a glass in his hand and raised it to his lips. Weber drank, then coughed, the strong whiskey burning his throat and washing away the last vestiges of his trance.

Weber coughed again, then wiped his lips.

"Are you all right?" Mary asked again.

Weber nodded and finally managed to speak. "Jesus, Mary. What the hell is going on in this town? Who would do something like this? Why?"

"I don't know, Jimmy." she told him. "I just don't know."

Weber's sense of duty returned and he looked toward the hallway, where a haggard looking Tommy Frost stood writing in a memo pad.

"We've got to call Parks' office," Weber said.

"It's been done," Mary said. "They've got some people flying up now."

Weber shook his head in disbelief. "This is all a nightmare, Mary. All of it."

Activity in the hallway drew his attention, as two paramedics wheeled out a stretcher, the form on it covered with a sheet. Weber felt what was left of his heart breaking. Suddenly he felt ill and stumbled to the sink. His stomach was empty, and all his spasms brought forth was a stinging bile.

In the early hours of the morning Robyn drove the Bronco back to Weber's cabin. He had been silent throughout the short ride, as he had been for the last hour or two, once he had dictated his report to her and a second one to an FBI agent. Like a sleepwalker, Robyn led the sheriff inside and into his bedroom. He fumbled with his gun belt, but couldn't make his fingers work. Robyn unbuckled the belt and laid it on Weber's dresser, then, like a parent with a sleepy child, helped him out of his clothes and into bed. She undressed and slipped under the covers, drawing him to her, and finally Weber allowed himself to let go, sobs shaking his body as he cried into her shoulder.

Chapter 20

The sound of a door closing just after 8 a.m. woke Weber from a troubled sleep, filled with images of dead bodies and blood spattered walls.

"Jimmy? Are you up?"

Debbie poked her head into Weber's bedroom, then drew back, blushing when she saw a naked, half-asleep Robyn curled up next to her brother.

"Oh, I'm sorry! I used my key and.... I just heard about Larry Parks and Miss Lucy. I...."

Robyn stirred and covered herself, smiling a combination of self-conscious embarrassment and sleepy greeting. Weber sat up, the comforter around his waist. "Give me a minute, Debbie."

"Sure." She closed the door and Weber pulled on jeans and slipped an old gray sweatshirt over his head. He leaned over and kissed Robyn.

"Sorry about that."

She shrugged it off, then her expression turned serious and she laid a hand alongside his face. "Are you okay, Jimmy?"

Weber nodded and then shrugged. "I'm alive. That's the best I can hope for this morning."

"I'll be right there," Robyn said as he left the bedroom.

Debbie was in the kitchen, pouring water into the top of Weber's Mr. Coffee. She turned and encircled his waist with her arms, hugging him tightly.

"Jimmy, I'm so sorry."

"Me too," Weber said, and felt his voice breaking.

Debbie drew back and looked up at him, her eyes sad.

"What's happening around here, Jimmy? Does this have to do with Mike and Phil being killed?"

"It has to be connected in some way," Weber told her. "But I can't figure out how yet. Miss Lucy had been calling the office all morning yesterday, but I was tied up on that accident out on the highway. I guess Parks got back into town and went up to see what she wanted, and walked in on something."

"But what, Jimmy? Why would anyone want to kill him, let alone Miss Lucy?"

Weber shook his head. "I don't know, kid. All I can think is that Miss Lucy either came up with something that would have tipped us to the killer, or at least whoever shot them *thought* she knew something."

"But she was just a harmless old lady in a wheelchair," Debbie argued. "What could she know?"

"Your guess is as good as mine," Weber said. "I know she spent a lot of time spying on Johnson's cabin. Maybe she saw someone or something, and the killer wanted to shut her up. That's the only thing that makes sense."

"None of it makes sense to me," Robyn said, walking into the kitchen in Weber's big terrycloth bathrobe. Even without makeup, her hair tousled, Weber thought she looked gorgeous. "How can anyone justify shooting people in cold blood? That old lady never hurt anyone in the world. And Parks..."

Robyn's voice trailed off, and there followed an awkward silence for a moment, as the two women sorted out the new dynamics in their relationship, given Robyn's involvement with Weber. Covering their discomfort with the mechanics of pouring coffee and getting cream and sugar, they finally settled in around the kitchen table.

"So," said Debbie, blowing into the coffee cup she held to her lips with both hands. "I didn't know you two were an item. I guess I'd better learn to knock from now on."

Robyn blushed again and Weber managed a wry grin. "I guess I could always leave a towel hanging on the doorknob."

Robyn kicked him under the table.

In a moment the brief gaiety was gone and Weber stared down into his coffee cup. "I just wish I would have gone up to that house instead of Parks. I might have..."

"You might have been killed, too," Debbie interrupted.

Both women shivered and Robyn placed a comforting hand on Weber's. The gesture wasn't lost on Debbie.

"I'd better call the office and check in," Weber continued. "We've got feds crawling all over the place. Maybe there's an update or something." He pushed his chair back and went into the living room to make the call.

"The feds there?" Weber asked.

"Oh yeah. In fact, Agent Sayers is standing right here and wants to talk to you."

Weber vaguely remembered Sayers from the chaos of the night before, Parks' Agent in Charge from Phoenix, a short man of about 50, who had seemed very pushy, given Weber's mental and emotional state at the scene. Weber's still fuzzy mind seemed to recall him finally telling the FBI man to stuff it, after he demanded yet another retelling of the facts leading up to the discovery of the shooting, what seemed like the fifth or sixth demand for the same information. Weber was too numb at the time to function properly. Chad had finally intervened, warning the federal lawman to back off, and sending Weber home to sleep. He made a mental note to thank his senior deputy the next time he saw him.

An agitated man's voice replaced Mary's on the telephone. "Sheriff Weber? Where the hell are you? We've got a murder investigation going on here, in case you've forgotten."

"Sayers? I just woke up. I'll be there as soon as I catch a shower."

"Do you think you might put a rush on that, Sheriff? I've got more to do than sit around here in Mayberry and watch your overweight deputy pick his nose."

Weber decided that he disliked Agent Sayers.

"That would be Deputy Archer. He's new and leaves a lot to be desired, I'm afraid."

"*You* leave a lot to be desired!" Sayers said. "This entire investigation leaves a lot to be desired. I can see why Parks felt so at home here. I never knew how he made it as a federal officer. He belonged back on the farm in Oklahoma, shoveling horse shit or whatever it is that his people do. Maybe if he'd have stayed there, he'd have been better off. Get a move on, will you, Sheriff? I'd really like to get this investigation wrapped up sometime this decade."

Before Weber could reply, there was a click and the line went dead.

The sheriff resisted the urge to give the receiver the finger, knowing it was futile, but thought better of it after a second or two and went ahead with the gesture. It didn't make him feel any better.

The Big Lake Sheriff's Office was buzzing with activity when Weber arrived. He was accosted twice between his Bronco and the door by newsmen from Phoenix, asking if he had any new information on the previous day's shootings. One bleached blonde television reporter blocked his way and stuck a microphone in his face. "Sheriff, we understand that your brother-in-law was one of the original murder victims, and that you were close to at least two other victims in this case. How are you feeling right now about that, Sheriff?"

He wanted to tell her that he was mad as hell, that he was exhausted and emotionally devastated. He wanted to tell her that her question was both stupid and cruel. But when he opened his mouth to speak, all Weber could do was utter a quick "No comment" and push the microphone out of his face. Brushing off other grasping hands and thrusting microphones, Weber escaped inside, where his deputies tried to go about their business, amid a small army of FBI agents.

"It's so nice of you to grace us with your presence, Sheriff!" said Agent Sayers sarcastically, looking up from a desk where he was sorting through photos taken the night before at the crime scene. "I *do* hope we haven't inconvenienced you with all this murder business!"

Sayers was a pasty faced man with thinning hair. Weber suspected his pallor was a result of too many years inside, parked behind a desk, instead of being out in the field doing real police work. The Sheriff bit back his response and ignored Sayers, turning to Mary.

"This place is a madhouse. Bring me up to speed, will you?"

"I've got Chad and Archer out on patrol," Mary told him. "Tommy's over at Miss Lucy's, keeping people away. There's been a lot of traffic out there. People get curious, you know."

Weber nodded and Sayers pushed himself between them.

"Sheriff, just how long is it going to take to get the real crime scene photos back that were shot with the 35mm camera? I can't tell a thing from these damn Polaroids! I can't believe you don't have a darkroom in this place."

"Look, Sayers," Weber said, trying to be reasonable. "This is a small town. We don't have all the resources you federal boys have. We've got a one hour photo lab in town we farm our work out to. We shot a dozen rolls of film and he's working on them right now. I don't really think we're going to see the shooter's name written in blood on the walls once we get the pictures back. I think I'd have noticed that when I was there. Give us a break, okay? We're doing the best we can with our limited resources."

"Your *best* is none too good," Sayers spat back. "Stupid hick town!"

Before Weber could respond, the FBI agent stormed over to a desk and began berating one of his men for some real or imagined infraction. All of Sayers' men looked harried and haggard. But instead of empathizing with them over the loss of a brother agent, Sayers was too busy enjoying his power trip.

"Now there goes one fine human being," Weber told Mary.

"He's an asshole," she shot back, scowling at Sayers' back.

Weber grinned at his friend's response and walked into his office, where the ever present stack of pink telephone message slips awaited him. Mary brought him coffee as he stood at the desk, sorting through them and throwing the ones from media callers away.

"Chet Wingate's called three or four times," Mary said. "He's steamed, as usual."

"Oh, I don't know about steamed," Weber told her. "I've always thought of Chet as half baked, myself."

Mary snorted and pointed to one message. "Laura Wilson called and I could barely understand her, she was crying so hard. I sent Chad up to her place, but she wouldn't open the door. She just told him to go away and said she needs to talk to you, and only you."

Weber shook his head. "I don't have time for her neurotic bullshit right now. If she calls back, try to find out what she needs."

"What about the mayor?"

"He'll just have to wait," Weber said.

The door banged opened and Sayers marched in imperiously. "Sheriff, how do I get to this Jesse Miller's place?"

"What do you want with Jesse?" Weber asked, trying to hide his impatience with Sayers' irritating attitude.

"What do I *want*? My God, man, are you really that inept! His sister has already admitted to one shooting, she pointed a rifle at Agent Parks, and she's been mixed up in this case from the start. She's our shooter, you imbecile! Since you seem to be too busy to notice what's going on around you, *someone* needs to wrap this thing up!"

"Now, just hold on a minute," said Weber. "I really don't believe that Tina Miller killed those two guards. They're a bunch of crazies, no question about that, but we don't know that Tina, or any of them, had anything to do with what happened yesterday. But I can tell you this - if a bunch of FBI agents show up at Jesse's place, someone is going to get hurt."

"No one got hurt when you went up there to arrest Tina Miller," Sayers argued. "Are you suggesting the Federal Bureau of Investigation can't do the same thing your podunk little police force did, Sheriff?"

"Look Sayers," Weber said, exasperated. "I was surprised as hell we didn't have a shooting when we arrested her. I think the only reason we didn't is because we *are* the 'podunk' little police force around here. Jesse's convinced that the United States government is after him. After Waco and Ruby Ridge, there's no way he's going to let the FBI near him!"

"I'll tell you what, Sheriff," sneered Sayers. "How about you stick to monitoring the school crossing, getting pussycats out of trees, and screwing that pretty little dispatcher of yours, and let me handle Jesse Miller?"

Weber had been wanting to hit someone ever since the first moment he looked into the back of the armored car and saw the bodies of the two murdered guards. The beating he had given Ernie Miller hadn't provided the relief he needed, and with the other bodies he'd seen in the last few days, his fuse was short. Agent Sayers' last comments struck the match to that fuse.

Afterward, as Mary shook her head and applied Band-aids to his skinned knuckles, snickering all the while, Weber decided that no matter what charges he might eventually face for battery upon a federal officer, it was damn well worth it.

There had been quite a flurry of activity in the Sheriff's office after Weber punched out Special Agent Sayers, and for a moment, Weber feared that it might escalate into a confrontation between his deputies and the FBI men. But, judging by the secret grins the federal officers were surreptitiously sending his way, while they tended to their boss's bloody nose, it appeared that Weber had only done something many of them had longed to do for quite a while. Sayers was seated in a chair in the outer office, head tilted back and a cold compress applied to his nose.

"I want that man arrested," he had sputtered, after two of his agents picked him up from the floor. "Lock him up right now! That woman's my witness."

"For what?" Mary Caitlin had demanded. "It's not Sheriff Weber's fault you tripped and fell on your face. I saw the whole thing!"

"You're a liar!" Sayers screamed at Mary. "You saw him hit me!"

"All I saw was you trip over the rug," Mary shot back. "And watch who you're calling a liar, buster!"

"Sir, calm down, sir," urged one of Sayers' men. "Let's get you looked at and get that bleeding stopped."

"I said arrest that man!" Sayers ordered, pointing a shaking finger in Weber's face.

"You get that finger out of my face or you're going to pull back a stump," Weber had warned him.

"Sir, come with us," Sayers' agent had pleaded. "You're only going to make things worse."

Finally the FBI men had managed to lead their superior out of Weber's office and tend to his wounds, though he continued to threaten Weber with every sort of criminal prosecution and recourse all the while.

"You okay, Jimmy?" Robyn asked, sticking her head inside Weber's door.

"Yeah. I guess that was a pretty stupid thing to do, huh?"

Robyn shrugged, then gave him a devilish grin. "I don't know. It depends on whether or not that hand you skinned up will support your weight tonight!"

Weber laughed heartily, and Robyn blew him a kiss and closed the door behind her. Almost immediately, Chad knocked and stepped inside.

"Well, Jimmy, it looks like they're going to do it. Sayers just ordered his men to go up to Jesse's place and arrest Tina. What do you want us to do?"

"I hope to hell they don't go up there," Weber said. "If they do, someone's going to get killed, sure as hell."

"I know it," Chad agreed.

"Look, I don't want any of our guys mixed up in this," Weber said. "Try to stall them while I call the mayor and Judge Ryman. Maybe someone can talk some sense into Sayers. I doubt he'll listen to me right now."

"Uh... Jimmy? We need to do something about Laura Wilson. She's called a half dozen times, at least, and sounds really upset."

"Okay," Weber sighed, picking up his telephone. "If she calls back, tell her I'll run up there as soon as I get done with this."

Mayor Wingate answered the phone and immediately went on the attack.

"Just where have you been, Sheriff? I've been calling all morning!"

"Chet, I've got a multiple murder case going on, I've got a damned FBI agent from Phoenix here, getting ready to go up to Jesse Miller's place and start a war, and I've got Laura Wilson calling me every five minutes with some crisis. Give me a break, will you?"

"Laura Wilson? Roger Wilson's wife? They're very influential citizens. What does she want?"

Weber thought it was just like Big Lake's mayor to consider the needs of a rich voter more important than a murder investigation, or the likelihood of a major confrontation between armed survivalists and the Federal Bureau of Investigation.

"Look, Chet. I need your help here, okay? Someone has to talk this idiot out of going up there and getting his fool self shot."

"Well, talk some sense into him," the mayor demanded. "After all, you're the Sheriff!"

"I don't think he's going to listen to me," Weber said.

"Well, why not?"

"Because I just punched him in the nose," Weber admitted.

"You what?" Wingate shrieked.

"Chet, it's a long story and I really don't have time to get into it right now, okay?"

"Listen, Sheriff," Wingate said. "Law enforcement is your job. This town pays you to keep the peace. Now, you do whatever you have to do to stop this impending bloodbath, then get yourself up to Roger Wilson's place and see what his wife wants. That's an order!"

Weber started to protest, but the mayor had already hung up on him. Judge Ryman wasn't in his office and the Sheriff tried his home without success. He called the courthouse back and left a message for the judge to call him back as soon as possible. Weber stared at the telephone a long moment, than pulled the local telephone directory from a drawer and searched for a number. Jesse Miller's gruff voice answered.

"Jesse, Sheriff Weber here."

"What do you want?" Jesse demanded.

"Look, Jesse, I called to warn you. You've probably already heard that the FBI agent investigating the armored car hijacking was shot last night."

"So what if I did? You going to try and pin that on us too?"

"Listen, Jesse. There's a whole crowd of FBI men up here, and they're looking for a quick way to solve the shooting. Their boss has decided that Tina is the most likely suspect. They're going to come up there after her. I want you to get her out of there. I want all of you to get out of there until I can get them stopped."

"Why should I believe you?" Jesse asked, suspiciously. "All you've done is hassle us, Sheriff. How do I know you're not setting us up?"

"Because I don't believe Tina did it," Weber told him. "And because I don't want to see a bunch of people get killed in my town. We've already had too many killings. Listen to me, Jesse. Clear out of there, just for a little while."

"This is our home," Jesse declared. "We've known the government would come after us sooner or later, and we're ready for them."

"Goddamn it, Jesse, listen to me! Someone's going to get killed! This doesn't have to happen. Just give me some time to talk some sense into them, okay?"

"Thanks for your call, Sheriff. I do appreciate it," Jesse said. "But we're not going anywhere. We'll stand firm and fight for our home."

The line went dead in Weber's hand, and the sheriff cursed and slammed the receiver down into its cradle. Almost immediately it rang again.

"Sorry, Jimmy. Laura Wilson on line two," Robyn told him.

Weber punched the button on his telephone and said "What is it, Laura?"

"Sheriff? I need to talk to you! It's important!" she said in a shaky voice.

"What is it, Laura? Things are real crazy here right now."

"I can't tell you over the phone. Can you come up here?"

"Laura, I can't get away right now. I can send a deputy back...."

"No!" she pleaded. "I need to tell you! I'm afraid!"

"Afraid of what, Laura?" Weber asked impatiently, rubbing his forehead. A headache was starting to build behind his eyebrows.

"I know something. Something about the shooting last night. I'm scared, Sheriff!"

"Okay, listen Laura, I'll be up there as soon as possible. Keep the doors locked and stay inside. I have to take care of something here first, then I'll be up."

Weber hung up the telephone and walked into the outer office. Sayers, a wad of cotton stuffed up his nose, was directing his men as they donned Kevlar vests and checked their weapons. The cotton batting had stopped the bleeding, but made his voice sound even more nasal than it had before. Weber caught the eye of one of the agents who had helped Sayers out of his office, and the man stepped into the hallway with the Sheriff.

"Listen, I didn't catch your name..."

"John Bebo, Sheriff."

"Agent Bebo, this is a mistake. I really don't think Tina Miller is our shooter. If you guys go up there, someone's going to die. Can you talk some sense into your boss?"

Bebo shook his head. "You saw how stubborn he is, Sheriff. And, I don't know if the guys would stand down anyway. Larry Parks has a lot of friends out there in that room."

"Damn it man, I feel the same way!" Weber said. "But getting a bunch of innocent people killed isn't going to do him any good. We have to stop this!"

Again Bebo shook his head. "Sorry, Sheriff. You may be right, but I'm not going to lose my job over this. We have our orders. If the Miller woman is innocent, she'll get her day in court."

"No she won't!" Weber argued. "Not this way. That bunch of loonies are just waiting for something like this! It's the big war they've been planning and hoping for."

"Well," said the FBI agent, looking him in the eye, "They're in luck, then. Because we're going up there!"

"Listen, Bebo. I just got off the phone with a woman who said she has some information on last night's shooting. Can you stall Sayers long enough for me to go talk to her?"

"I don't know," Bebo said, relenting only a bit. "How reliable's your citizen?"

Weber knew if he told Bebo that Laura Wilson was a diagnosed mental case and a killer herself, there was no way he could delay the FBI raid on Jesse Miller's compound.

"She's solid," the sheriff lied. "All I'm asking is for you to stall them for a half hour or so. Can you do it?"

"I don't know," Bebo admitted. "Haul ass, Sheriff. I'll do my best."

Weber gripped his arm for a moment, then headed for his Bronco.

The Bronco screeched to a stop and Weber strode up to Laura Wilson's house and stabbed the doorbell. He waited impatiently, then rapped on the heavy wood, sending ripples of pain from his already battered knuckles. "Laura? Sheriff Weber. Open the door!"

Weber heard shuffling on the other side of the door and then Laura Wilson called out "Are you alone, Sheriff?"

"Yes, Laura. Now open up! I don't have time to waste."

There was a rattling of bolts and then the door opened, revealing a disheveled Laura Wilson wrapped in an emerald green robe. Her usually perfectly coiffed hair was in disarray, her eyes red from crying.

An ugly blue/black bruise covered her forehead and the skin was split open, congealed blood showing in the wound. Weber stepped inside and pushed the door closed behind him.

"What happened to you, Laura?"

She burst into tears and leaned into Weber, wrapping her arms around him, sobbing heavily. He could feel the pressure of her breasts against his chest, and even in the present circumstances, Weber would have been lying to claim he wasn't aware of her effect on him. He held her for a moment or two, then pushed away and led her to a seat on the leather sofa in the great room.

"Laura, the FBI is getting ready to raid Jesse Miller's place. People are going to die out there if I don't get back and stop it. Now what happened last night?"

The redhead sobbed for a moment longer, then pulled tissues from a box on a glass-topped end table and blew her nose, finally seeming to get some control over herself.

"God, I need a drink! I'm so scared."

"Laura, talk to me, damn it!"

She sighed heavily and looked at Weber. "I lied to you when I said the thing between Phil Johnson and myself was just a casual fling."

Weber waited for her to go on, not saying anything.

"Oh, it started out that way," Laura continued. "But then, I don't know.... it got more serious. Phil had a way of getting to you, even though you knew he was just using you. I loaned him money two or three times. Not a lot, a couple of thousand dollars here and there. He always promised to pay me back, but he never did. I guess I knew he wouldn't."

Weber wanted to say that in his world a 'couple of thousand dollars here and there' was a significant amount of money, but held his tongue. He was impatient to hear what the woman had to say, half his mind occupied with what was happening with the FBI raiding party, while the other half tried to concentrate on what Laura was saying.

"Anyway, after Roger caught us, I wanted to end it with Phil but he wouldn't let go. I'd like to think it was because he cared for me, but the truth was, he just didn't want the money to stop coming in. So he started blackmailing me."

"How could he blackmail you?" Weber asked. "Your husband already knew about the affair."

She shook her head. "No, he didn't threaten to tell Roger anything.

You're right, what could he tell him he didn't already know? No, Phil threatened to tell the entire state."

Weber was confused and growing more impatient. He resisted the urge to shake her.

"What do you mean, Laura?"

"It's no secret Roger is planning to run for office next year. I never knew about it until after I tried to cut him off, but Phil had hidden a camera in his bedroom and taped us in bed. He showed me some photos from the videos and said if I stopped paying him, Roger's opponents would get the photos and tapes."

She used a tissue to wipe tears from her eyes. "Sheriff, whether you think I do or not, I *do* love my husband. I couldn't let what I had done with Phil ruin Roger's chance for election."

Weber wanted to ask her how she could profess to love Roger Wilson, yet carry on continual affairs with other men, but he reminded himself that Laura Wilson was mentally ill, and perhaps her version of love for her husband was the best she was capable of.

"Laura, did you kill Phil Johnson to stop him from blackmailing you?"

She laughed, an ironically sad sound, and when she spoke again, Weber knew it was the *real* Laura Wilson talking, not one of her many assumed identities.

"No, Sheriff. Though I'll admit it did cross my mind. But I didn't kill him or that other man. I had made up my mind to offer Phil one big lump sum of cash. Roger and I talked it over and hoped he would take it and go away."

"He never would have let go," Weber told her. "You were the goose with the golden egg."

Laura nodded. "I know. But it was our only option. Then the armored car got hijacked and Phil was dead and we thought it was all over and we were finally out of it. But we weren't."

"What do you mean?" Weber asked.

"The photos, Sheriff. And the tape Phil made them from. I went up to his cabin last Sunday night to try and find them, but they were gone. Or else he'd hidden them somewhere else."

At least Weber knew now who Miss Lucy had seen in Johnson's cabin. Or so he thought.

"Laura, did you take a gun from Johnson's night stand? And a condom package from the wastebasket next to the bed?"

She looked at him quizzically. "No, Sheriff. I just looked for the photos. When I couldn't find them, I left."

"How did you get in to the cabin?"

"I thought I'd have to crawl through a window or something, but the door was unlocked."

"Okay, what happened yesterday?"

"I decided to go back out there again, yesterday afternoon. I just *had* to find those photos, Sheriff! Roger's entire future is hanging on them. I thought maybe I could search better in the daylight."

Weber had to force himself to keep from tapping his foot impatiently at Laura's rambling statement. Before he could prompt her, she continued relating the events of the day before.

"Anyway, I went up to the cabin, but it was locked this time. I finally decided that maybe Phil's landlady had taken the pictures. He used to joke that she was spying on him all the time."

"She's in a wheelchair," Weber said. "There's no way she could have gotten into the cabin."

"I was desperate, Sheriff! I was grasping at straws," Laura said, "I didn't know what else to do. So I went up to the house."

"To Miss Lucy's house?" Weber asked cautiously, his full attention now riveted on the woman. He still hadn't dismissed Laura Wilson as a suspect in the earlier killings, and now she was admitting to being on the scene of the latest shooting.

"I drove up the house, and some dog was barking its head off inside the house. I knocked on the door but no one answered.

"What happened then?" Weber asked.

"The dog was still barking in the back of the house, and I started to go around to the back of the place and see if I could find a rear door. But when I came around the corner of the house, someone tried to kill me!"

"What happened?" Weber asked, growing more agitated by the second.

"As I came around the corner of the house, someone hit me with a club, or a baseball bat or something. It knocked me down and I guess I blacked out for a while. When I came to, I managed to pull myself up to a window and look inside. I saw that old woman there, in a big pool of blood. I was afraid whoever did it would come back. I managed to get back to my car and came home."

Her voice had been calm during the retelling of the attack, but now began to waver again. "Sheriff, whoever it was must think they killed me! If they find out I'm alive, they'll try it again. They must think I saw them!"

"Why didn't you call me?" Weber demanded.

"I thought she was already dead. There was nothing I could do for her. But if I called, the killer might know I was still alive. I was scared, Sheriff. Don't hate me for that!"

She grabbed Weber's hand, a frightened little girl, floundering in water well over her head. He knew it wasn't an act this time.

"Did you see who it was?" Weber asked.

She shook her head. "All I saw was a shape, then I passed out."

"Okay, Laura. Do you know how to use a gun?"

She nodded. "Roger insisted I learn since he's gone so much. I've got a pistol."

"I want you to get it and lock the door behind me. I have to get out to Jesse Miller's place, but I'm going to call a deputy to come up here and guard the place. Don't open the door to anyone."

"I don't want anyone to see me this way," Laura pleaded.

Weber wanted to tell her that there was no time for vanity, but didn't. "The deputy will stay outside. He'll just ask through the door if you're okay."

"Can't you stay, Sheriff?"

"No, Laura. I have to go. You'll be fine, just stay inside and keep the doors locked."

Weber started the Bronco and called into the Sheriff's Office. Robyn's voice was strained when she answered. "I want a deputy up at the Wilson house," Weber told her. "Tell him not to let anyone in the place but me."

"I don't have anyone available," Robyn replied. "They're all on their way up to Jesse Miller's place. There's been a shooting. Tina's dead."

Weber cursed with rage and frustration and raced toward the compound, siren screaming.

Chapter 21

Gunfire crackled as Weber bounced over the rutted road to Jesse Miller's compound. Two hundred yards from the gate, he stopped behind Buz's new Bronco. His deputy was crouched behind the front fender, a Mini-14 in his hands.

"What the hell happened, Buz?" Weber demanded.

"We tried to stop them from coming up," Buz said, his voice filled with frustration. "But Sayers ordered his men to go with him. Next thing we knew, they radioed for help and said shots had been fired. One of them shot Tina."

"Son of a bitch! Where's Sayers?"

Buz nodded toward a group of FBI agents clustered behind three agency cars just ahead. "Our guys are in the woods and watching the back end of the place."

Weber ran in a crouch toward the FBI agents, expecting the impact of a bullet at any second. By the time he got to the cover of their cars, he realized all the gunfire was coming from two FBI sharpshooters firing toward the compound.

"Hold your fire, goddamn it!" Weber ordered. "What the hell are you shooting at, anyway? There's no one in sight!"

"Covering fire, Sheriff," Sayers said. "We're keeping their heads down!" The FBI agent's voice was quavering and he seemed unaware that he was sitting in a muddy puddle of melted snow. The firing had stopped. Acrid gun smoke hung heavy in the air

"What did you do, you damned idiot?" Weber demanded.

"We were fired upon and we returned fire," Sayers said.

"Bullshit!"

Weber turned to see Agent Bebo, his clothing covered with mud.

"Shut up, Bebo!" Sayers ordered shrilly. "I'm in charge here!"

"Bullshit," Bebo said again. "You can *have* my damned retirement. I'm not covering this up, Sayers."

He turned to Weber. "The girl was a looney tune, just like you said, Sheriff. She came out of that bunker up there and was waving a rifle around, ordering us to leave. Next thing I knew, Sayers shot her."

"She was going to shoot us!" Sayers screamed. "I shot in self-defense!"

From the grim looks on the faces of the other FBI agents, Weber knew Sayers was lying. But he wondered how many would come forward and tell the truth like Bebo had done, once the smoke had cleared.

"She never pointed her weapon at any of us," Bebo said.

"Shut up, Bebo. That's an order!" Sayers shouted, but Weber ignored him.

"Anyone else hit?" Weber asked.

"No. They fired several shots at us after the girl went down, then stopped. The whole thing only lasted a minute or two," Bebo said. "We haven't seen them since."

"Where's Tina?"

Bebo pointed toward a pile of brush, and Weber spotted the woman's body. He took the FBI agent's portable radio and pushed the transmit button. "Attention, everyone. This is Sheriff Weber. Everyone is to hold their positions. I repeat, hold your positions. No one is to fire again, unless directly fired upon. That's an order!"

"You have no right to interfere with a federal operation," Sayers protested. "These men don't answer to you, Sheriff!"

Weber drew his Colt and pointed it at the agent. "You're under arrest for murder, Sayers. Bebo, cuff him!"

The FBI agent didn't hesitate, taking his senior agent's pistol and snapping handcuffs onto his wrists.

"I'll have your ass for this, Weber! I'll have both of you!" Sayers threatened.

Weber ignored him. "Have you got a cellular phone?"

Bebo nodded and opened the car door. He reached inside and withdrew a phone. Weber punched in Jesse Miller's number. The phone rang a long time before a woman finally answered.

"Mrs. Miller? It's Sheriff Jim Weber. Let me talk to Jesse, please."

"Tina's dead," said Jesse's wife. "The FBI done killed her."

"I know, Mrs. Miller. Let me talk to Jesse, please."

After a long time, Jesse came on the line.

"What do you want, Sheriff?"

"Jesse, I've arrested the FBI agent who shot your sister. Is anyone else hurt?"

"No. Just Tina."

"Okay, Jesse. You're not in any trouble. All you did was shoot back in self-defense. I don't think any court in the land will convict you of anything. No one out here has been hit. Let's end this right here."

Sayers started to open his mouth, but Bebo gripped him firmly by the throat, fingers digging deeply into the flesh, to cut off any outburst the man might make. Sayers flailed his arms wildly for a moment, then stopped resisting. Only then did Bebo relax his hold.

"No way, Sheriff!" Jesse said. "You just want us to come out, then they'll gun us down too! No, we'll stay here and take some of them with us.

"Damn it, Jesse! We've had our differences, but if I wanted you dead, I'd have done it when I had the chance! Come out before anyone else has to die."

"Come and get us!"

"Jesse, I'm coming in there. I'll be unarmed. I want to check on Tina. Maybe she's just hurt. Let me do that, okay?"

Jesse was silent, and Weber pushed on. "I'll be unarmed, Jesse. Maybe they can cover up shooting Tina. But they know they can't hurt you without killing me first, then all my men. There's no way they can cover that up!"

"I want the newspaper here," Jesse demanded. "Then you can come in. Not until."

"You got it," Weber said. "Just sit tight and don't do anything crazy." He pushed the END button on the telephone, then dialed his office. "Robyn, I want Paul Lewis from the newspaper up here, with a camera. Tell him to step on it!"

Thirty minutes later the newspaper editor was crouched behind a car with his camera while Weber stripped off his jacket, gun belt, and shirt. Though the snow had mostly melted off, goose bumps covered his skin in the chilly winter air. Weber called Jesse again.

"The newspaper is here, Jesse. I'm coming in, I'm unarmed."

"Come on in," Jesse said. "But one trick, Sheriff, and you're the first to die!"

Weber stood up and stepped out from the cover of the car, walking toward the gate with his arms held up. He crawled over the fence and walked to where Tina's body lay, a lever action 30-30 Winchester beside her.

Weber closed his eyes when he saw the perfect round bullet hole in her neck and knew there was no hope, but still he felt in vain for a pulse. For the first time he could remember, Tina Miller looked at peace. The sheriff wasn't a religious man, but he found himself hoping there was an afterlife, and if there was, that Tina Miller and the man she loved were together and happier than they had been in this world.

He walked on down the driveway, aware all the time that more than one weapon was trained on him. Finally, around a curve from the gate, Jesse Miller stepped out from behind a tree, a nylon stocked pump shotgun held at the ready. Ernie was beside him, armed with a scoped bolt action hunting rifle. Farther down the driveway, near the mobile homes, Jesse's two young sons stood with rifles.

"I'm unarmed, Jesse, just like I said." Weber turned slowly to show Jesse he wasn't carrying a weapon, being careful to keep his hands in plain sight all the while.

"They killed her, Sheriff," Jesse said, and Weber saw tears streaming down the big man's face.

"I know, Jesse. I've got the man who did it in custody. Let's end it here."

The big man shook his head. "Why? So they can kill the rest of us, too?"

Weber shook his head. "Jesse, I've got the newspaper out there. The FBI can't do a thing. Do it my way and we'll be able to tell the story the right way. But if you fight back and one lawman gets killed, or even hurt, they can twist it all around. They'll make you the bad guy. This way, public opinion's going to be on your side. It won't be a shootout with the FBI. The story will be about them coming to your home and killing Tina."

Jesse was still undecided, but Ernie spoke up. "Listen to the man, Jesse. He may be a cop, but he's telling the truth. I don't want to die here, Jesse."

"That's your problem," the other man snapped. "You're a coward, Ernie! I'm not afraid to die! Hell Ernie, except for when you're beating up on your old lady, Tina had more balls than you ever will!"

Ernie was rocked backward by Jesse's words, and Weber spoke up before he could reply.

"*I'm* afraid to die," Weber told Jesse. "So are your wife and kids, Jesse. Sure, they're full of your ideas, but they don't want to die for them. Tina didn't want to die, either. She wanted to have her baby and raise it.

Jesse, if we do it my way, the whole world knows Tina died defending her home. If you make this another Ruby Ridge, you'll all go down as just another bunch of nuts that took on the feds and lost. This way, you win. There are FBI agents out there who will tell the truth. Come on out, Jesse."

Weber knew he was lying. He knew that by the time the FBI's publicity people got done with the story, the Bureau would come out on top, and Tina Miller would be portrayed as a gun toting lunatic that had been killed assaulting federal officers. But he also knew the lie was the only way to save the lives of Jesse Miller and his family, and quite possibly the lives of some of the lawmen waiting outside the compound.

Weber had never considered himself much of a salesman, but right now he was selling his heart out. Trying to sell Jesse Miller on the value of truth over revenge, of life over death. Weber could only hope Jesse would buy what he was selling.

The big man looked at Weber a long time; fear, rage and indecision playing across his face. Finally, Jesse slowly lowered his weapon.

Chapter 22

The aftermath of the shooting of Tina Miller, as well as following up on the shootings of Miss Lucy Washburn and Larry Parks the day before, kept Weber busy the rest of the day. Robyn had left the office in the early evening, saying she needed to go to her house to tend to her cat and water the houseplants. It was nearly midnight by the time an exhausted Weber got back to his cabin, ate a bowl of cold cereal, and dragged himself into the shower. He collapsed on his bed without drying off, waking shivering sometime in the middle of the night and crawling under the down comforter.

The next morning, Weber woke feeling fairly rested, though it still felt like grains of sand were embedded on the undersides of his eyelids. While finishing his second cup of coffee, he ran a load of laundry. Stripping the bed in the guest bedroom, Weber spotted Larry Park's battered leather suitcase and overnight bag sitting next to the bed. Weber realized his friend must have stopped by the cabin to drop off his things when he had returned to town two days earlier, before continuing on to the Sheriff's office, and ultimately his encounter with a gunman at Miss Lucy's house.

Weber sat the two bags on the bed and unzipped the overnight bag. Inside were a shaving kit, deodorant, toothbrush and tube of toothpaste, and aftershave lotion. A zippered pistol case held a stainless Walther PPKS .380 semi-automatic pistol, with a spare loaded magazine. The only other item in the bag was a small 35mm pocket camera in a vinyl drawstring bag. Weber turned to the suitcase, opening it to reveal several sets of underwear, socks, three flannel shirts, and a pair of jeans. In a zippered compartment in the inside of the lid were several manila folders. Weber opened one and began to read.

"Well, it looks like we've wrapped this case up," said a senior FBI agent from Phoenix, when the sheriff walked into his office dressed in a forest green down vest over jeans and a red flannel shirt.

"What do you mean?"

Weber knew the Bureau's spin doctors were busy with their own special brand of the truth, and he was sure they would manage to put Sayers' actions in the best light.

"Sheriff, no matter how it all shakes out with Sayers killing that girl, she was our best suspect in the killings. She had motive - her husband was sleeping around on her, and that bunch of fanatics could use the money to finance their 'revolution.' We already know she shot up that saloon, so we have a demonstrated propensity for violence. And she's somebody those two guards would have stopped for, even against regulations. They had no reason to fear her, or suspect anything."

"So why did she shoot Larry Parks and Lucy Washburn?"

The agent smiled patiently at Weber, like a schoolteacher trying to explain a mathematical problem to a dim witted student who just wasn't getting it. "Sheriff, Parks was the enemy. He was the FBI! And he was getting too close to solving the case. So she took him out."

"What about the old woman? Why would she shoot her?"

The FBI man shook his head, still smiling, but sounding a trifle frustrated with Weber's failure to comprehend things from the official point of view. "Who knows, Sheriff? After all, she *was* a nut! Rational people like you and I can't be expected to understand what goes on inside the mind of someone like that."

"Then where's the money?" Weber argued.

This time the agent shrugged, and his voice took on an edge of exasperation. "Gone, probably. They either spent it on guns and the rest of their paramilitary hardware, or hid it somewhere. We'll run her brothers through interrogation, maybe they'll tell us where the rest is hidden, if there *is* any left."

Weber shook his head. "It won't work."

The FBI man's eyes narrowed. "What do you mean, Sheriff?"

"You're willing to stick it to a dead woman and the rest of her fruitcake family to cover your asses and close the book on a bunch of killings. It makes a tidy package, but it won't work."

"And just why *not?*" the government man demanded.

"Because Tina didn't kill anyone. She didn't hijack that armored car. The most you could blame her with is shooting up the Antler Inn and waving a gun around. That's not a federal offense, and it's damn sure not reason enough to kill her."

"Well, if Tina Miller didn't do it, who did?"

Weber stood up and headed for the door. "I'll let you read my report when I'm done."

Weber knocked, then let himself into Debbie's house. "Anyone home?"

The house was empty. Weber crossed to the bureau in the dining room and began to sort through Mike and Debbie Perkins' old bills and checkbooks. An hour later the front door opened and Debbie walked in.

"Jimmy! About time you found some time for me," she teased, then saw the pile of bills, canceled checks, invoices, and folders scattered around the dining room table. "What's all this?"

"Mike wasn't cheating on you, Debbie," Weber told her, nodding at the mess on the table. "This proves it."

She sighed in relief and sat down across from him, brushing her long blonde hair back from her face. "God, Jimmy, thank you! I don't know if I could have gone on with my life not knowing. I don't know if I could have trusted anyone ever again."

Weber looked back at the paperwork. "You got anything cold to drink, kid?"

"Sure," Debbie scooted her chair back and headed for the kitchen. "Beer, Pepsi or iced tea?"

"Pepsi's fine," Weber told her. "With all the feds around, I probably shouldn't have beer on my breath."

From the kitchen came the hiss of a pop top being opened, the tinkling of ice cubes in glasses, and then Debbie returned with two glasses of soda. She placed one in front of her brother and took her seat again.

"So, out with it, Jimmy! I'm relieved to know Mike wasn't cheating. It makes losing him a little easier. But how can you be sure?"

Weber looked at her. "Because *you* were cheating on him, Debbie."

There was a long silence while brother and sister stared into each other's eyes. Finally Debbie broke contact and burst out laughing, shaking her head, "Jimmy, you've been working *way* too hard!"

Weber shook his head. "No, Debbie. You were having an affair with Phil Johnson. You hijacked the armored car. You convinced Phil Johnson to kill Mike, then you killed him, and you did the shooting at Miss Lucy's the other day."

The look of shock that had come over Debbie's face was quickly replaced by anger. "This isn't funny, Jimmy! You can't believe I would kill my own husband, not to mention four other people, including a harmless old woman I've known all my life!"

"There were only two other people, Debbie."

"What?" She shook her head. "You're confusing me. I don't know what you're talking about, Jimmy. None of this makes sense!"

"There were only two other people killed, Debbie. Phil Johnson and Lucy Washburn. You said four. Where did you come up with the other two?"

Debbie waved her hand in exasperation. "I don't know, Jimmy! One, two, three... whatever!"

"You said four, because you thought you had killed Laura Wilson and Larry Parks, too, Debbie. But Parks is still alive. His blood pressure was so low I thought he was dead too, but he's a tough one. And you only knocked Laura out. Why didn't you shoot her, too? Did you run out of bullets?"

Debbie stood up and strode across the room to the telephone stand. "Jimmy, you're my brother and I love you. But get out of here right now or I'm calling one of your deputies to come and get you! You've cracked up or something. God knows you've been under enough stress! But Jimmy, you're scaring me!"

"No," Weber told her. "I wish I *was* crazy, Debbie. I wish this was all a bad dream. But it's not. The proof is all right here." He waved his hand at the papers on the table. "With everything going on, I forgot that Gila County was going to fax us up the copies of the motel receipts Mike was supposed to have signed. But they did, Debbie. And you knew they were coming. It wouldn't have taken much for you to intercept them. You have free run of the Sheriff's Office."

"What difference would the receipts make," Debbie demanded.

"You knew as soon as I saw them, I'd know it wasn't Mike's signature on them. I've seen his handwriting hundreds of times on his reports from volunteer duty. It wouldn't have taken me long to figure out it was Johnson's handwriting, not Mike's."

"Okay, so maybe Phil borrowed Mike's credit card, or stole it and used it, I don't know! That makes me a killer?"

"You said Mike paid all the bills, Debbie. But these canceled checks... you wrote almost all of them. You paid the Visa bills. You paid all the bills. If Mike would have seen the bills from the motel, he'd have known something was going on. Every motel room rental coincides with a date you said you were studying in Flagstaff. I imagine if I called the university library, no one would be able to confirm you were there."

Debbie jerked the drawer of the telephone stand open and pulled out a pack of cigarettes, trembling hands fumbling with a lighter. She finally got one lit and inhaled deeply, her face tight with anger.

"Okay, Sherlock Holmes," she said, blowing a cloud of blue smoke toward the ceiling. "What else makes you think I'm a killer?"

"The one question everyone had was why would Mike and Johnson stop the armored car, out there in the middle of nowhere, Debbie. It was against the rules. Today an FBI agent told me they would have stopped for Tina Miller, because she was Johnson's wife. They'd have stopped for you too, Debbie."

Debbie shook her head, a sad smile on her face. "Jimmy, *listen to me!* You're way off base here. I don't know where you came up with this crazy idea, but this is me, *Debbie!* I'm not some criminal! I know you loved Mike too, Jimmy. And then this thing with Parks. No wonder you're confused. But you have to stop this, Jimmy!"

Weber shook his head. "Parks left his suitcase at my cabin before he went up to Miss Lucy's, Debbie. He picked up the original motel receipts. He also talked to the woman at the motel. She's a nice old lady."

"There!" Debbie said, pointing a finger at her brother. "The woman at the motel identified Mike as being the one who rented the room!"

Weber shook his head and picked up a copy of the newspaper from the chair beside him.

"No Debbie, she identified the picture of the man who rented the room. The newspaper printed both men's photos, but they got the wrong names under the pictures. At first I thought it was a mistake on the newspaper's part, one that just played into your plan. But Parks caught on and left it in his notes. *You* were the one that sent them the photos, Debbie. I remember, because they called the office, and you said you'd send them photos you had. *You* switched the names, just in case."

Debbie picked up the telephone receiver. "That's it, Jimmy! Get out of here or I'm calling a deputy!"

Weber held up two canceled checks from the pile on the table. "You thought you had it all covered, Debbie. But you made a couple of real mistakes. These checks are for a storage garage in Show Low. If I called the Show Low police and they went and cut the lock open, would they find Phil Johnson's Jeep inside that garage, Debbie? The way I have it figured, you and Johnson set the hijack up and he stashed his Jeep in

Show Low. It would have been easy for you to take it, drive to the Canyon and stage the hijacking, then get back to class. It's less than an hour's drive each way. But you got greedy and double-crossed Johnson, too. *Why*, Debbie? Why did you do it?"

Debbie shook her head again, and hung up the telephone. She sighed and crushed her cigarette in an ashtray next to the telephone. She kept her back to Weber, spine rigid with anger.

"Why, Debbie?" he asked again.

When Debbie turned around finally, she held Phil Johnson's snub nosed .38 in her hand.

"*Why*? I'll tell you why! Because I was sick of this hick town! I was sick of Mike and his penny pinching ways. '*Don't spend money on clothes right now, Debbie. We have to watch our money until you graduate.*' Like a teacher's salary was going to make us rich!"

Weber kept his hands in plain sight on the table.

"When did it start with Johnson, Debbie?"

She shook her head. "Who cares? What does it matter? Last summer sometime. The old fart couldn't keep his pants zipped, and I guess his partner's wife was just too much of a challenge to resist. With Phil, it was all about the conquest. For me, it was a means to an end."

"Mike loved you more than anything, Debbie."

She sneered. "So what? He was never going to be anything but a small town hick. Between his hero worshiping you, and wanting to play cop, he didn't know there was a life outside Big Lake. Christ, Jimmy! You got to leave this place! I never did! All I ever wanted was out. I begged him to move, but he wouldn't listen to a word I said."

"You think $300,000 will get you a new life?" Weber asked her.

"Oh, I'm not *that* stupid," Debbie said. "But don't forget, Mike had a $250,000 life insurance policy, too. I figure between the two, I can go someplace and *live* for once."

"Why did you shoot Miss Lucy, and Parks?"

"The old bitch was always spying on Phil. We tried to be careful, but when I went there the other day, and then you mentioned something about her watching the cabin, I got worried. I looked out the window and there she was, at her window, watching me. I was sure she could identify me. Larry Parks just got there at the wrong time and I had to shoot him. As for that silly slut, Laura Wilson, she surprised me. I grabbed a piece of cordwood and smacked her. She looked dead to me!"

"Why did you take a chance on going to the cabin, Debbie? Was it the condom package?"

She smiled ruefully and nodded her head. "You're good, Jimmy, I'll give you that. The last thing I needed was for that old fool to get me pregnant! So we used the condoms. I forgot that I had opened the last one. I was afraid somehow someone would get my fingerprints off it. Plus, Phil had bragged to me about his little photography hobby. He was kinky. I wanted to be sure there weren't any photos of *me* there."

"Where are the photos now?" Weber asked.

"Oh, I burned them all in my fireplace. Sick, disgusting pervert! And all those silly women putting out to him! At least I had a reason all along."

"So now what?" Weber asked, his eyes locked on hers. "Are you going to kill me too, Debbie?"

She frowned. "Are you going to make me, Jimmy? I hope not. You're my brother, and I love you. Really, I do."

"I can't let you get away with it," Weber told her.

Debbie waved the revolver. "Come on, Jimmy! The FBI wants to stick it all on Tina Miller. All you have to do is let them! I can still go away, and no one will ever know!"

"*I'll* know, Debbie," Weber said. "I'm sorry, I can't let you do it."

Debbie pulled back the hammer of the .38 and stared at her brother. "Please don't make me shoot you, Jimmy."

"You'd really do it, wouldn't you?" he asked her.

Tears had begun to run down Debbie's cheeks, and she wiped her face with the back of one hand, the other keeping the gun pointed at Weber. "I couldn't kill you, Jimmy. But remember, you taught me to shoot. I'll hurt you enough to slow you down so I can get away."

"You should have paid more attention," Weber told her. "I also taught you to check every gun you pick up to make sure it's loaded. I searched the house and found the .38 in the telephone stand, and took the bullets out before you got home."

Debbie lowered the hammer and pushed the gun's cylinder release button to pop it open, then smiled wryly and tossed it on the table. "It doesn't make any difference, Jimmy. I know you. You love me too much to arrest me. I'm the only family you have left! You couldn't live with yourself if you did."

"I couldn't live with myself if I let you go," Weber told her.

Crying harder now, Debbie crossed to her brother and bent over, putting her hands on his shoulders. "Please, Jimmy!" she begged. "Give me one hour. I can pick up the money at the storage locker and be gone. No one has to know!"

Weber was crying too as he shook his head. "Debbie, I'll sell the house and my cabin to get you the best lawyers. But I just can't let you go."

"You son of a bitch!" Debbie snarled, slapping his face. As Weber recoiled from the blow, she snatched his Colt from his waistband and pointed it at him. "I know this one's loaded, Jimmy! Give me your handcuffs!"

Carefully Weber reached into his vest pocket and pulled out his handcuffs, his eyes locked on Debbie's. His hand brushed the butt of Parks' Walther .380. He thought he had a better than even chance, but he couldn't bring himself to pull the gun on his sister.

"Over there!" Debbie pointed toward the stairway. She followed Weber across the room and ordered him to lace his hands through the railing of the banister. Using one hand while she kept the Colt on him with the other, she managed to snap the cuffs onto his wrists. Finally Debbie stepped back and laid the .45 on an end table.

"I love you, Jimmy. By the time someone finds you, I'll be gone."

"You can't hide forever, Debbie."

She stepped close and kissed his cheek, then wiped tears away from her eyes. "I love you, Jimmy," she repeated. "Goodbye."

The tears blurring his vision prevented him from seeing her leave, but Weber heard the door close behind his sister, then the sound of her car pulling out of the driveway.

It took nearly an hour of pulling and kicking on the rungs of the heavy stair banister, but Weber finally managed to splinter the wood and free himself. His wrists were scraped raw from the effort, and he was panting for breath. He stumbled into the dining room and picked up what was left of the Pepsi Debbie had poured him earlier and drank deeply, letting the tepid soda wash away his thirst. The Sheriff wiped his eyes with the sleeves of his shirt and fumbled inside his jacket for his key ring. It took several attempts before he succeeded in unlocking the handcuffs. Then Weber shambled to the telephone and dialed a number.

"Robyn. It's Jimmy. Call the Show Low Police Department. Tell them Debbie Perkins is at the storage lockers on 5th Street and to arrest her for murder and armed robbery." Weber ignored Robyn's questions and hung up the telephone, then sank into a chair. He put his head down on his arms and wept.

Turn the page for a sneak preview of Nick Russell's newest book, *Big Lake Lynching* available in Janaury, 2012 in paperback or in the Amazon Kindle bookstore!

Big Lake Lynching

The tassel-eared Albert's squirrel scampered nimbly down the limb of the huge Ponderosa pine and paused when he came to the spot where the sun warmed the branch exactly to his liking. Eyes and ears alert for anything out of place, the animal spent several minutes looking for danger. His stomach was full, and now he needed to rest.

The night before, humans had intruded into the forest. The noise and smell of them had frightened away many of the small animals, sending them off in search of safer and quieter refuge until the trespassers were gone.

But the squirrel, an old scarred boar, had stayed in his tree. Long ago he had learned how to remain motionless for as long as was required, depending upon his pelt's natural camouflage to escape detection. Many younger, more nervous squirrels were not able to stand the strain and would often flee for safety. Sometimes they made it, but all too often their movement betrayed them and the long sticks the humans carried roared and spat fire, and the runners tumbled to the ground and were carried away. The old boar was never one to act in haste, a trait that had helped him survive in the wild for so long. He had watched many a human pass by below his tree, unseen by the eyes of the hunters.

Satisfied that he was safe from predators, he stretched out in the sun and let the warmth soak into his body, easing the stiff place that still ached where the hawk's sharp talons had pierced his hip so long ago. His eyelids grew heavy and he began to drowse.

Moments later an alien sound alerted him and he sprang to his feet. A giant shadow passed overhead and a roar more horrible than any cougar's call shook the still morning air. The squirrel forgot all the many lessons he had learned about holding in place and waiting until danger passed. This menace was too close and too horrible for any thoughts but blind escape from the exposed tree limb! His arthritic hip was forgotten as his panic carried him deep into the branches of the tree. Ducking behind a canopy of needles, he finally halted and flattened himself against the bark, every sense on full alert.

Overhead the terrible apparition roared again and flames shot upward through it as it drifted slowly past. The squirrel's ears picked up a new sound as the roaring subsided. The words of humans! But how could that be? Humans were ground creatures, not flying animals. Not a jay or a hawk, or even the feared owl! But there was no mistaking the sound. The old boar had heard it too many times. He flattened even closer to the rough bark of the pine tree.

"It's just beautiful, Nels! I never knew it could be so gorgeous up here!"

The sound was from a female human, but the veteran squirrel knew they could be just as deadly as the males. He held his position. Then the male spoke and he knew there were at least two of them.

"I told you it was grand! Look over there, see the mist coming off the water? Beautiful isn't it?"

The words were drowned out by another ear-splitting roar and huge belch of flame and the nightmare drifted farther past and started to glide down the gentle slope of the mountain toward the lake. Again, the words of the humans floated back on the morning air.

"What's that down there, Nels? Over there. It looks like..."

"What? Where? Oh... Oh shit! Oh, Jesus Christ! Oh my God!"

The female human screamed, a sound more terrifying than the roaring that went with the fiery flames. More terrifying than the call of a coyote or the screech of an owl bearing down on his tree. The old squirrel knew that he was going to die. He jumped from his hiding place and ran as fast as he could... ran like the days when he was a youngster so long ago. He reached the end of the branch and his legs pushed him off in a mighty leap. He expected any minute to hear the roar of the humans' fire sticks and feel himself being torn to pieces. But instead, he sailed across the gap to the waiting branches of another tree, clawed his way around its trunk and ran along a huge limb as far as it would take him, then leapt to a third tree, putting as much cover and distance between himself and the terrible flying humans behind him as he could.

But even then, over the pounding inside his head, he could still hear the terrible screams of the female human behind him. He was halfway down the other side of the mountain before he finally stopped in a great snag of branches high up in an ancient old Ponderosa to allow his heart to slow down again.

He couldn't hear the horrific noises anymore more, but the old boar would remember them for the rest of his days.

Chapter 1

The first time the telephone rang, Sheriff Jim Weber pulled his pillow over his head and hoped it was a dream. The second ring told him it wasn't a dream. At the third ring he cursed and groped for the handset on his nightstand, knocking it to the floor. Four rings and two expletives later, he finally managed to get the telephone to his ear.

"It's Sunday. Go away," mumbled Weber.

"Jimmy? Sheriff Weber? Uh... this is Archer. Your deputy?"

Weber groaned and rolled back over in bed. His head ached and his mouth tasted like rancid bacon grease. He belched and scratched at the whisker stubble on his face.

"I know who you are, Archer. I just don't know what you want. Go away. Call me later."

"Uh... Sheriff. We just got a call from Nels Lundgren on his cell phone. He sounded pretty upset."

Weber stretched and burrowed back down into the sheet. "Yeah? What's wrong with the Mad Viking this early in the morning? Someone drop another dog turd in a mailbox? Or did Old Man Foster finally shoot at his hot air balloon for scarin' his chickens out of laying eggs?"

"No sir, neither one, Sheriff. He said he found a body the other side of Cat Mountain. He said it looks like somebody got themself lynched."

The sheriff bolted upright in bed, wide awake now.

"Run that by me again, Archer. A body?"

"Yes, sir. He said him and Miz Gaylord was up in his balloon and they saw this body just hanging from a tree. They both sounded pretty upset, Sheriff."

Weber was out of bed and pulling on a pair of jeans. He jerked open a dresser drawer and grabbed socks and a t-shirt. "Where is he now, Archer?"

"Gee... I guess he's still hanging in the tree, Sheriff."

"No, Nels! Where was he calling from?" Weber had learned long ago that getting frustrated at Archer's bumbling attempts to communicate, or do anything else even remotely related to police work, was a lesson in futility. All it did was confuse Archer even more. But at times like this, it was hard to keep the agitation out of his voice.

"He said they was setting the balloon down as close to Rim Road as they could and waiting for the chase crew. Said if you was to drive out the road, you'd run into them. You want me to call in the rest of the guys, Sheriff?"

Weber considered the suggestion for just a moment as he buttoned a short sleeved plaid shirt. Summer weekends were demanding enough on his small staff without calling them out for what could be nothing more than a wild goose chase. If it was anyone else, he might have considered that possibility. But Nels Lundgren, Big Lake's postmaster and resident hot air balloon pilot, was a level headed veteran of the Gulf War, not given to hysterics or jumping to conclusions. If Lundgren said he had seen a body hanging from a tree, Weber believed there was indeed a body hanging from a tree.

"Let's see... Buz had the duty last night. Let him sleep. Call the others and tell them to meet me out there."

Weber hung up and was heading for the door before Archer could reply.

Even in late May, the mornings can be cool in Arizona's high country. Sitting at 9500 feet atop the Mogollon Rim, the small town of Big Lake lies hidden in the world's largest Ponderosa pine forest, where it isn't unheard of for frost to linger until the middle of April some years. At 7 a.m. this Sunday morning the sun had burned off the early morning chill, but there was still condensation on Weber's Bronco that quickly evaporated as he sped along Rim Road toward the back of Cat Mountain. Weber had flipped on his overhead emergency lights, but left the siren off. Aside from a few fishermen getting a late start, traffic was light. Most of the die-hard anglers were already on the water, it was still too early for the church crowd, and last night's drunks wouldn't be waking up for a couple of hours yet.

It took Weber twenty minutes to reach Lundgren's makeshift landing zone in a meadow between the side of Cat Mountain and the road. The white Ford crew cab pickup that served as the balloonist's chase vehicle was parked alongside the road and Lundgren and his grim-faced ground crew were just loading the balloon's big wicker basket onto the trailer. When the sheriff stopped behind the trailer, Tami Gaylord jumped out of the pickup and ran back to Weber's door, clutching his arm through the open window hard enough to make the sheriff wince.

Tami Gaylord would never be called a pretty woman under the best of circumstances. Today, with mascara running down her face and her hair in disarray, she looked more like a hysterical, overweight raccoon than the owner of a boutique that specialized in overpriced Native American art that only the tourists could be fooled into buying. Weber had never before seen Tami out of the multicolored shift dresses she wore every day. The jeans and flannel shirt she had on this morning did not flatter her plump figure.

"Oh, Sheriff! It was just awful!" She said, leaning inside his window and clutching his arm even harder. "You've got to do something!"

"I know, Tami. Just let me..."

"Please, Sheriff. You can't just leave him hanging up there. Do something!"

"I'm going to, Tami. But right now, I'm trying to get out of my truck! I have to do that first!"

Lonnie VanPelt, one of Lundgren's two man chase crew, saw the sheriff's predicament and took hold of Tami's arm and gently led her back to the pickup with soothing words. Weber met Lundgren at the back of the trailer.

"What do we have, Nels?"

The postmaster pointed up the side of the mountain. "We topped the ridge and were heading down the slope when we spotted him, Jimmy. Actually, Tami saw him first. I'd say he's maybe a hundred yards from the shore of Turtle Lake. He's hanging from a tree, naked and covered in blood."

"You sure it's a person? Not a deer some poacher strung up to butcher and then got scared off when he heard your balloon?"

Lundgren shook his head. "I've seen dead men before, Jimmy. This wasn't any deer."

The sound of a vehicle approaching at high speed caught their attention, and the men turned in time to see a marked Big Lake squad car round the last curve and head toward them.

"I sure hope you're right," Weber told the balloon pilot. "Those boys are going to be mighty pissed if we drug them out of bed and out here for nothing."

"Oh, it's something, all right," Lundgren assured him. "Something damned ugly, Jimmy."

Puffing with exertion from the climb up the steep mountainside, Weber, Lundgren, and Deputies Chad Summers and Tommy Frost emerged from the trees onto the bank of Turtle Lake and paused to catch their breath.

"Damn! I'm getting too old for this shit." Chad said, bent slightly forward, hands on his knees.

Weber took off his hat and wiped his brow with the back of his hand, then surveyed the far shoreline of the lake. Turtle Lake wasn't much of a lake, more a pond of about five acres occupying a flat shelf of land on the mountainside. It was shallow and muddy, home to a few catfish, crawdads and turtles. Fishermen, with all of Big Lake and neighboring Crescent Lake to choose from, ignored the small body of water in favor of easier access, deeper water, and the chance to bag trophy trout.

"Where is it?" he asked Lungren.

The postmaster pointed to a spot off to their right on the far shoreline.

"He's hanging from that big old snag," he said, indicating a lighting-struck spar that poked nakedly into the sky. "There's a little clearing and he's right there."

"At least it's not uphill," observed Tommy Frost.

"Too steep for you, kid?" asked Chad with a grin.

Tommy shook his head. "No, sir. I just don't want to have to lug you and a dead guy down off this mountain at the same time. You're not a kid anymore, you know."

Chad straightened up and stretched, wincing. "Oh, yeah. I know that. Hills like this remind me, I don't need your input, you pup."

"Let's check it out," Weber said, leading off as they picked their way over rocks and along the bank.

A few minutes later, Chad groaned as the group stepped into the small clearing beside the old snag tree. "Son-of-a-bitch! It's not a deer, that's for sure."

Tommy Frost turned away and vomited into a bush as the others looked up at the body, suspended by a length of cheap cotton clothesline from a limb of the bare tree, rocking ever so slightly in the breeze. Weber had to swallow hard not to do the same as he tried to shut out the sounds coming from his young deputy.

"Do you recognize him?" Weber asked of no one in particular.

"Who can tell?" Chad replied. "Someone really worked him over."

The body appeared to be a young Indian or Hispanic male, long black hair matted with blood hanging down over his face, which was so bloody it looked like he was wearing a red mask. The victim was naked, and the corpse was covered with contusions and welts.

"Somebody's gonna have to cut him down." Lundgren said.

"Not yet," Weber replied. "He's not going anywhere, and he's beyond help. Everybody spread out and see if we can find anything. You okay, Tommy?"

Tommy wiped a string of spittle from his pale face with a handkerchief and nodded. "Yeah, sorry."

"Nothing to be sorry about," Weber told him. "Every good lawman loses his cookies sooner or later. How about you see if you can raise the office on your radio and have Archer send out the EMTs and find Dolan."

Tommy nodded and pulled his portable radio from its belt clip as Weber moved off, searching for any clues as to how the body got where it was. Whoever had killed the young man didn't go out of their way to cover their tracks. There were three cigarette butts and the stub of a cigar on the ground under the victim. Weber was squatting down studying a trampled patch of grass at the edge of the clearing when Chad called his name.

The sheriff walked to where his deputy and Lundgren knelt, studying something in the weeds.

"What have you got?"

"Looks like we found his clothes," Lundgren said.

Weber crouched down and poked at a blue shirt with a stick, raising it just enough to peer at a worn pair of jeans underneath. A battered tennis shoe rested nearby. The clothes were soiled and damp from laying out overnight.

"No one touches anything until we get a camera up here," the sheriff ordered. He looked up as Tommy joined them. "You get hold of the office?"

"Yes, sir. Everybody's on the way. The EMTs told Archer there's an old logging road drops off the top of the ridge about a quarter mile south of here. Guy said he hadn't been up here in years, but they think they can get in at least part of the way."

"Place is crisscrossed with logging trails," Lundgren said. "You need to come up with me some morning, Jimmy. Give you a real bird's eye view of your territory."

The sheriff shook his head. "If I go up in the air, I want wings and motors to keep me up there. I get all the hot air I need from Chet Wingate."

Everyone grinned or nodded at the mention of Big Lake's mayor, an overweight martinet who was Archer's father and Weber's personal nemesis.

"Besides," Weber said with an evil grin, "If you're taking Tami Gaylord flying these days, I don't see how you'd have time to fit me into your schedule, Nels."

The balloonist blushed as Chad snickered. "Hey, what can I say? She won a flight at the Friends of the Library auction. Is it my fault if I'm a public spirited citizen who donates his time for charity?"

"You spend much time with that lady and we'll start thinking you're supporting Friends of Animals," Chad suggested. "What's she gone through now? Four husbands?"

"Something like that," Weber said. "Watch yourself, Nels old buddy. If we have a bad summer, she may end up marrying you just so she can divorce you and sell your balloon to raise enough money to keep her shop open."

"Doesn't it take two people consenting to get married?" the postmaster asked good-naturedly.

"I don't think so," Chad said. "After all, would four guys in a row volunteer to marry that?"

Their laughter was interrupted by a call over Tommy's radio. "Big Lake One, this is Three. Where are you guys?"

Weber took the radio from Tommy and keyed the microphone. "We're on the north side of the lake, Dolan. Look for a big old snag tree, we're under it."

"10-4, I've got it in sight."

Moments later, Deputy Dolan Reed joined them. He took in the scene...body hanging in the tree, the sheriff and the others studying the evidence they had found, and pulled a Nikon camera from his backpack.

"Didn't take you long to get here," Weber said, as Dolan began taking photos of the crime scene.

"Lucky you called when you did. I was heading out to the lake. Archer raised me on the radio just as I was getting ready to launch the boat."

"Sorry to spoil your day off," Weber said as Dolan crouched down to shoot a picture of the pile of clothing. "You get it?"

Dolan nodded and the sheriff started searching through the pockets as Dolan tilted his head toward where the victim still hung. "No problem. My day's still better than his, I guess."

The shirt pocket held only a flattened pack of chewing gum with two sticks left. The right front jeans pocket contained a key for a Ford and thirty cents in change. A back pocket held a worn leather wallet. Weber opened the wallet and began to sort through the contents: a business card from an automobile repair shop in Lakeside, another from a restaurant in Springerville, a photo of an overweight Indian woman, a White Mountain Apache tribal library card, $45 in cash, a folded slip of paper with the name Charles written above a telephone number with a Big Lake prefix, and an Arizona drivers license issued to Daniel Bell, with the address listed as a post office box in McNary, Arizona. The license described Bell as an Indian male, 23, 5'7" tall, and 135 pounds. Weber took the license and walked over to look up at the body. A breeze had moved the hair off part of his face. Take away the blood, bruises and the swelling from strangulation, and the body could very well be the man pictured on the drivers license.

"Ahhh... Sheriff?" Tommy Frost stood at his side.

Weber didn't answer, just continued to study the body.

"Sheriff, Dolan says he's got his pictures. It don't seem right, him hanging up there. Shouldn't we cut him down?"

Weber was still silent. The freckle-faced young deputy shuffled his feet uncomfortably, trying to ignore the buzzing of flies attracted to the smell of blood and avoid looking at the feet hanging in front of him at eye level. Finally the sheriff shook his head and looked at his young deputy. "Yeah, Tommy. Let's get him down."

The deputy nodded, then walked over to the tree. With a boost from Chad, he managed to pull himself up into a fork and then climbed out onto the limb the body was hanging from. Trying to avoid looking at the dead man, Tommy fumbled his folding Buck knife from the sheath on his belt, then grasped the rope and sliced through it. Weber and Chad eased the body to the ground, then stepped aside to allow Dolan to take more photographs. He was rewinding his second roll of film when the EMTs stumbled into the clearing amid a great crashing of brush.

Weber and his deputies stepped aside to allow the medics to load the body onto a stretcher. Weber was lighting up one of the strong cigars he relished and the rest of the world abhorred when Randy Clark, one of the EMTs, called him.

"Sheriff? Did you see this?"

Weber walked back to the stretcher. "What is it?"

Clark was a dark haired, stocky man of 40, who had seen a lot of blood and mayhem in fifteen years as a paramedic, but his round face was pale as he looked up from the body.

"All this blood," he waved a hand toward the dead man. "They scalped him, Sheriff."

For the second time that morning, the sound of Deputy Tommy Frost throwing up assaulted the morning air.